SPINNERS

BY THE SAME AUTHOR

SPINNERS

. . . .

A Novel

Anthony McCarten

William Morrow and Company, Inc.

New York

It is the policy of William Morrow and Company, Inc., and its imprints and
affiliates, recognizing the importance of preserving what has been written, to
print the books we publish on acid-free paper, and we exert our best efforts to
that end.

Library of Congress Cataloging-in-Publication Data

McCarten, Anthony, 1961–
Spinners : a novel / Anthony McCarten.
p.   cm.
ISBN 0-688-16303-3
I. Title.
PR9639.3.M195S65   1999
823—dc21   98-20792
CIP

Printed in the United States of America

First U.S. Edition

1 2 3 4 5 6 7 8 9 10

BOOK DESIGN BY CAROLINE CUNNINGHAM

www.williammorrow.com

for Petra

SPINNERS

One

FACTORY GIRLS

It was some time on Saturday night after work but before closing time down at the pub that Delia Chapman saw a spaceman. Well, that wasn't quite true. She saw ten of them. They stayed for about half an hour. And they took her on their vessel. They had silver suits and stainless-steel boots. The vessel was ultramodern and entirely impressive.

Delia had completed her third straight split shift in the smallgoods packing section at Borthwick's Freezing Works. Her body, therefore, was still at breakfast, her head at midnight, her internal clock as scrambled as an international flight attendant's, and although she was completely exhausted she was too confused to sleep. Still wearing her white factory clothes and gum boots, she left her family farmhouse on foot, bought a bag of hot chips at the Texacana Take-away Bar and wandered on the river road toward the highway leading out of town.

Who expected to see something like a spaceman in Opunake? Since Delia was unprepared for such a nationally significant experience she was, at best, clumsy in her observations. Two hours later she was able to report that she had had a nice time, seen some lights and a few shapes, and had received a dozen or so nonverbal commands. But beyond that, and when pressed for more explicit details, she could add only that her guests had been extremely polite throughout the incident and had treated her as if she were extremely important.

Only when the earliest and most amused reactions to Delia's claim had been voiced the next morning in the bakery, the betting shop and in the express lane at the New World supermarket, and only after people had purged their systems of terms like "silly bitch" and "stupid mole" and "total spinner," did any more open-minded appraisals begin.

Delia Chapman was sixteen years old. In her penultimate year of high school, she was one of a raft of light-headed young women to have taken summer jobs at Borthwick's. Requiring of its employees an inhuman rotation of day and night shifts as the seasonal kill reached its peak, it was known that 80 percent of the town's female population were being taxed to the point of near nervous collapse by the factory's unrelenting regimen. Delia's hysterical claim had therefore to be seen in the mitigating light of a record-breaking slaughter.

There were other theories why she would invent such a story. Delia Chapman was known to wear a Lakers NBA basketball cap wherever she went. Often she added to this a University of North Carolina T-shirt and imported sneakers, and with a Walkman player on her hip and gum in her mouth, she seemed to have become a living, breathing showcase of Americana. Could not the sighting of a spaceship, then, be viewed as just the next logical step in her metamorphosis into a Yank?

At the time of the visitation, put later by the town's resident policeman at approximately 9:20 P.M., most of the town was glued to a much-delayed broadcast of a rugby test match between

the All Blacks and England played at Twickenham: A bitter fight
for screening rights had left the area deprived of the live program
and those gathered in the public bar were tortured with the pent-
up passion of a day spent avoiding even a hint of the final result.

By 9:50, while the game was still in progress and the outcome
far from certain, Delia's life had been changed forever, but except
for the painfully dull boy at the Texacana who remembered that
Delia had bought one scoop of chips and declined vinegar, nobody could corroborate a single aspect of her strange story.

Harvey Watson, the local policeman, who also doubled as
Delia's weekend netball coach, used a gentle tone with her, more
akin to that of a priest hearing a confused confession, when he
drove her home an hour later that same night. Why was she telling him a story like this? Had she just seen a movie? Half of the
holiday movies and all the television shows nowadays were about
aliens; perhaps she'd been watching too many. He could tell right
away that she was in some kind of shock; she would feel better
if she told him the truth, he said. He could sense her internal
search for another story which could otherwise explain her tousled
hair, the bruises on her arm and the unfocused look in her eyes.
And yet something seemed to prevent her from finding an alternative explanation for her bewilderment. As her mouth opened,
her expression faltered. And when the words came out, they were
merely a reiteration.

"The ship was like um . . . kind of like a . . . ball of light, I
s'pose. A great ball of light. And it was sort of resting on a . . .
on a . . ."

"Yes, on a what?" he asked, craning forward. "Resting . . . ?"

"On a tripod."

Delia was not dressed for ambassadorial duties when she saw
the glorious visitation. How must she have seemed to these visitors, standing before them in her rubber boots, holding her bag
of chips? Her white uniform must have suggested that the human

race was a much more practical life-form than is really the case: a
pale breed, brown-haired, wide-eyed, uncertain, mute, compliant,
vegetarian and polite.

Delia represented billions that Saturday night.

. . . . .

Across town Delia's father sat in front of his television. Marty
Chapman understood that his daughter had gone to bed with the
same splitting headache which currently plagued him. His interest in sports, along with everything else, had dissipated in recent
years, and had wafted away like methylated spirits from an open
bottle. He watched a gardening program on channel two.

The propagation of dahlias in a hothouse environment was the
subject, and Marty watched it with a weary detachment, one leg
thrown over the arm of his chair while an unseen moth fought
for survival on the froth in his half-emptied glass of beer. On the
television an overweight English lady explained her blueprint for
cultivation. When the subject of the show switched and she began
to describe a pogrom for combating noxious weeds, he rose and
hit off the set. His house fell silent, and the fear of living his life
alone arose around him like a fog.

The underarms of his white shirt were stuck to his sides with
sweat, and his temples pounded. He decided to take an aspirin
and water with him up the stairs to his single widower's bed.

Before going up he went out onto his porch, which was bor-
dered with his late wife's flower pots, and urinated prolifically
onto the grass. His farm could use the liquid. In the distance
against the moonlight he saw his bony, dehydrated cattle on the
hills. In winter the lowland pastures flooded and were reduced to
vast mud flats thick with river silt; now, he had to contend with
an early drought and the hottest recorded Christmas season in
forty-two years. He did up his fly and rested against the door
frame, where his daughter's height was scratched in ten levels
from childhood to her maturity a year ago. He tugged his mud-

stiffened bootlaces free, wrenched the boots from his feet and left them outside to air.

At the top of the stairs Marty stopped outside his daughter's door. He did this mostly from habit. It was not unusual that he himself had banished her there, and so would stop to listen for sounds of rebellion from behind her closed door. His solution to the great mystery of solo parenthood was to be meticulous in his supervision of Delia. But where greater wisdom and experience would have permitted him to conserve his energies for those moments requiring his genuine concern, growing ignorance of his daughter's maturing nature kept him in a near-exhausted state of perpetual vigilance. Women had always been a mystery to him, and the taller his daughter became, the more restless and desperate grew his dilemma.

With his teeth Marty tore the aspirin from its foil wrapper, dropped it into the glass and watched its merciful white bubbles. He waited in pain as the tablet sank to the bottom and the glass clouded, foamed and then delivered the effervescing pill back to the surface, dwindled by then to a white medicinal fudge. He swallowed it quickly, and put his ear one last time to Delia's door. His full attention was given to this task, listening for sobs, or the radio, or tuneless singing to an unheard Walkman. He couldn't hear a thing. He knocked, and raised his voice, calling her name, but no reply came.

The often-repaired latch on Delia's door exploded into pieces.

The window was wide open. Marty Chapman could not tell how long his daughter had been gone. All women were beneath trust.

* * * * *

Phillip Sullivan had been driving all day as night fell. The trip had been uneventful, except for one incident in which he had overtaken a long line of slow-moving cars on the highway, blaring his horn to protest their sluggish pace. On a reckless passing maneuver, however, in which he overtook all eight vehicles in one sweep, he realized he had been honking at a funeral cortege. In his rearview mirror, he saw each mourner's car, headlights respectfully switched on, and when he passed the hearse at the front of the convoy, he received from the graven undertaker a look of such stinging rebuke that it seemed an augury from God. Phillip decided in that vertiginous moment that his life must change.

Sometimes a single look can be the seed of the most lasting changes; and, coming after a month of sobering events, this one motivated Phillip to conquer his fatal weakness—a rarely displayed but frightening temper—once and for all. Easing his foot off the accelerator, he resolved to renounce his hot-bloodedness and to replace with quiet patience the rage that had ruined his career.

The sun sank into the Tasman Sea to the west as he approached Taranaki. The conical peak of the mountain reared up 2,500 meters above the farmland, illuminated in passionate color in the long December evening. He stopped at a roadside picnic area in Patea, the heat bearable at last, ate a sandwich and watched the effect of nightfall upon the mountain. He consulted his AA map which lay on the passenger seat beside an extremely rare copy of Turgenev's *Sportsmen's Sketches*, and saw that he was almost at Hawera, only fifteen kilometers along the coast from Opunake.

Beyond Hawera Phillip passed a cut-rate traveling carnival, a motley collection of trucks and trailers set up in a paddock. The enterprise was tiny and ramshackle. He watched as a short man with bushy sideburns and tattooed arms carried antique segments of railway four or five times his own size. As a very small boy Phillip had ridden once on a ghost train; his mother, who believed in the bold confrontation of one's fears, had bought two tickets, hoping the ride might cure the boy of an infantile fear of the dark. But once inside the tunnels Phillip had fallen into a deep silence, not of terrified apoplexy, but of solid boredom.

Deafened by the screams of the other children Phillip could only observe the frailty of the illusions, the botched effects and the amateurism of the ride. The dangling skeletons were clearly made of plastic; the fires intended to burn sulfurously in the eyes of skulls were simply flashing red lights like those on the family stereo; and the one real human face, animating several characters by appearing on top of their shoulders in appropriate hats—a witch spitting curses, a rancid sailor swilling porter, a dungeoned loon in manacles pleading for royal justice—belonged to none other than the lady ticket seller, breathless and untalented, who audibly scampered around the outside of the structure plunging her variously costumed head into the darkness through a number of small holes in the wall. Crushed in tightly beside him, Phillip's mother believed that violent cathartic forces would cause her son to try to jump from the train in the darkness, so she gripped him firmly in a primitive initiation ceremony. But it wasn't fear. Phillip wanted to ponder the stupidity of others in peace. Why were people screaming? Did they see something that he could not? Was it possible—a question to fill a lifetime!—to experience a single event on many levels? It would take Phillip fifteen years to realize that a penchant for analysis was born in those dark passageways, that the ghost train experience had been his very first outing as a cynic, and that at the tender age of seven he had already been rerouted from daylight into those unlit catacombs which were the natural habitat of the intellectual.

Turning a corner, his car's headlights probing the intense darkness, he very nearly collided with a specter in white, standing in the middle of the road. It was a young woman, barely real, her arm raised to shield her eyes from his headlights. She made no attempt to move. Phillip's car had stopped only centimeters from her shins, his tires smoking, his heart in seizures. He sat forward in his seat to confirm the vision: shoulder-length brown hair, a white smock, bare legs channeled into white rubber boots. He gaped at her for several seconds before he got out of the car.

"I almost didn't see you." He caught his breath. "Are you . . . okay?"

Listlessly she looked back at him: wide-eyed, stoop-shouldered, bony, a reluctant beauty of about sixteen years. After several more moments, she asked in a voice barely above a whisper if he was going to the nearest town. She turned her face away and out of the light.

"I think the next town north is Opunake," he replied, studying her profile and noting a reluctance to talk.

"Oh," she said.

"Can I give you a ride there, then?"

She nodded after a second, ungrateful, strange.

"Do you know it?" he asked, losing patience.

She turned back to him. "What?"

"Do you know Opunake at all?"

Again, she nodded. "I live there."

These were the last words she spoke for the whole journey.

The road into the township swept in an arc between sea and mountain. Out of the corner of his eye, Phillip monitored the girl's small activities. Fingers, dirty under the nails, fidgeted constantly in her lap, knitted into a scrum one second and then climbed all over each other the next. She also smelled vaguely of mud, and of the country, of manure. The odor and her finger gymnastics combined to give him the impression that at any minute she would burst out with a sensational explanation of what had happened to her. But nothing came. Whatever her story, he was unworthy of it.

In an effort to fill the awkward silence, he gave an exact figure to the number of kilometers he had driven that day, and inquired about the state of the old Opunake Public Library, casually mentioning that he would soon mastermind its long-awaited re-opening. Reportedly, the building was no more than a shoebox, he told her, and from his correspondence he understood that for ten years it had sat across the road from the council chambers,

abandoned, serving only as a greenhouse for cobwebs, as a mansion for mice, as an aviary.

But nothing drew a response, or even a turn of her pretty head.

Almost for his own enjoyment, he then began to describe the long list of desirable new books, classics and translations, encyclopedias and reference magazines, which would be among his first orders to the national library service in Wellington. All were volumes he deemed essential to a half-decent library, and it would be his responsibility, he told her, to present the town of Opunake with a comprehensive list of titles and to place within each rural's grasp the treasure trove they had for so long been denied.

Delia Chapman formed no opinion at all of this young man as they drove in the shadow of the mountain, only that the antiseptic smell of his cologne reminded her of being at the dentist's.

, , , , ,

Opunake looked to be in the grip of a civil emergency. All along the main street cars were abandoned. The even rows of clapboard shops were dark. The streets were empty. Stretched between power poles overhead were the banners of tawdry Christmas lights, many bulbs defunct so that the festive message was impaired: Candles had no flame; MERRY XMAS no X; a Santa no head.

Phillip pulled up in front of the White Hart Hotel, the only vibrant feature of the town.

His passenger did not stir.

, , , , ,

Sergeant Harvey Watson was feeling distinctly under the weather. He had not been sleeping well since his vasectomy, and was not looking forward to this evening's public meeting. The townspeople, bloated and sunburned, were still gathered in the public bar of the White Hart Hotel after the disastrous rugby test.

The sergeant had anticipated a great victory and had seen in it an opportunity to speak to a captive and good-tempered audience. This wish had not been granted. After the All Blacks' shock defeat, the crowd was in a murderous mood. Incensed by the bunglings of the French referee, they had no tolerance for further bad news of an official nature. Harvey would need to be very forthright in such a climate of dismay, and he longed to be at home with his wife, his police hat hanging on the back of the door, secure in his bed and succumbing to the devastations of sleep.

He mingled with the more irascible patrons at the bar, shaking hands, consoling the most depressed sports fans and reforging old alliances like a seasoned politician, turning down offers of a drink and instead whipping up a constituency of goodwill before his speech. He concealed his sleeplessness well, as he concealed all details pertaining to his recent surgery. In a town such as this, the notion of a vasectomy was still considered avant-garde. Indeed, he had made sure that it be conducted out of town, and in utmost secrecy. It had taken only half an hour, and apart from a small yet distressing deposit of blood the next morning in his abundant white underwear, his routine had been otherwise undisturbed. As a peacekeeper in a small town, Watson knew very well how people expanded personal peculiarities into grounds for vicious prejudice. So it was doubly important that as the town's sole police officer he be far above rumor and dissent.

"Now let me have your attention," he said, and the crowd in the bar gradually fell silent.

"I know you're all wondering why I've called this public meeting. I can now tell you. As you know, we've had a lot of problems in trying to slow down highway traffic coming around the mountain on the way to New Plymouth. Traditionally these drivers, many of them businessmen, have had no respect for people who live in a small town such as this, and for a long time I have made it my personal responsibility to address the problem by sitting out in my car for many long hours on the edge of town with radar facilities. Unfortunately, I've only ever had limited success. Smart-ass collaborators coming the other way have tended to alert oncoming traffic farther down the road to my presence and I've largely failed to find a vantage point where I can set up my equipment and remain unseen. Now, from Wellington, I have received news that . . ." and here he drew out an impressive sheath of government papers and raised them into the air. "I have been advised that we are earmarked for a speed camera."

There was a unanimous look of incomprehension around the room. Watson continued his prolepsis.

"Now for those of you who don't know, these speed cameras take high-quality night and day photographs of speed-limit violators, regardless of who they are. One of these cameras will initially be placed on the southern highway out of town for a trial period of a year. Now I know that up till now I have been lenient on local residents in favor of pursuing the out-of-town freak who shoots through here willy-nilly, but with this speed camera we enter a new era of nondiscrimination."

Again the sergeant's statement seemed to have no impact whatsoever. The wall of somber faces looked at him as if he were a complete stranger—though as the town's only netball coach he was responsible for the training and general fitness of many of their daughters.

"And so I have called you all together to alert you to this fact, because I don't want you coming back to me at some later stage with your speeding tickets, asking for them to be torn up. I won't be able to do that. Once the camera has furtively taken your picture, there is nothing on heaven or earth that can be done. Everything from the camera will be processed and sent to Wellington. Times have changed."

After a final silence, the first objection was voiced. Whittaker, the barber and tobacconist, asked whether Wellington could also process a quick clout by a sledgehammer in the middle of the night. Watson replied that reckless destruction of police property was a criminal offense and anyone with that sort of impulse should consider the consequences.

At that point a tide of pent-up disgust with this and a thousand other perceived invasions of the townspeople's privacy erupted across the bar, threatening a repeat of the riots of nine years earlier when two of the four assembly lines at the freezing works had been shut down in defiance of the union. The interior of the White Hart Hotel had been largely demolished on that occasion and much of the mahogany decor had never regained its former glory. Even the once twelve-pointed antler horns above the bar were reduced to a series of pathetic stumps. It was, in a way, the last act of the union before its deregulation.

But Watson was already picking up his hat and making his way toward the side door which led to the car park. At the door he stopped and turned, assured of his escape route. He raised both hands.

"Now settle down. If you just lay off the gas, none of you will have anything to worry about. The only people who need to be concerned about this are the lawbreakers."

With that, he slipped out and shut the door behind him. The sound of public rancor became a soft rumble. When he reached his patrol car, the only word he articulated was "Fuck." Someone had slashed his front-right tire.

The gentle tap on his shoulder from behind made the sergeant jump out of his skin.

, , , , ,

Phillip Sullivan led Sergeant Watson around to his Ford out on the main street. When they got to his vehicle, Phillip had to explain that the young woman he'd described was no longer in his car.

"She was here a minute ago," he protested as both heads peered into the car's interior.

"And you say you didn't get her name?"

"No."

"Then maybe I'd better get yours. Don't you reckon?"

Watson fixed a firm but tired look on the stranger. He was in no mood for a midnight calamity. Every cell in his body appealed to him for sleep, and this woolly story of a mercy dash with an unnamed woman was a hideous substitute. The matter of his own slashed tire was far more pressing, as was the first indication of an unpopularity he could professionally ill afford.

"All right, where do you think she went?"

"I don't know," said Phillip.

"You don't know?"

"No."

Phillip looked down the road to where it disappeared into darkness.

, , , ,

At the crowded bar, Delia quickly found a drink in her hand, thanks to the generosity of the pub owner's wife, Lucille, who, having no daughters of her own, was eternally patient with the sentimental dilemmas of young women.

By this time, the pub's patrons had split up into small groups around the room, beginning at the back with the remote farmers who drove massive V-8 Holden Commodores and were therefore the most threatened by the camera proposal, and continuing in an arc of diminishing resentment to the older women at the bar who were mostly members of the local bowling club and rarely drove at all, and never with any haste.

"Are you all right there, Delia, love? You look a bit pasty. Get that drink down you, put a bit of color back in your cheeks." Lucille often ignored the underage drinking laws, exercising her own judgment.

"Ta." Delia raised the glass. No sooner had it touched her lips than two huge young men flanked her on either side and a third draped his head over her left shoulder.

"Oi," said one.

"Oi oi," said another.

"Oi oi oi," completed the third.

With rehearsed precision three empty beer glasses struck the bar top at the same moment, their owners so indivisible from each other that the young men's heads appeared to sprout from the same body—a three-headed six-armed beer-drinking Medusa, and the bane of all of Opunake's young women. Although they behaved like teenagers, they were, in fact, well over thirty, their common mix of buoyancy and cultivated stupidity keeping them in a state of perpetual juvenility.

"Deeeee . . ." began one, as if he were in a choir.

". . . eeee . . ." sang the second.

". . . lliiiaaa!" sang the third.

The weight of the three hefty forearms fell across her shoulders, and forced her to lean forward over the bar. She shut her eyes.

It was this precise kind of boozy machismo that made her loathe being a teenager. Since the onset of puberty, she had tried to delay her own flowering by cutting her hair short, wearing shapeless clothes, and developing a stooped and slouching walk to fend off the slavish eyes of local boys. Yet despite her best efforts, these tactics backfired on her. The only effect of this camouflage was to throw her startling qualities into greater relief, and in the fever of acquisition created by all things unattainable they drove her price higher still.

"Leave her alone, you boys!" shouted the pub owner's wife. "I'm serious. Leave her alone. Go on. Now!"

Lucille, heeded by everybody and everything, guided Delia to the quiet end of the bar as the young men departed.

Delia was never going to marry either, never. Fortunately, she had been spared the humiliation of having a sexual appetite. Sex, in her mind, would be like letting an eel from the river take liberties with you: unthinkable. No matter how long the queue of hopefuls or how vicious the slander that she was a snotty bitch who had her legs welded together, she was an implacable iron maiden. And everything had been running to plan, sexually speaking, until her impulse to go and get a bag of chips just a few hours before.

"Where have you been? Are you all right?" Lucille asked.

"Mmm."

"You've got marks all over your clothes. Smells like some sort of manure."

"I just slipped over. I think I did. I'm all right. Thanks. I'm okay."

When Sergeant Harvey Watson reentered with Phillip Sullivan beside him, silence scattered like birdseed across the bar, giving rise to a moment's confusion. Phillip was the first to spy Delia in the corner, her back turned on them, drinking quietly on her own. Without a word Watson crossed the floor with official haste and guided her back through the crowd to exit through the side door.

The locals, who had been holding their breath, erupted into a renewed flurry of consultation and discord as the door closed.

, , , , ,

In order to satisfy his curiosity about the girl, Phillip had offered to change Watson's tire, while the officer talked to Delia under the discreet light of a streetlamp some distance away.

Phillip jacked up the patrol car until the lacerated tire lifted off the ground. When he looked over, he saw that Delia was now speaking, and Watson seemed to be accepting silently whatever was being said to him. His hands never left his hips, and his head turned only occasionally, to check that no one was secretly creeping up on them.

Phillip pulled the wheel from its hub and placed the four chrome nuts in the hubcap. He went to the trunk to find the spare tire.

Watson was shaking his head now, scratching behind his ear and displaying signs of irritation at what he was being told. He turned from Delia, walked three paces away and then returned to ask a new question. She lit a cigarette and Phillip could not decide whether she was deeply upset or utterly unaffected by the conversation.

Phillip finished the job, fastened the last nut tightly, replaced the hubcap. He wiped his hands and made a polite slow movement toward the two of them, and so heard the officer admonishing, "Now look, Delia, that's enough of this nonsense. I want you to . . . I want you, listen to me, Jesus . . ." The officer's well-lit face was showing signs of high color, while Delia's was in strict shadow, her mood still indiscernible.

Watson came over to Phillip.

"You finished? Thanks a lot. Well look, I'll, ah . . . I'll get her home."

Phillip nodded and looked at Delia. She kept her back turned, puffing on a cigarette in the cone of light from the streetlamp. He was about to step forward to say good-bye to her, his weight shifting to his toes, when the sergeant's hand came down heavily on his shoulder. Watson was shaking his head with such potent authority that Phillip nodded and at once walked back to his car, where he turned the key, revved the engine to a fever pitch and pulled out onto the road.

Back under the streetlamp, the sergeant watched the car move into darkness, sighing heavily. Then and there he made a vow to himself never to mention a word of what he'd been told to another human soul—with the exception of his wife, with whom he shared everything.

"Okay, let's go over this again, Delia. From the beginning. And for God's sake, this time, please, please try and be a bit serious."

. . . . .

In his living room, Opunake's mayor, Jim Sullivan, was organizing his scrapbook of recent municipal celebrations when his wife called out to him that his nephew had arrived and was waiting out on the porch.

He went to the screen door carrying a glue pot, and stood looking at the boy through the mesh. A cloud of moths almost obscured the unadmitted visitor.

Sullivan had been dreading Phillip's arrival for some hours, and his nephew's lateness further disinclined him to invite him indoors. For two years, reports had filtered back to the mayor of the young man's mediocre military record. Now, with Phillip's most recent military disgrace still large in Sullivan's mind, a dishonorable discharge as a result of a kitchen brawl in which one man was maimed, he could feign no interest at all in the boy. Only as a favor to his dear sister had he agreed to find a place for his nephew "somewhere on the municipal payroll" and so had conjured up for him a small and meaningless job, an extension of Phillip's work in the army: the reopening and running of Opunake's tiny library. In a town where few people read anything more serious than the Sunday tabloids or pulp romances, the new job could hardly be more irrelevant.

"You're here, then."

"Uncle Jim."

Sullivan nodded, keeping his reception cool. "Well, Flo has sorted out some bedding in the trailer around the back. We've put the power on. It should do you for a while, until you find a place of your own. We'll talk in the morning. At least you found your way here. Everything all right?"

"Fine. I won't come in."

"How's that sister of mine?"

"Fine."

The mayor explored the boy's face for a family likeness. He saw some hope in the jawline, a familial hawkishness, a slightly beaked nose: All the rest derived from that gutless interloper who was Phillip's father, and the overall effect was unlikable. The young man had been a kid the last time Sullivan had seen him, and even then was patently not a team player. A stand-backish child with a marshmallow handshake; the army had been an appalling choice. Sullivan could imagine the scenario: a corner-bunk kid from day one, unable to forge comradeship, clean and humorless, a drill-sergeant favorite. Every barrack sought a butt for its pranks, and Jim Sullivan did not need to be told how his nephew had been goaded and harangued and steered, hour by hour—God help the poor bastard—toward a Discharge for Extreme Violence Against a Fellow Soldier, all over the nonissue of a dispute over the seating plan in the mess hall: It need only be noted that the boy's character was flawed from the first. He had not lived up to the promise of that dynastic jawline.

"All right then. The trailer's around the back. I'll jack up a council flat for ya maybe, but that should do for now."

Phillip nodded and stepped back into the darkness with his bag, leaving the screen empty but for the moths.

The concept of collage had recently impressed itself upon the mayor, and it was with this in mind that he returned to his scrapbook, not stopping to consider that his nephew might require a hot drink or food after his long journey.

The trailer would suffice for a while. It stood in a far corner of the property under a plum tree, wheel-less, a relic set up on concrete blocks, an early statement from the mayor that Phillip was being punished. Phillip smiled and found the knob, opened the rusty refrigerator-sized door, and stepped inside to a dank aroma of mildew and rot. He pulled his sleeping bag out of its sack at once, not wishing to check his surroundings, and lay down on the narrow and armpit-scented berth in the dark, his nose pressed into the rancid potpourri of a degenerating mattress. A mosquito bit him on the arm in the dark before audibly escaping, and the area quickly swelled; but a quarter hour later, and still deep in dislocated thought, Phillip had the great satisfaction of terminating the same buzzing insect, blindly mashing it dead on his forearm: It gave up the stolen blood at once, unusable and contaminated now, his own corpuscles mixed with those drawn from a dog's ass, no doubt, but back at least where they belonged.

, , , , ,

The sergeant drove Delia home. His patrol car bucked as it shot off the road onto the unpaved drive that led up to a simple white wooden farmhouse, half concealed from view by pohutukawa trees.

Marty Chapman was standing on the porch as the car arrived, and Harvey Watson again had to summon his energies, marshal his wits and further postpone his entry into the delicious haven of sleep.

Delia Chapman walked straight past her father and went inside. The two men could argue the details. Watson did his best to defuse the tension, but he knew that with Marty Chapman one was always dealing with the unknown. He tried taking a tangent, and discussed the upcoming netball game against an invitation team of female schoolteachers from Hawera:

"Delia remains the best goal-shoot in the entire district."

But Marty wanted an explanation. Why was his daughter being delivered home in a police car? What the hell had she done now?

The sergeant started to explain that he had merely passed Delia on the road and thought it unsafe for her to be out walking so late. Certainly he had no official complaint. And there was no cause for alarm of any kind. Furthermore, it was getting late and—as he realized he'd been saying all night—it was time everyone went to bed.

When Marty Chapman received this information silently and declared with a fixed expression that he needed no more excuses, Watson returned to his car. The sergeant did not walk away with an easy conscience, however, and thought that whatever happened in the ensuing minutes between Marty and Delia under the guise of disciplinary action had better be within the strictest bounds of the law and in keeping with higher moral principles. This consideration was not without basis. On two occasions in the past year, he had noticed that his prized goal-shoot had

bruises on her arms and legs, and his suspicions as to their origin
needed no further fuel. He was sworn to protect the innocent,
and even if his jurisdiction was questionable once the front door
was closed, he would not hesitate to invade the delicate chemistry
of a family unit to exercise his authority. From experience, he
knew that evenings of high drama like this seldom ended with
the departure of the police.

Watson left the house and headed home just below legal speed.

, , , , ,

Marty Chapman had had enough. He sat in his downstairs
armchair with the window open, wearing only his pajama pants.
He was staring at the blank TV screen and wondering what next
to do. Despite the aspirin, his headache had intensified. Delia
was up in her room and her door with the broken lock was closed.

With headphones over her ears, Delia listened to a tape on her
Walkman. Her walls were covered with posters of the New
Zealand netball team in action over a victorious fifteen-year period, and her own awards, medals, ribbons and citations were
pinned in a neat display over her bed. It was a childish collage
which she had already outgrown but was still some months away
from taking down. When the tape finished, she took off the headphones but did not turn the light off or lie down on the bed.
Instead, she took off her soiled clothes which really did smell of
dung, went to the wardrobe and selected a dress which she'd not
worn for several months. She put it on and looked at herself in
the mirror. As she sat down, gazing at her reflection, it was as if
she were waiting for someone, or something, and only the sound
of their arrival would break her trance. And then someone did
arrive.

The already broken latch permitted her father to enter with ease.

"So what's all this about?" He was strained by humiliation and
his own irrelevance. He was capable only of hearing words which
would further justify his anger.

"Harvey gave me a lift," she said.

"Where were you?"

Then she told him about the first man, the stranger. A bag of chips. The highway. Marty was unhappy: All this was no excuse for being out. He wanted to know the name of the young man, but she didn't have a name for him. She was old enough to take care of herself, she argued. Eventually he left the room and she lay on the bed in her summer dress, legs curled up, looking at the ceiling which kept from her the multitudes of quietly raging galaxies beyond.

. . . . .

Harvey Watson's careful and near-silent glide into his garage was to no avail. His wife had been awakened an hour earlier by the erratic alarm on their replica Queen Anne carriage clock. When Watson crept into their bedroom, naked and quiet as a church mouse, she was already resting on one elbow and waiting for him.

He sat on the edge of the bed, disconsolate, and rewound the clock. He would have to be up again in four hours. His eyes were sore and his back ached. He was in no mood to talk.

"How did it go?"

"Fine. A few grumbles. Mainly fine."

"Tell me about it, then. Who was there? What happened?"

"It was fine. Over in ten minutes."

"Then why are you so late?"

Watson sighed from deep within himself. Without even resetting the alarm he put down the clock and jettisoned his last hopes for the simple peace of his bed.

But perhaps it was best. Margaret, his sweetheart, his wife and sole confidante of eight years, a big-city girl and divorced mother of two before meeting her "big old cop," was the only one capable of comforting him in times of real trial. Being a one-man police force was a lonely profession, and loneliness could easily father despair.

"If I tell you something, you have to swear to keep this strictly to yourself. It's police business. Okay?"

In the half-light his wife did not bat an eyelid. For eight years he had prefaced every bedtime conversation with such a request, and for eight years she had stared innocently back at him, no such promise ever coming. It was a historical grievance: She refused to have her bedroom shrunk to a witness box, where nightly she would have to swear some oath to her own husband! Where was basic trust? When would he realize that such insults kept them from finding true sincerity in their marriage?

For his part, Watson knew very well the strengths and weaknesses of the woman who had delayed marrying him for four years out of a common distaste for policemen. He knew that the life she had inherited was a largely monotonous one compared to his own incident-filled career, and that in an effort to keep her brain from atrophying and to exercise daily her prodigious memory, she had compensated for her lack of vocation by trading with others in the most virulent gossip. He knew all of this, yet he continued to reveal to her the most confidential aspects of his work. It was, in effect, a belated reward for the sacrifices she had agreed to make in marrying him.

"Jim Sullivan's nephew, Phillip or something, who is apparently going to reopen the old public library or something, drove into town a couple of hours ago . . . with Marty Chapman's girl, Delia."

"Delia?"

"Showed up at the pub. You're not going to believe this."

"What?"

"She was in a bit of a state. Been found by Jim's nephew wandering out on the highway south of town in a daze apparently."

"What had happened?"

"I dunno."

"Did you talk to Delia?"

"Mmm."

"What did she say?"

"I blame that father of hers."

"Why?"

"He's a psychopath, that's why. She's terrified of him. No wonder the girl has the odd problem."

"Harvey? What is it?"

"I talked to her."

"Yes."

"I . . ." he said. "She . . ."

"What happened?!"

"She said . . ."

"For God's sake, Harvey!"

"Out there in a field . . . Look, I've gotta get to sleep. I've gotta get up again in four hours!"

"Something happened out in a field?"

"Let's forget it. She'd had some sort of fall or something, I'm sure of it."

"What did she tell you?"

"She just said she'd seen a spaceship out there in the field and one of the blokes got off it and took her on board or something for half an hour or so and then let her go."

"What?"

"She's gotta play netball for me next Saturday. I don't want this to get out. Oh . . . and I turned the oven off, I can't eat those chips tonight."

"A what? A . . . spaceship?" Her laughter was loud.

"Margaret, it could have been anything. It could have been a lot of things. She's not a liar. And she's not a lunatic."

"But hang on, you said she was taken on board!"

"Anyway, the last thing I need is this getting out. She's a good girl. Nicest girl on the team."

Margaret lay back, her hand on Watson's shoulder. "She's just having you on, Harvey! She's pulling your leg, darling."

"I don't want anyone to know. All right, Margaret? I don't

care if there are a hundred fucking spaceships straight from Mars landing out there right now, Delia's had a hard enough time with that father of hers."

"Did you tell him about it?" She laughed again.

"Of course not. In a day she'll have forgotten all about it."

"She must have been drunk."

"She was sober and deadly serious. Everything I said to talk her out of it, she'd just say, 'I don't care if you don't believe me.' "

"She's mad, just like her mother, God rest her soul. That whole family, I'm telling you. There's something going on out on that farm. Young girls don't start saying this sort of thing without reason, Harvey."

Watson got into bed. Margaret started kissing him. Soon he responded with ancient determination, drew himself on top of her and started to move in slow motion, until she stopped him with a sweet kiss on his lips and pulled out four silk scarves from under the pillow.

"Oh, not now, Margaret," said Watson, consulting the Queen Anne carriage clock. "Oh, please. It's nearly, Jesus, look . . . two in the morning. I haven't slept in weeks."

"All right," she whispered seductively. "I'll be easy on you. I'll let you tie them loosely."

He paused, arrested and imprisoned in a life of service. With his big hands, he took the silky cords from his wife, and in a patient, loving regimen began to fasten one scarf to each corner of their marriage bed.

Two

. . . .

SEX

In the first electric pulse of activity on Sunday morning, the lights simultaneously came on in the Church of Our Lady of Perpetual Succor and the tobacconist's shop across the street. As Agnes Whittaker set the morning's tabloid billboard beside the barber pole, she looked up, rubbed sleep from her eyes and saw the first milk tanker lumbering out of town, belching black diesel. The putrid smell mingled with the odor of fried bacon from the cafeteria of the Sahara Desert Motor Inn one block behind her. She retreated inside, repulsed by aromas, and found that her husband was once again breaking the trading laws by cutting the priest's hair on a Sunday.

For over twenty-five years the single barber's chair had sat at the back of the tobacconist's shop, and all that time, and with minimal skill, Whittaker had persevered in his secondary function as barber. But with the recent opening in town of a fully equipped and modern hair salon, advertising the delirious slogan "Hair Concepts" and providing free hand moisturizer for even its male clients—an utterly unforeseeable advance—Whittaker had no option but to face the violent facts of his obsolescence. It also left him in no position to turn down the priest's request for a haircut once every quarter before Sunday Mass, as any haircutting business at all was a miracle.

Father James O'Brien's graying locks fell in drifts onto the checkered linoleum with the autumnal splendor of a man whose life was spent in grace. As a sense of his skull reemerged for the first time in months, the man of prayer studied an out-of-date newspaper.

"You didn't come to the meeting last night, Father?" Whittaker asked, quickly reproducing his trademark haircut, a perfect facsimile of every one he had ever given.

"I hope I didn't miss anything." O'Brien's voice was rich and dignified.

"Oh, just another invasion into our way of life by government forces."

"I s'pose so," said the priest, turning to the sports section, pausing for a second before dispensing his next comment. "It does seem as though a rather specious and second-rate rule of accountancy, namely that of showing a profit, has overtaken yet another sacred area of our nation's life."

The barber nodded as he began on the back of the priest's head, where his scissors, now out of sight, rapidly snipped pure air to create the illusion of professionalism. For several years Whittaker had noticed that the most memorable elements of their Sunday-morning conversations had a remarkable habit of reappearing a few hours later in the Sunday sermon. That he should provide the priest with an opportunity to rehearse the dispensation of God's wisdom was an honor he did not take lightly. The barber laughed. "You can say that again, Father."

"I just might." O'Brien smiled at his own reflection in the mirror.

Whittaker left the haircut for a moment, and in his capacity as tobacconist sold a tabloid newspaper and a pack of Horizon cigarettes to a customer at the front counter. While selling a paper to a meat worker, he first heard the story which was to occupy his customers for many months to come. The news of Delia's sighting had traveled to his door by an impressive skein of connections, and made him chuckle in disbelief. Silly bitch.

An hour before dawn, at 6:15 A.M., it had first entered the public domain when the milkman, making his gridlike deliveries through the streets, encountered the sergeant's wife at her gate. A quick conversation, as she took her bottles, insured the story's rapid proliferation.

By 7:26 A.M., the contagion had spread. The milkman moved from door to door like a pollinating bee among flowers. From the Delaneys to the Rudjovics he went. The Clapcotts received a record twelve liters and so heard the story at their threshold.

By 8 A.M., a good portion of the southwestern corner of Opunake, from Simon Street to the south and Hubbard Place to the east, was bubbling with derision. Had the story risen from among the ranks of the youngest children, it could have been stopped quickly with a parental slap of admonishment. But this story was percolating down from the adults. The police had been alerted, and police matters were primarily of adult interest. The transmission of Delia's story could not be stemmed.

Churchgoers were heading for the church by 8:15. This was when young Lucinda Evans, an eccentric and rather overweight apprentice of the black arts, who worked on the same assembly line as Delia Chapman at Borthwick's Freezing Works, grasped the news and took it northward.

To make the 8:25 whistle, a rendezvous she seldom achieved, Lucinda's path to work led her through the landscaped court of the state housing project on Harrison Street, a cluster of three-story apartment blocks surrounding a concrete square. She was spotted at once by her colleague Deborah Kerr, who was looking out of the window while brushing her teeth just as Lucinda passed.

"Hey, Cinda!" Deborah shouted down, her froth-filled mouth dribbling suds.

Lucinda stopped, looked up, waved. She was already dressed in her factory whites. "Hey!" she called, breathless.

"What's going on?" Deborah often received news from her co-worker in this manner and at this hour, which always annoyed the neighbors, especially on a Sunday.

"Delia Chapman's seen a spaceman!" Lucinda announced.

"What?" Deborah doubted her own ears.

"Delia said she saw a spaceman!"

A head popped out from the third-story window opposite. "Keep the bloody noise down will ya?" It was old Percy in his undershirt, armpit hair like twin bushes of barley.

"You keep it down," returned Lucinda, irritated by the protest.

Deborah Kerr wanted an immediate explanation. "She said she saw what?"

"A spaceman. She reported it to Harvey. Last night."

"Who did?" It was another voice, from the adjoining block, wanting details.

"Delia Chapman," hailed Lucinda. "Told the cops." Everyone used the word cops in the plural, knowing very well it meant only Harvey.

"You're fuckin' joking!"

"Am not. Said she saw ten of them."

"She fuckin' didn't!" yelled Deborah Kerr, stunned, her toothbrush now in storage in her cheek.

"That's it!" Percy had his shirt on now. "You stay where you are. I'm coming down. Foulmouthed little so-and-so."

"Fuck off," Lucinda responded, augmenting the phrase with two fingers.

Percy was on his way down as Lucinda repeated all the information from the beginning, to a growing gallery of people at their windows.

"Talk to you at work," finished Deborah, closing the window as Percy emerged onto the forecourt, tottering with age.

"Right," said Lucinda, and quickly outran the old coot.

Finally the news had reached barber Whittaker, who, upon hearing it and finding it inconsistent with traditional values, linked it immediately in his mind, if somewhat obscurely, with the fabulous advent of hand moisturizers. He returned to Father O'Brien to confess the outlandishness.

The priest nodded, his shiny temples now exposed, not as shocked as Whittaker expected him to be. In fact, the priest, nodding knowingly, believed that this sort of thing should be expected nowadays. Visions of spacemen, in epidemic revival, were the great fin de siècle fantasy, he said, the antebellum delusion. But the cause was simple, almost banal—namely, a failure of the imagination to deal with the weight of spiritual questions posed by a new century. At such a definitive time in history, he reasoned, our ancient need to talk to God had reasserted itself. However, that primal impulse to look toward the heavens for answers was warped by the technological age into this present phenomenon: God was displaced by a spaceman.

The priest liked this image very much, but as he looked up to view his reflection in the mirror his expression clouded. Not only had the haircut aged him greatly, but without his collar he no longer looked like a priest at all.

. . . . .

In the cafeteria of the Sahara Desert Motor Inn, and distant from all this, Phillip ate fried eggs. Around him other customers read the Sunday papers with quiet zeal amid the pervasive smell of fried bacon.

From his table in the corner he could read the headlines, and gleaned a complex picture of the universe. A two-headed cow born in Hawera: A photograph showed twin heads. An elderly woman jumped five stories from a burning building: SURVIVED was the headline. Thieves had broken into a mansion last night in the Bay of Islands and made off with four guard dogs. Somewhere else a drunk fell into the bear cage at a zoo: GRIZZLY NIGHT WITH YOGI, the front page proclaimed. It could have read: "Unappetizing." The proprietor of the motor inn came over with a jug of boiling water and refilled Phillip's metal teapot; he winked then moved to the next table.

In Phillip's pocket rested the key to the Opunake Public Library. He had driven past it twenty minutes earlier. It was a small wooden building isolated on a lawn, across the road from the council chambers and beside the dental clinic. It was in need of paint and, by his uncle's account, of a new tin roof before the rain came. Against all expectations, Phillip was hoping to make a success of his job. He had already been up for two hours, dressing with an infantryman's precision in the cramped trailer behind his uncle's house. Keen to make a favorable impression, he did not want to be late on his first morning, even if it was Sunday.

Leaving his breakfast half eaten, he walked to work.

, , , ,

The sudden ventilation from the open door disrupted years of dust; the shaft of light split the interior of the old library with a solid celestial beam. Moving through the decrepit odor of dried book bindings, Phillip threw open the rotten curtains, some of which tore off in his hand. Daylight filled the room. It was an alarming sight. Because of the leaky roof, damp and mildew had ruined a full third of the books. The worst affected had been alternately rained on, dried out in summer, then rained on again, and many were now swollen to twice their original size: Their cardboard covers had begun to buckle and contort, and at random a book had been forced forward by its swelling neighbors. This movement, which had taken a decade, was an incalculably slow reversal of the action which had so casually shelved them all those years before. Phillip ran his hand along their spines, forcing the rogue books back into alignment, canceling the years of excruciating struggle. It was his first act of librarianship.

Dust as fine as talcum powder settled on his lungs, and his coughs stirred up miniature typhoons. He could not raise the sash window. Needing a heavy object to assist him, he used *Jude the Obscure*. With a solid thump, which caused the book to disintegrate in his hand, he forced the window open, and the draft pulled flowing rivers of dust out into the fresh air. As visibility improved, he gained a full impression of the job ahead of him.

The shrunken skeleton of a dead cat lay on the Issues desk. Sickened, it had come here to die. Its last act had been to climb up onto the sheet of glass covering the tabletop. Phillip wrapped the desiccated corpse in old newspapers and dropped it into the litter bin outside. He found a molting broom with only half its bristles left, and began to sweep the room. A catalog of alternative uses for an abandoned public library quickly revealed itself.

A mausoleum for pets aside, the broken window in the stack room had been a point of entry for numerous illicit lovers; an old rug was spread on the floor beside a melted candle, burned matches, stubbed-out cigarettes; and dozens of condom wrappers had drifted into a corner. He wondered what scandals were concealed here: crimes of youth, gender, adultery, or perhaps all three. As he studied the evidence, he drew rapid conclusions. In another corner a *Playboy* magazine still lay open, marking some youth's solitary erotic education. And on the floor of the entranceway, inscribed in chalk, was an inverted pentagram: What better place in a small town to summon spooks, and so, in clandestine séances, drive terror into young hearts? With his foot he quickly erased the devil's symbol.

Clearly, the library had not been abandoned at all. Armies of misfits had turned this into a parlor of nefarious pleasures, and had come and gone through a broken window, leaving only a vague forensic record. He brushed the floor clean, abruptly ending an era. And then among the debris he found an old OPEN sign. He dusted it with his sleeve, set it in the window, and with no further ceremony opened the small library for proper business.

, , , , ,

As she walked to work, once again in her gum boots and white overcoat, Delia Chapman looked up suddenly, having sensed a disturbance in the air above her. The cobalt-blue sky was momentarily empty, but as she waited one more second her premonition was satisfied.

Just above her head, a jet fighter no sooner appeared than it disappeared, flying so low it seemed to endanger the flagpole on the municipal clock tower. As it scorched across the sky, its flight path made the aircraft seem immense and fleeting. Only several seconds after the plane had gone did the thunder from its engines boom and rattle windows. By the time all other onlookers stopped and looked up, the craft was almost in another province. Delia felt she must have been alone in seeing it. She lit a cigarette and walked toward the freezing works. Her route took her past the Mobil petrol station.

, , , , ,

Flanked by petrol pumps, Max Hardy reprimanded his only mechanic and pump attendant, Gilbert Haines, for incompetence.

"I'm just going over some of the repair jobs you've done, and you've undercharged a hundred and fifty dollars."

Gilbert was filling a car with petrol from emergency stocks while Max waved old invoices at him. Gilbert was small, stunted, with very thin limbs. He was cheerful but routinely dirty. A human coat hanger for soiled laundry, he won admiration and engendered disdain in equal measure and often at the same time. The smile plastered on his face since birth was all that stopped him from falling into an abyss of loneliness. He made women uneasy: This was his fatal flaw. His sensitivity made him a candidate for love, but it was not sufficient in itself to overcome the opposing emotions he inspired: those of sympathy and guilt.

Gilbert was profoundly distracted by Delia as she walked by, a pristine vision in white. Blood raced to his empty soul.

His obsession with this girl was growing far beyond his control. Straining inside him like a starved beast was a passion which demanded to be fed. He knew, as most unrequited lovers do, that it wouldn't be long now until the beast, needing sustenance, would turn upon its master.

He had been in love with Delia Chapman ever since he had seen her hitting a shuttlecock in the high school gymnasium when she was barely thirteen, on tiptoe, biting her tongue. Two years older than Delia, he had ejected himself from school at fifteen to train as a mechanic. Now grease was so ingrained into his thin fingers they had become reptilian.

"Undercharged?"

"Gilbert!"

"Mmm?"

"Are you listening to me? I said you've undercharged this customer!"

"Be back in a second."

Max was incredulous.

Leaving the pump nozzle in the car, Gilbert crossed the road and hurried after Delia.

She stopped for him. "Hi," she said.

"What's going on? Delia? I need to talk to you. What happened last night? What did you tell Sergeant Watson?"

She was amazed that he could know about it. Gilbert quickly told her that most of the town was already fully briefed. She hurried away impatiently. He ran to intercept her.

"Delia? Please—"

He stopped several paces in front of her.

"Delia? Dee-lia!"

He had planted his heels, waiting for his grandstanding to take effect, but she simply stepped around him and disappeared down the street as he watched, leaving him to consider the small impression he had made, and had always made, in her life. And inside his chest, the starving beast licked again at his livid heart, sniffed with hot breath and wet muzzle, bared its fangs and in a second tore off a chunk of his heart. Pain. For the first time, Gilbert Haines felt the misery and full force of unreciprocated passion.

Max grabbed his arm. "What's the matter? Don't run away when I'm talking to you, okay?!"

Gilbert was mesmerized.

"Gilbert? Are you all right? Your mind isn't on the job at all these days. You've undercharged this customer a hundred and fifty dollars. Stop being so fucking generous at my expense, okay? Well, what have you got to say?"

Gilbert apologized. "I'll be okay."

Max fixed a look of wisdom upon him. "If you've got women problems, leave them at home. That's all there is to it."

Gilbert nodded. But what Max said next, and with brutal nonchalance, made him fully conscious, and he stared at his employer with new respect. "For example, you wouldn't know to look at me, but Jenny left me yesterday . . . twenty-seven years . . . over . . . she just shot through. And I bet you didn't notice a thing, did you?"

It was true. Max turned and walked away in utterly undiscernible pain.

. . . . .

The after-hours return box had become a nest for brown mice. Phillip was cleaning it out when Delia Chapman walked up to him and, without stopping or catching his eye, dropped a book into the box.

She was wearing the same clothes as on the previous night,

with one exception. Around her neck was a surgical-style hygiene mask.

He was unable to speak. Only when she was rounding the corner five meters away did ten or more questions spring to mind.

He put his hand into the return box and drew out the book. It was a manual: *Teach Yourself to Read*. A glance at the flyleaf revealed that it had been issued eleven years earlier, and bore the stamp: Opunake Public Library.

Phillip was utterly perplexed. He could not remember mentioning to the girl an opening day for the library. In fact, he had surprised himself how quickly he had been able to open for business. He also knew that in the ten years prior to this moment, not a single overdue book had been dropped into the return box— not unless it had been totally eaten by successive generations of mice. How could this strange girl, then, have known that when she returned a book on this Sunday morning, at this precise moment, a librarian would finally be on duty to receive it?

He had gone to bed the previous night plagued by thoughts of Delia. He hadn't thought of her at all this morning. After this incident, however, he would find it hard to think about anything or anyone else.

. . . . .

The mayor awoke with a roaring in his ears and tried to pull on his shoes. He made a mental note to complain to both the Ministry of Defence and the Strategic Training Division of the Royal Air Force. He went into the living room to ask his wife for the shoehorn. Florence Sullivan was sitting at the rolltop desk writing to her sister-in-law to tell her that Phillip had arrived and was at this very moment inspecting the new library.

"Don't wear those shoes. You know as well as I do you get in a bad mood when you wear them."

"They cost me a hundred and fifty bucks. If I don't wear them on days like this, when am I going to wear them?"

"It's in the nugget box by the back door."

Jim Sullivan pulled the large brass shoehorn from the box and sat on the step, trying to force his foot into one of the Italian shoes. He'd rashly bought them during a Rome stopover on their return from London to New Zealand. The shoes had been greatly discounted and were available only in an unpopular size. Against Florence's advice, he had grandly produced his credit card in the Via del Corso, and even then the shoes had made him totter like a penguin, so that she had to look away.

The heel of the shoe ripped completely as he now applied additional force. "Fuck's sake," he cursed, hurling the shoehorn across the room, followed quickly by the tortured shoe. He returned to the living room to ask his wife where his Irish brogues were hidden, cursing as he went, and making a mental note to add "expensive Italian shoes" to his next insurance claim.

. . . . .

Later that morning, Sergeant Harvey Watson sat in the window of the Sahara Desert Motor Inn cafeteria and ordered a consummate breakfast of fried livers and steamed whitebreads. The smell guaranteed that the surrounding tables remained empty.

He was halfway through a book, *Championship Netball.* Several complex insights into this beloved game, which he had not yet fully digested, were being admirably expressed by the Australian authority. Page by page, it gained the dimensions of a tour de force, and twice he flipped to the biography on the flyleaf to read more about its author. The advantages of a left-wing spearhead attack were being discussed with the most vibrant clarity, while the merits of the running pass in a 3–4–3 front configuration were advanced in stunning prose. It produced such a rapture of partial understanding in the sergeant that, sure of having found a new bible, he felt inclined to call his team together right then to test the revolutionary moves.

"How's the breakfast?" asked Harry, the proprietor, bringing over more toast in the hope of imposing on the officer's thoughts.

"The kitchen smells like you killed a cat out there."

Harry cleaned up the table as Watson read and buttered a triangle of toast without looking.

"Good book?"

"Mmm."

Harry poured more tea into the cup. "Funny about Delia Chapman."

"Mmm." Watson didn't look up.

"Madness in the family, goes without saying."

"Madness . . ." The word percolated through the netball jargon. "Madness? Who? Who's mad?"

"Delia Chapman."

"What do you know about Delia Chapman?"

"Just what I heard."

"What did you hear, Harry?"

The sergeant's altered manner alerted Harry to the thinness of the ice he was standing on, and he backed off.

"Nothing."

"What did you hear? What's everyone saying?"

"It's just what I heard."

"Don't muck me round."

"Jesus, I dunno. I just heard . . . could be wrong . . ."

"Keep going."

". . . spaceship?" Harry shrugged and looked at the sergeant with the watery eyes of an innocent victim of circumstance.

"Who told you?" Watson demanded.

"Is it true?"

"Who told you that, Harry?"

"Who told me? I'm not sure. I just heard it around. It's going around. I do a lot of breakfasts, Harv."

Watson pushed the plate away, his mind now off food.

"Around," he muttered with a rising bad mood. "Around? Well, it can't have been around for all that long, mate. It's only nine o'clock in the fuckin' morning!"

"Well, that's a long time round here."

Watson snapped a look at Harry, who, he had to admit, had never spoken a truer word in his life.

"Well, she never said anything of the sort," clarified the sergeant for the record, hoping that this too would go around with the same velocity. "And I ought to know because I found her. So you can tell anyone who comes in here spreading that sort of thing that they've got the wrong end of the stick. All right?"

"Fine."

"Because all that happened was that she was out . . . walking. You can't trust anyone anymore."

"Never could."

"You'd think you'd learn, eh? You can't tell anyone anything."

"So is it true?"

"Is what true?"

"That Delia said she saw this spaceship thing?"

The sergeant lost his temper. "I thought I just told you, Harry! I just told you she didn't."

"You did. You did. Yeah. I know, Harv. But you've gotta admit it. Kid going around in a place like this saying she's been visited by . . . and gone on board . . ."

The sergeant fixed Harry with a powerful stare. "This sort of thing shouldn't be going around, Harry. You hear me? It's not right."

Harry nodded. "So it's true then, is it?"

"It doesn't matter if it's true. Delia's a good kid. She doesn't need this getting around."

Harry nodded again instantly, receiving all the confirmation he needed. "Anything I can do?"

The sergeant looked up. "I s'pose there's no point in telling you to keep this to yourself."

"Good as done. If it helps. Bit of a dag though, all this."

Watson studied Harry, whose wry smile at that moment said everything that could be said about cats which had been let out of the bag.

"She's the best goal-shoot in the whole province, Harry."

"No discussion there."

"Just got a fertile imagination, like all of them at that age."

"All it is, I s'pose."

"But if we let people get their hooks into her . . ." Watson shook his head, foreseeing the future as if it lay just beyond the gravel car park.

"It should never have got out, Harvey. Any idea who it was?"

The sergeant got up and left the cafeteria, sickened slightly by the richness of his breakfast, and by the small but millionfold misdemeanors made by ordinary people in the name of having something to talk about. It was as tragic in its way as a high school reunion.

, , , , ,

The factory whistle at Borthwick's Freezing Works called in the early-morning workers, and as the men and women in white climbed metal steps in rubber boots they beat out the same leaden arpeggio that had underscored so many quiet Sundays. The annual killing season was seeing a frenetic slaughter of livestock in a record effort to maintain quota, and the factory's five assembly lines were operating at maximum capacity seven days a week.

In the far corner of the killing room, to the sound of ripsaws, the first severed cows' heads of the day came through swing doors on a conveyor belt. Two meters apart, the heads moved forward at the pace of a lazy walk though green pastures, each one almost alive but for its eyes glazed with a membrane of death. They were a ghostly, meandering herd and Delia, as she passed through, half expected one to moo.

The cows' bodies had taken a different route. After the killing floor, they were trapped by the skinning machine. In one move, it peeled each carcass like a banana. Delia pulled her face mask over her nose, blotting out all impressions, and hurried on. From there, she passed on to the butchers' floor: lines of sixty men and women in white smocks and gum boots working on the parade of carcasses, skillfully and with seemingly little effect flicking their knives at each beast as it glided by. Yet with each incision, the meat was being imperceptibly weakened so that toward the end of the line, where only half a dozen butchers remained, just the smallest nick saw perfect sections of the animal tumble into plastic bins. The last butcher at the end of the line miraculously dealt with a skeleton. The profuse blood ran into a delta of gutters which eventually led out of the building to be diluted in the river.

In the packing room, two dozen girls prepared themselves for the parade of excised hearts. This was a sterile zone. Their hair was tucked under white caps and they were instructed to be alert to the ever-present possibility of contaminants. Years before, a whole season's production had been quarantined because of a variety of scalp lice found in the stock. In this slaughterhouse, the girls had to stay as clean as Japanese geisha, and pack 120 hearts an hour into lined cardboard boxes for shipment.

"Did you hear about Dee? Saw a spaceman."

"Yeah, right."

"She did."

"Rubbish. When?"

"Did so. Last night."

"Oh, yeah. Come off it."

"What did she say she saw?" asked Yvonne McKay, arriving late.

"Serious. She told the cops. Serious."

"Told them what?"

The girls barely looked up when Delia came in with her mask on and her eyes downcast. She pulled on her rubber gloves with a snap, and waited for the conveyor belts to start up. She looked toward the hatch leading from the butchers' floor through which the hearts would come. She wanted to keep her mind on the job. She hadn't slept more than an hour last night, and could easily fail to keep up with the endless flow of organs.

Across the other side of the room, the girls stood around savoring the morning's hottest story, enjoying their last moments of freedom before the conveyor belts called them to work. Delia didn't join them. She stayed where she was. And after five minutes, five minutes filled with screams and shouts, the floor manager walked in waving her hands as if shooing pigeons. The larger group broke up, leaving a core of four young women who refused to move until the belts rolled.

"What's the matter with you all?" the floor manager shouted.

"Seen spacemen, haven't we? Big ugly ones. Looked a bit like you, actually."

The floor manager was not amused. "Has anybody seen Lucinda Evans?"

The girls shrugged. Lucinda had gone out for a smoke.

"Probably late again," said Deborah Kerr. "Time you fired her, I reckon."

Bearing a screen star's name, Deborah felt it necessary to be glowingly preeminent. She wore legendary white stilettos when not in gum boots, and under her cap she had thin permed hair which, when unleashed, fell in a torrent to her waist. Blue mascara coated her lashes so that they came to resemble curled flies' legs under the weight of repeated applications. She was widely admired and widely imitated. Almost all of her wardrobe choices were copied by the town's other young women, and even her improvisation with accessories caused a scramble. A gratuitous safety pin in her jeans would initiate a near stampede of young imitators. A radical change in her lipstick color created a ripple effect so that within a week it had become the standard in the bars and at the cinema. Deborah was considered exceptionally worldly, and she was the first girl working at Borthwick's to decide to leave school and live in her own flat. This decision had been quickly emulated by Lucinda, who also felt more mature than the others.

Deborah Kerr and Delia Chapman had been best friends from their earliest school days, although Deborah was a year older. It was a friendship founded initially on the girlhood pleasure of dressing up in their mothers' clothes, transforming themselves from pigtailed midgets into exotic and dangerous femmes fatales. But over the years, their friendship had needed to find fresh points of intersection. Until recently, it had rested on a fragile three-cornered premise: First, they had been on the same netball teams since they were ten years old and now shared the position of goal-shoot. Second, they were the two prettiest girls in the team, a seldom contested fact. It even said so in the bus stop on Cuthbert Street, and so it had to be true; under the Statue of the Unidentified Soldier, a similar declaration had been scratched into the green paint of the park bench: D and D are SPUNKY, written within the outline of a heart.

Being an aesthete, Deborah had decided early that an ally was preferable to a competitor in looks and romance. She felt that if they were seen together constantly, their allure would somehow, synergistically, be more than doubled: They would be elevated to near goddesses. Delia, however, was merely grateful for Deborah's company and for having someone who could attract the bulk of the wolf whistles from Opunake's sex-mad young men. Then third and last, there was still the chance that they might share rare moments when only the understanding ear and forthright word of the other could relieve or avert a crisis. No one else would suffice. As kids, they had got under each other's skins early, and such sympathy cannot easily be reversed.

Deborah's loud suggestion across the factory floor that Lucinda Evans should be fired was quickly endorsed by Suzy Jackson, who quickly told a joke when the floor manager was out of earshot. Suzy was a Maori girl from a tribal farm, and was the fourth core member of the clique. If she ever spoiled her jokes, it was because she laughed so hard anticipating the punch line that she completely obliterated it when it came.

"Okay," she said. "Here's another one. Okay . . . What happens if a bird shits on your car?"

Yvonne McKay didn't know. Deborah didn't know. Suzy was already beginning to laugh. "Don't invite her out again!" Yvonne laughed hardest. "Don't invite her out again." Deborah managed a smile.

Delia, across the room, turned around to see the cause of the laughter, and the huge conveyor belt rumbled into action. She drew her first empty box closer as the meat came toward her.

Yvonne's high laugh was the last to die down. She was timid and shy, a little over five feet tall and had the lamentable habit of repeating the last interesting thing anyone said. "Don't invite her out again!" She had a simple, joy-wanting heart, which her friends read like a book. She was also Delia's cousin, but had inherited none of the Chapman good looks. She bore the traits of the McKay side, the ectomorphic branch of the family.

The doors of the packing room burst open. Lucinda Evans came in, extinguishing a cigarette, larger than life, still belting up her smock and tucking ragged curls inside her cap.

Lucinda was one of the largest girls in town. She was the seventh child of a seventh child, a fact she endowed with great mystical significance. She was a walking showcase of the body-piercer's art, wore custom-made clothes, and had no fewer than nine rings in each ear—one for each year of her life, she said—and an oyster shell stud in each nostril, signifying with eccentric symbolism that she was born in the second zodiac month under Aquarius rising. Not well informed enough to be an initiate in the black arts, her amateur witchcraftery was merely one quirky step away from a childhood taste for ghost stories. She painted her fingernails black on the thirteenth of each month, and with no grasp of their atavistic value, she carried a Tarot deck in her handbag. She wrote phone numbers and shopping lists on them.

Unwilling to view her as an impostor, however, the smaller children in her neighborhood held her up as an example of what a real witch must look like, and played Halloween-like games around her house when incense and eerie New Age music drifted out through her defiantly purple curtains at night. But to the studded and jewelry-saddled Lucinda, her self-mutilations had higher meaning. She openly claimed access to spiritual planes, and by her own reckoning had an ancient gypsy soul. She knew of two previous incarnations of herself: a Celtic prince in fourth-century Ireland and a nineteenth-century whore in the Pigalle district of Paris, a city from where, she romantically postulated, all great whores hailed. One night, when a drunken farmhand stumbled home with her, he swore the next day, and with a blood-drained face, that her bedroom contained huge jars of cultivated spiders. This was believed at once. But he did not stop there. Lucinda had also wanted to tie him up, and the lad was in no doubt that this was merely a start to her debauchery. Although his friends recognized in this claim a huge element of wishful thinking, they did not discredit a word, especially in view of one previous incident: Lucinda's well-documented abduction of more than a dozen neighborhood cats. Although Sergeant Watson was eventually to accept Lucinda's story that the disappeared animals had come to her freely and had simply refused to leave when she fed them tuna and soya milk upon demand, the town preferred to believe the twelve felines had been detained for some kind of sick agenda. Each owner would swear long afterward that his pet had been tampered with, had undergone shifts in personality, and from then on permanently possessed a chilling, almost human glint in its eyes.

Every community has a designated freak, and Lucinda had nominated and then elected herself as Opunake's.

"What do you think?" Lucinda asked eagerly.

"About what?" answered Suzy without looking up, still relishing her joke.

"Didn't Deborah tell you about Delia, then?" whispered Lucinda, with an aura of clairvoyance.

"Course I did," said Deborah.

"Course she did," added Suzy.

"She told Harvey Watson that she . . . that she had . . . did you hear this?"

"We know," the others replied in unison, trying to exclude her.

"She had sex with them," Lucinda announced.

"What?"

"What?"

"What?"

Three jaws crashed like plummeting elevators.

"Had sex with them."

"No!"

"No!"

"She didn't!"

"Did!"

"Bullshit!"

"She reported it. To Harvey. Had sex. That's what she told him."

The reaction of the group took several seconds to crystallize. There was a moment of silent astonishment in which expressions froze. Four refrigerated looks were focused on Lucinda Evans, the bearer of news. New insights had been provided.

Deborah Kerr, as was the custom, became their eventual spokesperson: "That's not what you told me."

"Yeah. That's what I heard." Lucinda sunbathed in the attention.

"Don't be ridiculous!"

"You're taking the piss."

"Who told you that?!"

Lucinda told them she'd heard it from Rita, who had heard it off Marjorie. Marjorie had credibility. Marjorie was staunch. She was married with two kiddies. Marjorie had heard it from Delia herself. Delia had been walking to work. Marjorie wouldn't lie. "It's true," protested Lucinda.

"What did she say?"

"Dee went and told the police. Spilled her guts. Made a proper report and everything! Harvey had to type it up. She said she had sex with a whole lot of them!" Lucinda was finding it difficult to disguise a hint of envy.

"Sex with who?" asked Yvonne, who was slow to catch on.

"With the spacemen!" they repeated in chorus.

Suzy, Deborah and Yvonne looked at each other.

"Fuckin' hell," said Deborah.

"She didn't," said Suzy.

"Yeah, yeah, she did." Lucinda's excitement was ready to bubble over. "That's what she told Harvey."

As if fire had broken out, as if sirens had gone off, as if lives would be lost and the end of the world had come, the four young women ran across the packing-room floor toward Delia whose mask was drawn up over her face. Was it true? Did she really say it? They gathered around their friend in a circle, grabbing her, turning her around and stopping her work. Did she really tell the cops that? Quick, answer! Because this would be the best thing that had ever happened. She would be a complete star, and famous forever.

Then Delia fulfilled every expectation with the glorious words, "What if I did?"

"You're having us on."

Dying for it to be true, the four were still holding back until it was doubly confirmed. They had to be sure. Delia had to be asked again, then they would be ready to canonize her. It would be the craziest thing anyone had ever done. It would be the best thing anyone had ever done.

"I told him what I saw."

Deborah didn't want any confusion. She cautioned against an uproar. "Shut up," she said. There was an additional point she

wanted clarified for the record before an era of anarchy could
be unleashed.

"You told Harvey that . . . now hang on, you told Harvey . . .
okay . . . that you had sex with a . . . you told him *that*? *Sex*?"

Delia didn't feel the need to reply.

"Excellent," whispered Lucinda Evans after an awestruck
pause, excited for all of them.

"I can't believe it!" shrieked Deborah.

Delia shrugged.

A collective scream arose. It echoed about the room. Those
otherwise engaged or late to arrive were drawn to the circle to
join with the babble of voices, the deluge, a hundred questions at
once, an unanswerable storm, with Delia in its eye, swirling words
rotating around her.

That Delia should have conceived of such a brilliant stunt was
beyond mere words of praise. She deserved a medal for courage.
Most of the girls had more than a few embarrassing blemishes
on their private records. Each had been picked up by Sergeant
Watson at some time or other and been questioned. But none
had invented an answer that was even half as good as this. All
comparisons failed. Delia had trumped everyone.

Delia went back to work, wrapping and packing, unmoved by
her celebrity status. Open mouths surrounded her.

The only exception was Deborah. In the absence of further
dialogue she said, "Fair enough." The others looked to her for
guidance in a time of confusion. "Fair enough," she repeated.
"What's the big deal? She saw a spaceship. Good on her. She had
sex with them while she was on board. So? Woulda done the
same myself."

Brows furrowed, incomprehension now directed at Deborah.
"What are you all staring at?" she reprimanded. "Who's to say it
couldn't happen?"

Before Deborah's statement could be exposed as a joke or a
piece of sarcasm, however, a shout came from across the floor.

"Hey!" The floor manager was clapping her hands in the door-way. The conveyor belts were about to go around a second time, and mounting hearts were ready to spill onto the floor. The inquisition had to be postponed.

Only Lucinda Evans remained a second longer. "So, what about insemination? Did they inseminate you?"

"Evans!" shouted the manager in a reprimanding roar, sending Lucinda scurrying finally to her post.

For the next four hours, the hands of the factory girls might well have been busy in the monotony of packing and wrapping, but their heads were turned rigidly in the direction of Delia Chapman.

Unbelievable!

Too excellent for words!

Brilliant!

, , , , ,

"You heard me, I want to borrow the Bible."

The old woman had been the second person to see the OPEN sign on the library door, while walking to church. Standing on the street, she'd put on her glasses and noted with virtually no surprise that library hours had been resumed. Opening her purse, she withdrew a crumbling library card.

Phillip was trying to explain to her that it had been only an hour since he'd allowed the first air inside these walls for ten years, and he was neither administratively prepared to handle her request nor certain that he even had a copy. Also, it was Sunday. He could not officially issue a book on a Sunday. He was as polite as he could be, but the state of the library had thrown him into turmoil.

The old woman stared at him with dignified outrage. It should be clear to anyone with eyes in his head, she said, that she was a senior member of this library, and it was exactly because it was Sunday that she wanted such a book. "Who wants the Bible on

a Monday?" Moreover, the notion that the library might not possess the Bible was immoral and "simply ridiculous in a Christian
town." She concluded with rustic wisdom, "A library without a
Bible has got no business existing."

Phillip agreed to look at the files.

He pulled open the drawer marked Bac to Chr and blew away
dust. His fingers walked through the sepia-colored cards, flicking
from Bach to Chronology but he couldn't find Bible. Hoping
he'd simply missed it in his haste, he went through the cards
again. No reference to the book existed. As a last resort, he went
to the T's, hoping it had been ineptly filed under The Bible, and
at this moment he was rescued by his uncle, the mayor.

Jim Sullivan immediately detected drawn knives. He drew his
suit jacket over his stomach, fastening one button. A collection
of rehearsed postures made him instantly appear taller than he
was. In a second, he lost all informality and achieved a lofty grace
that was almost presidential.

The old matriarch was pleased to be able to consult a higher
authority, and finally accepted the mayor's apologies, complete
with a personal pledge that a suitable Bible would be found as
soon as possible. While he helpfully dusted lint off her jacket, he
guaranteed that notification of its arrival would be sent to her the
second the book appeared. He then asked Phillip quickly to check
against records that her address had not changed in the intervening years, which was unnecessary, since it had not changed in
seven decades, but this precaution lent the proceedings an aura
of stupendous efficiency. Finally the mayor ushered her out and
waved good-bye.

Phillip stood speechless.

Sullivan advised his nephew that the first lesson of public office
was to look after the old ones. At any price. They might seem
feeble and rickety and half dead, but they were as sleepless as rats
and they could nibble at the foundations until the entire town
collapsed.

"So how's it going?" asked Sullivan, swiftly changing the subject.

"Just cleaning up at this stage."

"Good. When can you open?"

"A few days. Perhaps I shouldn't have displayed the 'Open' sign so soon."

"No. The sooner the better. Because besides the new Aquatic Center, I see this as the other half of the town renewal program. This is a new era. Let me tell you something. Tourists gravitate to two things: water and books. You see them all over the world—beaches and bookstores. That's what they want."

"The only problem is . . . there aren't a lot of books," Phillip remarked.

"No books?"

"No. Not on the shelves. And not compared with the files. See for yourself. And then a lot of them are water damaged."

Sullivan looked around at the library. It took a few seconds for his mental picture of the library as it had been in its heyday to dissipate and for the chaos that now lay before him to sink in. He was shocked. The place was as desolate as a mortuary. "Good Lord, what happened?"

His memory had been frozen at the morning of the inaugural opening thirty-two years before. New books, glistening and uniform, had lined every shelf, so many books that three trucks had had to carry them. Then a young man, he had helped to paint the interior himself, and every wooden beam had been new and ready for a hundred years of service.

"Everything turns to shit," he complained. "You know what this does? This makes me feel very old."

He asked Phillip if he had any immediate thoughts, and seemed depressed.

"Well, the good news is that the last librarian you had did the worst job I've ever seen, and because of this she might just have saved the library."

"What are you talking about?"

"Well, I've only had a quick look at the files, but . . . I'd say the good news is that most of the books which were originally on the shelves have been accidentally saved."

"Saved?"

"They're still out on loan."

"What do you mean?"

"People never returned the books they borrowed."

"It's true. They never return them," the mayor affirmed.

"I'd say as many as ninety percent of the library's entire stocks are still out there somewhere."

"Bullshit!"

"That's several hundred books the town has paid for."

"Ninety percent?" the mayor repeated, dazed.

"Take a look. Every card in this catalog represents a book." Phillip pulled open drawer after drawer in the cabinet to prove the glaring disparity. "Which is just as well, because the rain would have destroyed them completely if they had been returned."

The mayor passed his hand through his graying hair and said, "Well, that's farmers for you. They're not going to come all the way into town because they've got overdue library books. It was the same with the elections. They wanted to vote but they wouldn't come into town." He walked to the window and looked out. "What can we do?"

Phillip shut the file drawers. "I'd like to get some overdue reminder cards printed, send them out."

"Good. Yes. Do it."

"But it's been ten years. I don't know how many of these books they'll still have. After a certain time, library books tend to get donated to the church gala."

Phillip was right again.

The mayor turned. "Then we bill them for total replacement. Invoice them for the full amount. We won't sanction theft of town property." He pondered. "Ninety percent?"

"I think so."

"First the cards. Then we invoice."

The mayor walked out. He was late for the last service at the church where he also held a position as a lay minister.

Phillip returned to his work. Earlier, he had discovered that the library contained the complete works of only two authors, Neville Shute and Alistair MacLean. He thought MacLean a pulp writer, but he did not mind that so much shelf space should be allotted to Neville Shute, believing he had written some valuable books on the topic of human courage, and at least one classic in *A Town Like Alice*. Born in 1899, on the cusp of a new century, Shute had described a double world-war era with maximum economy, and had directly influenced Phillip's decision to join the army. War was a dramatic opportunity. The great issues were at stake: life and death and good and evil. By toughening the body, you toughened the mind: War was spiritual and intellectual. You literally attacked life, placed it in the crosshair of your rifle, and in return life surrendered meaning. Phillip reasoned, quite seriously, that by joining the army he could conduct a near-mathematical examination of his own soul.

Now decommissioned, and found to be wanting, Phillip did not forget the nights he had spent reading Shute, his literary hero, who had made a fortune out of bestsellers that titillated readers with the thought that greatness was much closer to every soldier's reach than any civilian's. Phillip lowered his head to his work. What potential was there for greatness in working in the Opunake Public Library? He tore off a piece of Sellotape and applied it to a ripped page.

Three

. . . .

WE SEE GHOSTS

A spaceship landed. In a clearing, the door opened. Perhaps it's called a hatch. Anyway, an indistinct figure appeared in the doorway. The ship could not really be likened to a saucer. It was more of a torpedo, a sausage. She was invited on board. She went. No, that's not quite right. She was drawn.

Inside, she remembered very little. There were lights, shapes. But these lights and shapes were kind of fuzzy, like seeing them through vapor, or a goldfish bowl. At some point, she was horizontal. She couldn't remember lying down. It was more as if she had remained upright and the ship had tilted around her, but that was impossible! There was a face above her. Features—but a blur, like everything else.

After that she was released.

They didn't hurt her at all.

That was all.

That was it, really.

. . . . .

"Well, all I can say," said Deborah Kerr in the canteen with Delia at smoko, "is you must have been pissed . . . I mean *really* pissed."

She sat down beside Delia in the corner, drinking coffee from a Styrofoam cup. "And I mean blotto, right off your head. So you went inside. For twenty minutes, was it? So . . . what was that like, then?" Deborah's expression showed she was humoring her friend and potential rival. "Millions of knobs? Computers every-where, I s'pose? They always have them, don't they. Wall to wall. So you had a good look around, did you? What was it like? Or don't you remember that part? Tell you what I woulda done. I'da brought something back with me—I dunno, a ray gun or some-thing. Something from the future anyway. But nobody's ever done that, have they? All these people that've been taken on board." Deborah laughed. "Then they . . . what? . . . They told you they had to get going, but how about a quick shag before they took off? So? You dropped your knickers then, did ya? Dee? Come on, I promise I won't tell any of those other stupid tarts. You bonked one, or two, or what? Then the spaceship just flew off? It just . . . woosh? Or did it—"

"It rose," said Delia, sipping her coffee unflustered.

"Oh. I see. It rose. Well, fuck me."

"Just forget it. Don't worry about it, all right? Piss off back to the others. I'm telling you I saw it. I don't expect you to believe me."

"No. I really wanna know." Deborah turned away and stole a glance over her shoulder at the other girls across the room. She gave them a wink. "So," she said. "So . . . it rose. Okay, it rose. And then just flew off?"

"Then it was over." Delia turned and faced Deborah for the first time. "Look, why don't you go back to the others? They're waiting for you. Then you can all have a big laugh, all right? But you don't know what it was like."

"Hey listen, they don't need me over there to have a big laugh, Dee. They've been having a pretty big one all morning, in case you didn't notice."

"Yeah. I noticed."

"Well, then . . ."

"Well, then . . . *what?*"

"Cut the crap, Delia. What's all this about?"

"Pass me the sugar."

Deborah passed her the sugar without taking her eyes off her friend, without relieving the pressure. "You've got a lot of guts, anyway, I'll give you that. Telling the cops something like that."

Delia stirred sugar into her coffee. "Have I?"

"Yeah. You have."

"It happened."

"Oh, give us a break. You don't actually believe that, Dee, do ya?"

"You can think what you like. I'm not joking."

They both smoked in silence.

"You're stark raving."

"I didn't ask it to happen."

"It didn't happen, Delia!"

"All right, it didn't. Happy?" They locked eyes. "Go and tell everyone it didn't happen."

"I don't need to."

They had reached a stalemate. Delia broke it. "It could happen to you."

She had a look of such resolute firmness that Deborah started shaking her head.

"You know what," said Deborah. "I can see right through this, Delia Chapman. Why don't you just tell me who you were with and get it over with." Delia lifted the Styrofoam cup to her lips and drank. "Because you'll never get anyone to believe this. Anyway," she concluded, "only Americans see spacemen."

It was true; Delia had secretly to concede this. Mostly Yanks saw spacemen. They imagined close encounters at the drop of a hat, especially whenever they were depressed, or had insomnia, or were on some kind of pill. She had read this. But you needed to be from Minnesota or Nebraska, from somewhere named Wabash or Garfield County, or one of those towns called Two Forks if you wanted to say that you saw spacemen. New Zealanders were different. They saw ghosts, not UFOs; poltergeists, the odd devil and the ever-improbable witch. The distinctions were subtle but clear, Deborah was saying.

"We see ghosts, we *don't see E fuckin' T, okay?!*"

Delia had stopped responding. But Deborah had one more thing to add. "So next time you wanna shag someone, make it Casper the Fucking Ghost."

Delia remained silent. Neither confirm nor deny was her policy. She would let the theories spiral out like cream through coffee, like a Milky Way of argument, like a galaxy.

, , , ,

"Some of the girls are saying that you said you had sex with more than one of them."

Lucinda Evans was taking an open shower beside Delia in Borthwick's changing rooms. Lucinda was shampooing her hair, rivers of lather meandering down her ample flesh. Suds streamed over her face, forcing her to keep her eyes bunched shut. Both girls had worked through the night on the last shift.

Delia didn't like showers.

"They're saying that you told Deborah you had sex with quite a few of them while you were on board. Is it true? Dee? You didn't really, did you?"

Delia finally gave in. She shut off the water, and either from a desire to tell the whole truth or merely to titillate Lucinda's already overfertile imagination, said, "They don't do it like we do. It's completely different. They do it with heat waves."

Delia left Lucinda standing with her mouth open but unable to open her eyes under the stream of soap.

Dripping wet, Lucinda followed Delia into the locker room. As Delia dressed, she sat beside her, wrapped in towels, and talking in excited tones.

"Heat waves?"

"That's all I'm gonna say. Okay?" Delia already regretted what she had said. She could see it becoming another snowball. She would have to keep her mouth shut.

"Okay. But how do you mean heat waves?"

"I just told you, that's it."

"Right."

Lucinda considered the concept of heat waves in silence for a moment, trying to visualize it—rays of energy inducing a trance-like state—then said, "Far out."

"I gotta go," said Delia, quickly pulling on her boots, her hair untoweled.

"Yeah . . . okay . . ." Lucinda gazed blankly into space, trying to simulate in her mind the kind of heat and the form of wave that could possibly substitute for sex.

"See ya," said Delia, and walked out, leaving Lucinda deep in an erotic quandary.

, , , , ,

Delia had survived the day. She walked home in a fresh uniform, gum boots clomping on the pavement. Having generated the sort of excitement among her friends normally produced only by a conflagration of parties, music, alcohol and sexual intrigue, she chose a back route out of the factory, anticipating a gathering outside. It was to no avail. A dozen factory girls dropped cigarettes and swamped her as she tried to cross the car park.

Delia had no choice but to talk. She tried to satisfy most questions. Everyone wanted to know something, a juicy tidbit, a saucy aspect of the sexual encounter. In response, she tried to be as accurate as she could. If she was going to tell the story, she wanted to tell it right. She met every question with a straight answer, giving rise to shrieks, laughter and repeated "come-off-its." Whether Delia had started adding her own tiny exaggerations, or whether her memory was slowly fading, the story seemed to improve in the retelling.

Then just when she seemed almost to be enjoying the moment, she became remote, her attention diverted, and her voice faltered. Her audience pushed forward, waiting for her next word, wondering what new mesmerism might be delaying her. But it was a momentary hiccup and the next moment she became generous again. Cajoled and prodded into a further bout of recollections, she transported her listeners to a clearing by the river known to all, just in time for the arrival of the glowing vessel bearing ambassadors of uncertain origin, and for the moment of alien contact. She conveyed her audience to a breathless plateau of curiosity: Mouths hung agape, envy mixed with astonishment. They thought: It's true. The wildest rumors were true. Delia Chapman was going around talking shit. It was brilliant!

, , , ,

Margaret Watson's guilt was so acute that she cleaned the fridge right down to the vegetable rack. She preferred this to facing her husband, who was sitting at the kitchen table watching her. His rage had melted into mere exhaustion.

"Why did you do it?" His tone was severe.

"I don't know. I don't know. I just don't." She was close to tears.

"I expressly . . . I expressly—"

"I know. I *know.*"

"I thought I made it—"

"You did. You did."

"—absolutely clear—"

"Don't go on!"

"And by nightfall the entire province will be talking about this. I hope you know that."

"I'm sorry."

"As if I haven't enough on my plate."

"Perhaps it did happen?" said Margaret, in an effort to sidetrack him. The ploy was utterly defensive.

"What?"

"Perhaps something did land."

"Land?"

"Who knows."

Margaret did not take her head out of the fridge to say this, and her voice was oddly amplified. The sergeant was thus unable to fire her a withering look. "Don't be ridiculous," he said. "Your mind is refrigerating."

"There's one way to find out" came her enhanced reply. "If you want to settle this, and stop the story from growing any bigger."

"I don't need to settle anything."

"Go out to the edge of town where she said it happened. There's bound to still be some sign. You know, of a ship. If it's true."

"What's the matter with you? You think I should dignify this crazy story with a serious investigation? I'm treating this as suspicious, not science bloody fiction!"

Margaret emerged with a filthy squeegee cloth. She rinsed it in the sink.

"It was Trish Gumley's idea," she continued. "She suggested a group of us go out and have a look."

The sergeant's arm swiped across the table, relocating the vegetables onto the floor. "No one is going out there to check on anything! You, me, Trish bloody Gumley or anybody, is that clear? I'm not turning this into one of your amateur dramatic evenings."

"It was just a thought."

"Not a good one, Margaret!"

"Because if you don't do it by tonight, the forecast is for rain."

"Rain?" The sergeant was utterly lost.

"Yes. That's the forecast, anyway."

"What the hell are you talking about?"

"Well, obviously the rain could remove any sign of the . . . of the craft."

The intricate tapestry of marriage has many threads, and it is perhaps the challenge of a lifelong alliance to resist pulling the loose ones when they emerge. Rather, it is imperative to patiently tuck them back into the fabric of matrimony with calm acceptance, and thereby avert the suspicion that a small thread, once pulled, has no end.

"I'm not going out there," said the sergeant with formidable control. "And I won't turn my office into an object of ridicule and public amusement."

"Because you know how gossip runs," said Margaret.

This stopped him. "No. Tell me," he said, deferring to his wife's expertise in this area.

"They'll all take one side for a while. They'll all agree that Delia Chapman has gone haywire. But then in a week, there will be a backlash."

"Oh. A backlash?"

"A few people saying, 'Hang on a minute. What if she wasn't lying? Who really knows about this sort of thing? The universe is so big, et cetera . . . maybe something did land?' "

The sergeant's expression had frozen, set like stiffened jelly.

"I can't believe this is happening."

His wife continued. "And to control this, you'll need to be able to say you went out there before it rained and you found nothing. That's the irrefutable proof. It's all I'm saying. When it rains, you'll have lost your chance."

The sergeant was rising from his seat.

"That's it. I don't want to talk about this anymore."

"Okay. But if it rains—"

"It is not going to rain! I read the forecast this morning. And the drought won't break for at least another week, maybe two."

After a great silence, the sergeant's wife capitulated. "Okay, have it your way." In return, she escaped further admonition for her role as a gossip. The sergeant returned to work.

Margaret squeezed bloodred beet juice from her sponge into the bucket of water. She gathered the suppurating vegetables from the floor, removed the rotten leaves and began to reinstate them in the clean refrigerator.

, , , , ,

That afternoon it rained so suddenly and with such ferocity that the river flooded and even swept away a frail bridge.

Marty Chapman waited for the rain on the porch of his house. His daughter was late home from work. Sitting in a rattan armchair, he'd been watching with farmer's eyes as the clouds amassed all morning. In the afternoon, the sky had become so dark that he was sure any second his feet would be wet, but then the clouds dispersed again.

But by late afternoon the storm had recongregated, and an unmistakable vibration came up from the ground through his chair. He put out the palm of his hand beyond the eaves to receive the first drop. It was the size of a quail's egg, and indicated rains of massive proportions.

The first roll of thunder shook the foundations of the house; then the rain came, advancing in a wall over the hills, scattering sheep and cattle as it rolled forward, overwhelming the house and bringing on a premature evening.

Marty switched on the lights in the living room. He stepped into the kitchen and poured himself a whiskey from the bottle he kept above the sink. Then he went back to the living room to watch it rain beyond the open door.

He had already discovered that Delia had made a statement to Sergeant Watson. He had overheard the news at the co-op ma-

chine shop while picking up a twisted plowshare. His back had
been turned on the two farmers, and his grief and humiliation
were compounded by their chuckles of incomprehension and ill-
timed reference to the dead woman whose disquieted spirit still
filled Marty's house, inhabiting the rooms in an eternal whisper,
his eternal middle-aged bride whose dead perfumes were detect-
able even now, two years later. Often when entering a room, and
in a cloud of confusion brought on by these odors, he would expect to see her, or glimpse her shadow escaping through the door.

He had no definite plan to reprimand Delia, but it was a situation which called for extraordinary measures, this was certain. For
the last two years he had imposed upon the household a Victorian
level of privacy because of the tragedy which had been visited
upon him. This had now been breached. The erosion, begun by
the wife, had been completed by the daughter.

Because of his wife's spectacular discovery of the power of cyanide, he had no one with whom to discuss the correct parental
response to this crisis. What did he, after all, an old-style widower, a man of few words and most of them practical, know about
teenage girls? In a perfect world his wife would be present to step
in, banishing him outside with a wave and yelling to him, "I'll
take care of this, Marty!" He would then make the pretense of
resenting her orders, and fake walking off gruffly, mock-
slamming a door in a demonstration of anger but secretly breathing sighs of relief, quite happy to be irrelevant again, escaping
toward some farmyard practicality, a solid comprehensible problem. This was how the family had worked. Before the cyanide.

In the armchair again, he reached for the family photo album
only half full of photographs: Deeming them too expensive, he
had restricted the taking of them to special occasions. His wife's
face looked back at him from the first page, a portrait in her
twenties when they first met, wearing a straw hat. Picture by picture their marital story was retold: the faded romantic smiles of
courtship, she gripping the crook of his arm, the exhausted smiles

of a bride on his arm again, then Delia abruptly with them, thin and shy, and them all in shorts together at a Coromandel beach. Still youthful then, beside a rowboat, her wifely hair was cut mannishly short for the first time as the seriousness of life began to impress itself, photo by photo, on both their faces, the grip on the crook of his arm abandoned.

A thousand waves of information leaped from each photo and he let them address him, looking for answers. His hands were always in his pockets and hers folded under her breasts. The broken calm of her fortieth year was there to decode in a forced smile, the twig-snap of the first sign of trouble, the strange behavior which he had tried to ignore. Even her sleepless nights could be found in a Christmas-dinner shot—the first prescriptions from the doctor, precious little food on her plate. Around this time he recalled, as if a whole album had been devoted to them, the small bottles appearing in bathroom cabinets and on dressing tables to help her rest. And then the slippage into lithium and lunacy which followed, marked only by a growing absence on the pages as she grew unphotographable. He did not want these memories preserved, but their omission only made them doubly vivid.

Present there were all the times he couldn't take her anywhere for fear of what she might do or say, that gentle, almost peaceful glissando into a no-man's-land—and all this, all of it, for no medical reason that could ever be established.

He took to the bottle in private, not captured by any camera, growing just as confused and withdrawn and vicious as when she had first found him, first saved him from himself, humanizing him the way a woman will.

And then, after nearly ten years of being lost to him, ten years of mad and frightening behavior in which he sometimes wanted to bash out his own brains against the brick wall behind the milk shed in sheer bunch-fisted despair and self-hatred, came a vertiginous gust of magic: Right out of the blue she came back to him, his old Christine. The impossible had happened. And he remembered her face as if it were in Kodacolor, just as it had been when she came down to breakfast on that strange momentous morning, a calm serenity returned to her face, the wrinkles miraculously ironed, a look of penetrating insight reinstated in her sad eyes, and this marvelous image happening on the exact day that Marty casually decided to clear his property of possums once and for all by way of poison.

She rose on that clear and pleasant morning, when he was so full of joy he could hardly bear to leave her, and she cleared away breakfast, left the kitchen by the back door, and chose for herself an animal's death, the way of rodents and vermin, a terrible grue-some choice which not even crazy people make, but which all the locals said proved she was not right in the head. And on the last page of the album was her pitiful legacy: a funeral service card, *In Memoriam,* her long hair restored in the photograph under a yellow straw hat, and in italics beneath: *At Rest.* Not so for Marty, how-ever, examining the card in his armchair as it rained down in a vast deluge, revisiting the mystery he would now never solve: Just where on earth had this pretty girl with the long brown hair gone?

So what was he doing raking over these coals, what was the point of opening this album night after night? What Marty could see, book in work-thick hand, and as clear as a bell, was the un-fortunate story of a man whose limited gifts were no remedy for his wife's million dissatisfactions. And how incredibly small were the things that precipitated this fatal sequence. But what he didn't see, night after endless night, and no matter how hard he scoured his album for clues, was how responsible he was for the way his wife finished up: a piece of meat on the banks of a river. His memory, self-protective by nature, drew back from delivering any verdict.

Perhaps when his daughter arrived home he would know in-stinctively what to do, the answer surprising him. The right way to handle a teenage girl might still present itself if only he trusted himself. But Delia was late. And this made him angry.

While he sipped whiskey, he half imagined and half saw his wife walking through the rain toward the front gate. On the porch, she paused as she always did, as real ghosts must always do when they approach the precincts of the living. Silently, as usual, he invited her to climb the three small steps to the porch, to speak directly to him and explain once again her ruinous departure. But, as usual, she kept her wary distance just on the other side of the gate, an inconclusive outline in the angling rain.

When Delia walked into the house, she could not see her father anywhere. She was drenched and shook the water out of her hair. All the doors were open and every light was burning. Insects swirled around the bulbs in sensational torrents. From the bathroom she took a towel and went to the bedroom where she dried her hair, idly surveying the faded memorabilia pinned to her wall. It really was high time she took it down, all the stupid pennants, the badges and ribbons for which she no longer felt any pride.

And then there he was, etched in the doorway. The expression on her father's face, reflected in the mirror, made her stumble a few steps backward from the glass, but toward him.

He moved forward, and delivered the first deliberate and anticipated blow to the side of her wet head, knocking her to the floor.

He stood over her, his demonstration of correctional discipline under way.

, , , , ,

When Marty Chapman's fury expired, Delia was sore in so many places that the pain seemed diffused as though by an anesthetic. She could feel blood rushing to points on her face and on her ribs and shins, but she was removed from it, numb. She could feel the elastic pulse at many points, already forming domes of blue skin as she lay on the floor beside the bed with her legs drawn up. Her hair obscured her face and her eyes were closed. She was concentrating. She was wondering what she'd done, concluding she must have been very bad.

Her father had gone downstairs. She heard doors slamming below, vibrating up through the floorboards of her room. He was already exhibiting signs of the remorse that followed his violent outbursts. In the morning he would make her breakfast: It was always this way. It would be waiting for her when she came down. The toast would be buttered, a thick spread right to the corners. It was a nonverbal admission that he was a bad man, but that there was nothing he could do about it. Soon she would have saved enough money to be independent, and then she would leave him. That was all they could hope for.

In the indefinable humiliation of being beaten up by your own father, there was always the thought that you had done this to yourself, and Delia didn't blame her father. Father and daughter were two parts of a whole, after all. Just as the daughter's error sprang first from the father's failure to properly train her, making it his error, so the father's violence could be seen as the daughter's own guilty verdict, making the violence her own. The moment she had knowingly defied him, her pain became self-inflicted.

She lay on the carpet of faded damask rose and waited for time to pass, forcing herself once again to consider the timeless virtues of patience.

Patience had rescued her all her life. Years before, during her mother's frequent attempts to throw kettles of boiling water over her father whenever he was drunk, Delia would bind herself to the bony maternal thigh like a runner bean, and withstand the tempest and storm of her mother's insane rage until her father withdrew in defeat and went to sleep outside in the lean-to. Between maternal madness and paternal incompetence she learned the tender mercies of patience, of waiting for hurricanes to vent themselves, as clearly as she had also learned to hide the electrical cord of the kettle to prevent the disfigurement of her father.

Now from her father's room came the sound of footsteps pacing in ritual contrition. She tried to move on a wave of aches, and drew herself up from the floor with the uncertainty of an infant.

She crawled to the bathroom and locked the door. It was now the only door in the house with a lock on it.

She turned the shower taps on full until the room filled with steam, and with her eyes closed against the streaming water she visualized dead meat coming toward her in a slow, dull procession.

And then the blows materialized again, but after them, half in dream, in the humid atmosphere of the shower, images of her visitation: the flash of a man's forearm replaced with the gentle unfurling of a small white hand, a crashing blow to her head and her sudden blindness dissolving gently into an invitational gesture to step toward the light. The sight and smell of her own blood became subordinate to an experience of color and unknown odors and beyond that, or part of it, diaphanous people. Where the blows had driven her down, her memory now—and where it failed, her imagination also—lifted her up. She stood in the shower stream, her memory restored at last.

A figure had moved toward her through a pool of light—perhaps it was made of the light itself. Who expected, when you took a walk because you couldn't sleep, to be approached by a figure, the epitome of an angel, graceful, calm, his skin in the moon glow as white as milk, a beautiful body, she had to admit it (and she normally hated to think about men's bodies), his face more beautiful than any she had seen before, almost a woman's. She felt a warmth immediately, and an intelligence; yes, she felt his intelligence too, even if he never spoke. And when he reached out his hand to her, suggesting she follow him toward the light, what could she do? She followed. So what?

Delia shut off the water and used three towels to dry herself, patting lightly around the darkening bruises. She did not tremble. Wrapped in the largest towel, she walked from the bathroom to her bedroom like a crowned princess. She closed the door and did not come out till the following afternoon.

RAINS, AND A DEAD COW

Mayor Jim Sullivan had a very intimate recurring dream. In it he went to the bathroom, locked himself inside so that he would not be interrupted, undid his fly and began to pee. The satisfying stream of urine thudded into the bottom of the bowl. He watched it for a while and then let his eye wander upward. Gazing at washing flapping on the line and a darkening sky through the slightly open window, he eventually noted that his urination was showing no sign whatsoever of slackening. In fact, it had become the longest pee he could ever remember having. He told himself he was imagining it, but the terrifying thought occurred: What if the stream never stops? And, miraculously, as a full minute passed, the stream showed no sign of abating. A minute became two minutes. He stood helpless, urine flowing from him as if a water main had burst. His wife called for him, already missing her husband, and he lied to her from behind the closed door, shouting back in a voice of cloaked panic that he was just solving a plumbing problem. But, in truth, the mayor had become a prisoner of a bizarre and infinite emission. He tried several times to pinch his penis, to stem the ongoing flow, but the pain and pressure were unbearable, and he was forced to resume his phantasmagoric urination. It was as if all the water in the world were being siphoned through his body, and he would never again leave his own bathroom. . . .

The mayor awoke.

Outside it was raining.

The heaviest summer rains in a decade plunged the Opunake Borough Council into a therapeutic panic. Rivers instantly broke their banks, mud slides blocked roads, and the excavated site for the new Aquatic Center filled months ahead of time, becoming a disaster area, a muddy lagoon, a home to wild ducks and floating rubbish bags.

With only brief respites in two weeks of almost continuous rain, people learned to compress their business into the limited available time. The empty streets would fill with people in a minute. A whole week's Christmas shopping would be conducted in a flurry. Public events which had been repeatedly canceled were conducted quickly in a truncated form. A Plunket clinic for new mothers was inaugurated under pessimistic umbrellas, and a simplified sports day was held at the primary school. Father O'Brien made the most of a clear sky, and rapidly mourned and buried three people in the churchyard in one such hiatus.

Christmas Day itself was a nonevent, dampened by torrential rains and by Borthwick's, which refused everyone a day off, effectively killing the festive season.

Mayor Sullivan had been waiting some time to publicly launch his tourist campaign, and four recent postponements were jeopardizing the projected January 5 start date for construction of the Aquatic Center.

After the last delay he'd summoned a special session of the council, deciding that the ceremony would take place at the site of the excavations at midday on Friday, "come hell or high water."

As he looked out his office window on the Friday morning and consulted his watch, he realized that the latter condition would apply.

The entire council, and nobody else, gathered at the edge of the unwelcome lake in the rain. The faces of the members were so lowered against the weather that many never took their eyes off their shoes. The mayor spoke quickly but forcefully, avoiding formalities, words flowing from his mouth as if they were an aspect of the season. But in laying the first brick, he slipped on the muddy bank and very nearly shot down into the reservoir. He was spared this indignity only by digging in deep with his ceremonial trowel, which acted as a brake and prevented his slide into the mire, and then being assisted back up the bank by a chain of councillors linking arms. Wiping mud from his trousers he tried again to lay the brick, and succeeded this time in setting it beside the surveyor's peg, pronouncing the tourist campaign and the Aquatic Center officially launched. He was obediently applauded. Finally, a billboard showing an idealized drawing of the Aquatic Center dominated by the serpentine tower of a hydro-slide was pushed into the soft mud. The mayor tossed the trowel into the center of the dike and walked off, making a mental note to conduct all further campaign launches in chambers. The small crowd dispersed.

, , , , ,

During a tea break at the petrol station, Gilbert Haines sat in Max's office trying to perfect one of the many card tricks which began with the universal request: "Pick a card, any card."

His mind was only half on the illusion, and he had been unable to retrieve even one of the cards his employer had selected. The mercury in the office thermometer had sunk to ten degrees, and the single-bar heater was proving impotent against the sudden cold snap. Sitting behind a stack of oily ledgers, eyeglasses tenuously riding on his forehead, Max tapped occasionally at a calculator and stabbed receipts onto a nail.

"And you know why you should forget her? She's a spinner."

"I know that."

"Heard the stories. Save yourself the grief. Trouble's her middle name. Capital T, Gilbert. *Capital* T."

"Mmm," he muttered.

"You listening to me, or what?"

"Mmm." He held up a single card. "Was this your card?"

Max shook his head.

Gilbert had been violently depressed since the rumors about Delia had reached him five days before. He weighed a slight 110 pounds and was losing weight every day as his grief compounded with worry.

Max had become deeply concerned at the almost entropic effects the rumors were having on his employee. Absenteeism two days this week; lethargy; his complexion had lost its color and dark hoops had grown under his eyes. But in the last twenty-four hours the decline had reached a dangerous low. Gilbert was refusing to eat at all. He had not touched the lunch of fish and chips which Max had spread out on the desktop. He'd had to wrap the chips in bread and actually place them in Gilbert's hand before his employee would mechanically take a bite.

Man to man, Max said, he couldn't understand why Gilbert had such loyalty to a girl who, by all reports, had humiliated him a dozen times in public. And more fundamentally, he couldn't understand why such a fuss was being made over a girl who was only okay-looking. Extreme beauty might warrant this dangerous level of distraction, but not this kid: a battered sparrow of a girl, a nice mouth perhaps, eyes, he could imagine a potential scenario; but nothing about her was remotely arousing.

What Max failed to appreciate, however, was that to a young man as coated in sump residue and axle grease as Gilbert was,

Delia Chapman was a glowing vestal beauty, one vowed to chastity, a shining and pure mirage, as uncontaminated as a newborn baby.

Still, Max tried to be patient, at least for the sake of business. Gilbert was a good mechanic, not to be lost.

"But you probably won't listen to me, so my next advice, if you still want her, is . . ."

Gilbert had been waiting for this. He looked up, his face animated for the first time in days.

"Pay her some more attention. Flowers. Little presents she doesn't expect. My guess is this whole space-encounter thing is a cry for attention."

Gilbert considered this advice and offered the cards facedown in a fan. "Pick another card."

Max stopped adding the invoices, picked a card, memorized it and reinserted it into the pack. Gilbert closed the fan and cut the cards with one hand, three times. Then he began a series of precise manipulations designed, he told Max, to invoke the image of the chosen card in the mind of the magician, a cunning trick requiring both telepathy and a knowledge of the fundamentals of prestidigitation.

"I can't get her out of my head, Max," Gilbert interrupted himself in the middle of his complex trick.

Max nodded. "I've seen it on TV. People don't feel appreciated. They feel worthless. Lots of people. There's a statistic but I can't remember it. And when they feel like this . . . when they feel completely worthless . . . they start *seeing* shit."

"She won't even talk to me!"

"That's one of the symptoms, apparently."

Gilbert was trying hard to process Max's diagnosis: his last hope. "So . . . so you're saying," he interpolated, "that because she maybe feels worthless, that this is why she's not talking to me? That . . . what? . . . that because she doesn't feel appreciated, she's ignoring me? Is that what you're saying?"

"It's not necessarily that complicated, Gilbert. Could be she just doesn't like you."

"What?" Gilbert looked horrified.

"Look at my wife. Married twenty-seven years. Suddenly decides she doesn't like me. It takes twenty-seven years to work that out? It happens, Gilbert. There're no fuckin' rules. No fuckin' rules at all."

"What can I do?" muttered Gilbert, in view of the world's interminable disorder.

"Forget her. Just forget her. She doesn't exist. But if you can't do that . . . then you have to make her feel special."

"Thanks," said Gilbert devoutly.

Max pulled an invoice off the rusty nail with a rip and smoothed it on the desk with his hand until it became readable. "People just don't feel special. We're ignored, then we're taken for granted, then we're abandoned. Is it any wonder we start seeing things?"

It was unclear to Gilbert whether Max was talking about himself, his wife, Gilbert, Delia, or someone else altogether.

Gilbert said he'd try the new strategy. "Five of Clubs?" he finally asked, holding up the fateful card.

The look on Max's face was answer enough. Magic was a long apprenticeship. Nothing worth doing came easily. Nothing worth having simply materialized in front of you. You just had to persevere in the face of cynicism, inadequacy and defeat.

. . . . .

Deborah Kerr had discovered Opunake's new librarian, and approved of what she saw. She watched as he painted the old library sign. Standing on the lush grass, she wore a favorably killer top, black bra straps splendidly revealed, bare around the waist, high heels. She chewed Wrigley's with malicious intensity. She walked up to Phillip with a singular aim: that of acquiring him.

"Excellent," she said.

He turned.

"You're opening up again. Great. I adore books. Love to read, me." She lied through her photogenic teeth. "Can't get enough, actually." She smiled, gum clenched in her film-star smile. She liked to play. If he could handle it, then he was worthy; if not, he would cease to be of interest. "In bed," she said.

"Oh? Good," the librarian replied.

He was an acceptable height for Deborah, six-one, six-two, part Maori, she thought, with a nice near-hairless complexion, even-toothed like her; their children would be orthodontically well endowed, smooth-cheeked, slim; their grandchildren would still have something of his umber skin. In essence, he was symmetrical, which was more than could be said for most of the other young men in town: droopy-eyed, ears at different levels, lopsided grins, caved-in postures, uncouth—and these were just her recent boyfriends. Phillip would do nicely.

Deborah said, "So when can I get in?"

"A couple of days."

"Really?"

"Hope so."

"Cool," she said. "I'm on ice."

, , , ,

"Just an idea," said Suzy Jackson, who was responding to Deborah's verdict that "stuffing up the conveyor belt" by way of sabotage wouldn't be worth the risk.

"Not a bad idea though," conceded Deborah. "I'm so friggin bored I feel like one of these cows."

Meat. Morning, noon and night. Here it came: meat, meat and still more meat. It seemed unlikely there could be a single animal left in the country which had not been brought to the Borthwick's Freezing Works and slaughtered.

Suzy Jackson's suggestion of sabotaging the conveyor belt was a simple attempt to explode this boredom. The conveyor belt was their enemy. But Delia didn't mind the work. Her secret was to keep her mind on the job. That way you got through the day: It was an old factory trick. The moment you let your thoughts stray, you were lost and Friday night would never come; the clock would freeze stiff. But if you trained your thoughts on the next heart coming toward you and nothing more, on correctly picking up that single heart, and then on wrapping it economically in a single sheet of cellophane and setting it in a single tray, then you drifted through the day in a trance which defeated the boredom. You couldn't kill time. If you tried, it killed you first, because it became all you thought about. You could only let it lull you. This was what she had learned over the summer.

Delia listened to the usual talk, but didn't make any suggestions about what the girls should do this Friday night.

A lightning discussion over possible alternatives ended with the usual decision: to meet up and go out somewhere. The somewhere presupposed several options, which there weren't. The single idea was to station themselves for hours in front of the Texacana Take-away Bar and spurn undesirable young men in roving cars: In a town the size of Opunake, this meant spurning the same men over and over again; but the ritual was as harmless as it was deadening. Delia was invited to join them as a token of renewed acceptance, and she nodded her lukewarm agreement before returning to her mantra: Take it, wrap it, pack it. Again. Here it came, meat. To take, to wrap, to pack. She quickly sank back into a trance.

, , , , ,

Phillip had spent the first part of the morning at the files, alphabetizing and identifying unreturned books and their borrowers; the second part he devoted to writing overdue notices for a mail out.

When he had finished, he fashioned a rain hat out of a plastic bag and ran across the main street to the post office. It was empty.

He rang the bell while a radio played "How Sweet It Is to Be Loved by You."

As in every other shop in town, an unofficial holiday atmosphere had imposed itself as a result of the weather. The postmistress came to the counter carrying her teacup, looking relaxed and untrammeled.

"Hello," said Phillip.

"Morning," said the postmistress.

"I need some stamps."

"How many?"

"I'm not sure."

"Then we have a problem, don't we?"

Phillip lifted the box under his arm, placed it on the counter and started counting the rows of small red cards he had prepared. The postmistress waited, sipped her tea and watched without curiosity. After a significant period Phillip completed the tally and announced, "Four hundred and eighty-five."

The postmistress showed no interest. "Local or international?"

"Local. Around here."

"I know what local means. I'll have to rubber-stamp them." She took one of the red cards from the box and read: Opunake Public Library Overdue Reminder Notice.

"Don't expect to be popular," she said, and disappeared to the back with her cup of tea.

Phillip looked out the window and felt as if he were the only fish in a peculiar aquarium.

. . . . .

There was one overdue notice which Phillip had decided to deliver in person. His motives were impure. He had looked up the Chapman family status in his catalog that first morning when Delia had returned her book, and had been indecently delighted to find Mr. Martin Chapman to be in violation, on four counts. It was, however, the man's daughter he really hoped to see.

Driving his Ford with sleeves rolled to his elbows, Phillip threw the steering wheel in both directions to navigate the pot-holes and fallen trees along the country road, his head striking the roof with each large convulsion of the car. The unpaved road climbed toward the snow-capped cone of Mount Taranaki. Rising straight from the plains, it seemed to Phillip an impossible upheaval, reminding him of an infantryman's tent held up by a central pole. At regular intervals along the roadside lay animals drowned in the flash flood. On the carcasses, carrion birds marked their ownership but leaped into flight as Phillip passed, red sinews dangling from their beaks, swooping by his windshield in a flash of entrails.

The defunct library records showed Martin Chapman to be middle-aged, with a penchant for crime novels, particularly violent ones. Phillip had in mind the apocalyptic words of his uncle: Watch out for the old, they're as sleepless as rats.

The Chapman letterbox was an old iron milk urn on a post leaning at forty-five degrees. Phillip turned into the drive, juddering across the cattle stop, and headed up the tree-lined drive. A man who had clearly aged badly during the years in which the library had been out of service came onto the porch of the farm-house as he turned off the engine.

Phillip approached, and noticed a shotgun leaning against the railing.

"I've come for the books," he announced awkwardly.

"What books?"

"The overdue library books."

"What library?"

"The Opunake Public Library."

"Bullshit," the farmer barked. "That closed ages ago. I know where you're from. Well, you can tell your bosses from me that they'll have to take me out of here feetfirst, because that's the only way I'm leaving." He fixed an inscrutable glare on Phillip, then looked up into the gray sky. "Uh-oh, I think I can see those ducks coming back. Better keep your head down, my aim's a bit cockeyed these days."

Phillip could see no ducks, either in the air or on the ground, and he realized that metaphor was well within the reach of so avid and profligate a borrower.

Chapman picked up the shotgun.

Phillip stood in the slush of the drive, bookless. The nervous waiting game seemed to him insane considering the banality of his mission, which could have been conducted with less ambiguity through the post. However, he showed himself to be quite fearless—a remnant of his military training—and called the farmer's bluff. He gave the man no encouragement, but neither did he retreat.

"The library has been reopened," Phillip called, "and I've been given the authority to reclaim overdue books."

Considering this, Marty Chapman asked, "Exactly what library books are you talking about?"

Phillip took a tentative step toward him, and pulled out the overdue card on which were listed the bloodthirsty titles: *Dead Train, Dead Halt, Rivers of Death, Night of the Assassins,* all by Alistair MacLean. He handed the card to Chapman, who oddly held it at arm's reach to read. After a minute he seemed to remember.

"Oh, these," he said, then added paradoxically, "never had them. You've made a mistake."

Phillip didn't push his luck, and asked Mr. Chapman if he would please bring the books out.

"I told you. Never had them. Never saw them."

"Then I'll have to invoice you for them."

"No point in doing that. Won't pay it."

"Your signature is on the lending card."

"Never had them. You people are all the same."

"I'll leave the list of books with you."

As Phillip watched, Marty ceremoniously tore the list into

pieces and let the confetti float from the porch into the mud. Then he walked past Phillip and said, "Go in and look for yourself, if you like."

Phillip, baffled, stood in the mud and watched Chapman walk out onto his rain-soaked holding.

Phillip tentatively pulled open the screen door and stepped inside. Dark. Cool. The ticking of a clock. The sound of the refrigerator rattling from the kitchen. Old furniture, very old.

He looked around the room, but could not see a bookshelf. A pile of newspapers lay beside a reticulated potbelly stove.

"Hello?" he called, hoping to be answered by the thin creature who had once been alive in his headlights. He heard the clock. Tick tock. But no answer.

He walked straight into the well-ordered kitchen, but found no books there and so returned to the living room, scanning the walls a second time. He saw only proof of three generations of family life arranged with the hierarchical tidiness of an ancestral home. Brass pots hung on the wall from a time when a coal stove had heated them. Velvet-inlayed antique chairs fitted the tastes of a deceased grandmother.

In the doorway, he turned and looked up the stairs, paused and nervously began to climb them. At the top, he caught his breath, surprised by his reflection in a mirror—the face of an intruder, his eyes wide with a fear of being caught, and with the adrenal thrill of intrusion. He smoothed his hair, aware that at any second she might come out of a room, stop and stare at him, and say, "Hello." On the wooden surface of a sideboard sat a man's hairbrush, upturned, a comb planted neatly in its bristles, and a dozen buttons, none matching. He pulled out the drawers and found a rural telephone directory, a bag of screws. In another, he foraged and found an old watch without a strap, and several Christmas cards shedding glitter. He went into the master bedroom, his eye prepared for any number of war novels. The room was spare and its few objects were arranged with symmetrical precision. He found one book under the bed, *The Rearing and Management of Domestic Beef,* in reprint: A quick inspection showed it to be a private copy, and he slid it back into its haunt.

He left the room and stood outside another door for a moment. Her room. He entered, with his heart booming.

It was the room of a girl younger than Delia: A box of stuffed animals was pushed against the wall, the relations of the lone teddy bear which sat, legs splayed, on the single bed; the powder-blue walls were covered with triangular netball pennants and, in one corner, a map of North America. But there were also signs of maturity: a bra of a modest size was tossed on the floor, make-up was strewn on the dresser, and on shelves backed with mirror several dozen miniature colored bottles were multiplied to infinity in the glass. He opened a tiny vial and smelled its pungent per-fume, but it was not her smell.

This was that most romantic of rooms: the room of somebody in the final stage of leaving behind the toys of childhood in favor of the paraphernalia of an adult, a brief twilight that might last only until the next spring cleaning. Unable to suppress his curios-ity, he opened the drawers on the frail pretext of looking for books, and found her signature American T-shirts, torn jeans and multicolored underwear which he did well not to touch. He quickly closed them, noting, however, bows and barrettes, a dozen more bras, a bikini. He got down on his knees to peer under the bed. His nostrils filled with the odor of old leather before he found a punctured netball.

A poster of Brad Pitt looking destitute and sitting sidesaddle on a Harley-Davidson overhung a study desk on which were stacked the room's only books. A manual of logarithms. Three textbooks: biology, mathematics, geography. He opened an exer-cise book. Her handwriting was infantile. He closed it. Above the bed, along with the pennants, were several awards, medals, ribbons and citations for netball. He studied a poster of the New Zealand netball team and, beside it, a small dated photograph of

Delia. She was happy, on one foot, off-balance, about to receive the ball during some game. Her face was young and bright. These were the best faces, he thought; bright and innocent ones with a purity about them. These were the only faces which gave back to you the emotions and the sense of relief that made life bearable. When you woke up in the middle of the night, a face like this could save you; by day too you could screen yourself from darker thoughts by turning your eyes on it. Grief and fear could be repudiated by beauty because it was the finest distraction: wanting to have good looks at your side was never merely superficial. It was humanity's most popular insurance policy against the night.

On the way out Phillip noted that the latch on the door was broken.

No one accosted him as he left the house, and he drove away with nothing of what he had officially sought, but with several mental prizes which were far more compelling than any of the B-grade novels on his list. His compensation for the lost books was the assuaging of a rising curiosity, and the thrill of having been a ghost in the rooms of a stranger.

, , , , ,

That night Phillip went for a walk that took him out of town, toward Mount Taranaki.

He'd been reading about the dormant volcano and its history, reaching back to its prime around 2000 B.C. It was a significant date, the numerical twin of the present, equally relative to Jesus.

Walking down a road he kicked stones, and in microcosmic replay of the volcanic eruptions which had deposited giant boulders in the fields of Opunake, his small pebbles settled among the grass.

He walked for half an hour through the latest epidemic of frogs which had sprung up after the rains and which now proclaimed their annexed territory across the muddy fields, then turned off the road to follow a sign, HISTORIC GUN EMPLACEMENT. He paused for a moment to read the history of the huge gun, now a relic, which had been given to the district to repel the Japanese but was fired only once, amicably, in 1946 to placate the Returned Servicemen's Association.

From the top of the hill, he surveyed the farmland sweeping toward the coast. From lithographs in his library he knew that a vast tree-choked swamp had been transformed by five generations of farming families into this smooth 5,000-acre lawn which could have supported croquet and bowls but which instead served docile herds of sheep and cattle. He filled his lungs with damp evening air and coughed. Then he walked back down the hill.

Returning to town by a different route Phillip stopped beside a grove of trees in a field near the highway. He had noticed a strong light shining from the other side of the grove, throwing a curved penumbra up into the reddening sky. He quickly calculated a number of possible causes, but nothing fully explained it. Curious, he stepped forward, pushing back branches as he moved toward the origin of the light. With each step he became bathed in a glow ever more intense and revelatory. On the outer edge of the trees he finally held foliage from his eyes, his face lit up like an actor's, and he could not stop his imagination from prematurely dictating a single word: *spaceship.* But he was ahead of himself. Flooded in spotlights was a mystery of modern times, but not the enigma he had anticipated. A speed camera was being hoisted into its final position on top of a four-meter pole. Workers labored under it, and Phillip could see Sergeant Watson leaning on the fender of his patrol car, arms crossed, barking instructions to the men.

He watched a moment longer, saw the camera passed upward through three sets of hands to where it would be bolted in place, its sleepless eye directed down the highway, and then quietly withdrew into the trees, undetected.

As he slipped away, telling himself to relax, he could still hear the sergeant calling "Easy!" every few seconds until the warbling of the frogs took over again.

. . . . .

What is a vasectomy, after all? The severing of a tube, a useless tube at that, if fathering is not to be permitted, Sergeant Watson thought. It had no far-reaching impact on him. Was he any less a husband now that he could no longer produce even a drop of live baby batter? Or any less a policeman since the doctor had applied his scalpel? Perhaps it made him a better man, helping him to focus more on the living rather than the unborn. Like a priest. It had not harmed his sex life, that was for sure. Quite the contrary. Margaret, at whose behest he had submitted to the operation—accepting her decision that two full-grown children by an earlier marriage were quite enough for her—that sweet divorcée Margaret had turned into a menopausal tiger. Endless sexual congress was to be his compensation for his sacrificed fatherhood, and in as much as he was too exhausted to accurately evaluate the tradeoff, it had been a wild success. Yes, the doctor had warned him that in a certain percentage of men sex could seem meaningless for a time, and that a mood of pointlessness might pervade the act itself, but Watson would admit to none of this. He had never had it so good! No pitter-patter of little feet would ever ring down his hallway, but there were silk scarves stuffed under his mattress! Never would he find old chewing gum indented with cute infant toothprints in the backseat of his Corolla, but he had enough dirty talk ringing in his ears to fill a naval frigate.

Of course there were moments of regret, which were to be expected, but in no way were they responsible for his regular lunchtime visits to a local playground to sit between mothers and watch their toddlers grapple with the swings and roundabouts, and they had even less to do with his having adopted three African girls under the World Vision Aid Scheme at a price of three dollars a week: He kept their photos in the glove compartment of his patrol car purely by accident. Besides, he had his netball team. If he fantasized, he had twelve lovely and adoring daughters already.

It had been a slow day up to this point. Prior to the erection of the speed camera, he had made his official presence felt around town. His primary aim had been the propagation of calm. Years of experience had taught him that his most important daily duty was to walk the main street wearing a serene expression. He had done this, as usual, with both hands in his pockets, effecting a tranquil nonchalance, his hat tipped back so no one would fail to see the half measure of a smile. He stopped now and then to talk to shoppers with the dormant authority of a retired magistrate, and even bought an apple from a Chinese fruiterer, not to eat but simply to toss from hand to hand. By the time he retied his laces on the steps of the county offices and compared his watch with the town clock, he had once again given his constituency a near-perfect portrayal of aimlessness.

During this routine, he also calmed himself in readiness for the activation of the speed camera. He hoped it would be an advance, and not a cause of division. There would be a chorus of grumbles when the first new-look speeding tickets fell into local letterboxes. His phone would ring. He would be asked to make exceptions, as usual. Friends, family, hard times. He had always weakened before, seen life as give and take: This one was sick or this one had a father in the hospital; this one was broke and the dole hadn't come through this week. He often looked the other way. Now it would be out of his hands. People would have to appeal to a machine. He hoped he could sleep more soundly. And he hoped for peace in the modern world. The vas deferens. That was the name of the tube. The little nick had no effect on him.

When he got back to the station from the highway, he received a phone call from a local farmer. Roger Philpott had something urgent the sergeant should see. Watson was told to prepare himself for the unexpected.

, , , , ,

In the fading light, in the center of her barley field, stood Daphne Philpott with hands firmly planted on her hips. She was looking at the ground just in front of her feet. Roger Philpott, beside her, was waiting to hear what the sergeant had to say before speaking himself. Watson was merely dumbstruck.

A murmur of sighs had given way to an awesome silence as they looked at a perfect circle of flattened barley. The area was some six meters in diameter, and was scorched around its circumference. In the center of the circle lay a dead and badly flattened cow. The cow's ribs had obviously been crushed.

After an oppressive period of deliberation in which Watson turned on his flashlight and shone a beam around the ludicrously blackened rim and over the trammeled cow, he damned it as an unimpressive forgery, the work of an imbecile. It did not excite him in the least. "This isn't even funny," he said.

"No it's not," agreed Daphne Philpott. "That heifer was worth five hundred bucks."

Roger elbowed his wife, as if money was hardly relevant at a time like this.

Watson switched off his flashlight. It was clear to him that such a pitiful counterfeit could have been made in any of a dozen ways, even by the tread of human feet and the use of a domestic inflammable, and for the most part the entire enterprise was extremely amateur. "Some dickhead," he said. But if one aspect deserved a moment's reflection, it was the dead cow, which would have required seven full-grown men to move even an inch. Yet no visible signs of activity were present, neither vehicle tracks nor signs of a large group effort, leaving only the unpleasant conjecture that the cow had somehow attained its pancakelike dimensions right there in the center of the barley circle, presumably as a result of the application of pressure from above. Put plainly, something could have landed on it.

For this disastrous reason alone, the sergeant saw danger in releasing details. The cow factor, not easily explained, could inflame idle imaginations, of which there was no shortage. A certain discretion would therefore be asked of the Philpotts, a code of silence imposed. He saw his opportunity in Roger.

"Daphne, can I have a quick word with Roger alone, please? Would you mind? Just for a second."

They watched Daphne walk back to the house across the barley field employing a breaststroke motion, any trace of her path vanishing after a few seconds as the reeds closed behind her.

"What I want you to do is to keep this to yourself."

"I'm quite happy to do that," said the farmer.

"Do I have to say why?"

Philpott shook his head, proving that many years had passed since Watson had needed to tell him anything twice.

"Obviously, someone thinks they're being humorous."

"Wouldn't look like this anyway, would it," Roger mused, "if a flying saucer had landed?"

Watson looked at his contemporary. "Why is that?"

"It wouldn't look like this. If something had landed." Roger was waving his index finger over the flattened area with a contemplative expression. "Anything realistic would have to leave a much bigger mark than this. They think there's no life in this solar system, right, so it would've had to come from—I dunno, another solar system. But this mark, right, isn't big enough for even your basic commercial chopper to land."

Watson gave him one of his looks. "Roger, okay? *Nothing landed.*"

"I know. I'm just saying."

"Don't."

"Okay."

"It's just . . ." Roger tailed off.

Watson shot him a look. "It's just, what?"

Roger shrugged. "Nothing, but I s'pose you've gotta know."

"Yes?" Watson was beginning to lose patience. The day had been long enough.

"Daff and me . . ."

"Yeah?"

"Well, me and Daff . . ."

"I've heard this part, Roger!"

"We think we heard something. We heard something weird."

"What do you mean, weird?"

"Well, y'know . . ."

"No, I do not know."

"High-pitched noise. It was a high-pitched noise."

"What are you trying to tell me, Roger?"

"Nothing."

"That you heard a spaceship?"

"I'm not saying anything. But who knows."

"What are you implying?"

"Well . . ."

"Well, what?"

"Well . . . it wasn't a million miles, I s'pose, from a *spaceship noise.*"

"Shut up. Or I'll shoot you, Roger. I have a gun in the car."

"The dogs started going mad," Philpott continued, ignoring the fickle threat.

Watson held up his hand. "You ever heard a spaceship before?"

"No."

"You haven't. No. So how the fuck do you know what a spaceship sounds like?"

"From the movies, I guess."

"Roger, they *invent* that sound. Nobody knows how a spaceship sounds."

"It's a high-pitched noise—"

"Roger, shut the fuck up."

Watson's patience was fully deployed, and his sweaty blue police shirt was attaching itself to his skin as he raised his arms to push Roger backward several meters.

"You heard a high-pitched noise in the middle of the night? *You left your TV on, Roger!*"

"Harvey . . ."

"Your TV was on!"

"If it was just the noise, maybe, but then we come out here this morning, checking the irrigation trenches, and we find—"

"I thought you just said this mark isn't big enough for something from another galaxy!"

"I'm not a scientist!"

"I'm prepared to arrest you, Roger, if you tell anyone about this."

"I'm not actually saying it was a spaceship. You don't have to yell."

"What are you saying, Roger?"

"There's the Pentagon."

As he left the site of the hoax, Harvey Watson lost his bearings and found that the barley resisted him in a way which hadn't been apparent when Daphne had gracefully left the scene. The fibrous stalks seized his wrists, tugging at him with a serpentine strength, refusing to let him pass easily and threatening to drag him under. Roger Philpott, watching from the clearing, was able to see only the top of the policeman's blue hat, which appeared to drift away supported on the surface of the waving grass.

, , , ,

The next morning the narrow road leading up to the Philpotts' farm became a dramatic motorway.

Car after car flew off the asphalt into the loose gravel of the farm road, only to struggle for purchase on the steep unpaved incline. The resulting jam of stalled cars kept the area's tow trucks in constant use.

On the town boundary the speed camera, only twelve hours old, clicked with the regularity of a school-bus conductor's punch. It recorded so many violations of the law that the roll of film inside it, capable of photographing fifty misdemeanors, had to be twice replaced by Sergeant Watson that morning.

Many of the town's shops, and all of those providing non-essential services, sported sudden BACK IN HALF AN HOUR cards on their doors. The tobacconist and the priest could not be found. Father O'Brien cut short a christening and eloquently reduced the ceremony to a quick renunciation of the devil. He wished to witness firsthand a genuine theological quandary. Even before he saw the landing site, he'd decided to address it in the following Sunday's sermon.

The streets of Opunake emptied. Even a government road gang, contracted to paint a continuous 1,000-kilometer-long center line on State Highway 3, absented itself from its duties. Their trucks lay idle at the sides of the highway, shovels ditched and sunk into the gravel, the abandoned line an exclamation point. Only the funereal flow of slaughtered animals in the freezing works continued unabated.

The procession of people to the barley field, welcomed by the Philpotts, insured that the number gathered in an arc around the landing pad seldom dropped below twenty. Daphne Philpott and her husband presided over the enigma, keeping order and exercising a moderating influence on those intent on wild conjecture and denunciatory comment, dutifully reinforcing the police viewpoint that vandals were the most likely perpetrators, and yet keeping alive the entirely contradictory theory that a number of organizations, including the Pentagon, worked in many covert ways which could not always be immediately interpreted.

Father O'Brien quickly arrived and restrained himself from sprinkling holy water on the ground, not wanting to inflame imaginations. Deborah Kerr's father got down on his hands and knees, and in a forensic effort to detect if a whiff of fuel remained, sniffed the ground like a bloodhound. But most found the attempt to fool them laughable. To cite one inconsistency, you could easily see that the barley was bent over in a westward direction across the entire surface, and it was clear that a flying saucer, like a landing helicopter, would drive the barley out from the center like spokes on a wheel. The circumference of the circle was also poorly singed. Only in random clumps was it blackened properly, almost as if the counterfeiter had had trouble lighting the wet barley or had run out of matches. A child, it was agreed, could have done a better job. Yet imaginations were stirred. A dozen practical suggestions were offered as to how the illusion could be improved upon, and the Philpotts had to stop several farmers from entering into the center of the circle to lecture the crowd. The site, Roger Philpott said, had to be kept in its original state as police evidence.

The only inscrutable mystery was the cow. With its crushed ribs and no evidence in the barley of the telltale movement of the heavy machinery or men who had moved it, there remained only the pernicious possibilities that it had been crushed from above, or, barring this, had somehow plummeted from the skies. No one dared to suggest the latter view out loud.

Unnoticed by most people, eye pressed to a camera, an unknown journalist took his finger off the shutter-release button. The man, in his late forties, sporting a lank ponytail unsuited to his age and with a small but memorable cleft in the tip of his nose, captured on film Opunake citizens gathered like a public gallery around a putting green. None knew he had been photographed. The journalist used a wide-angle lens which foreshortened the picture, distorting the dead cow to look immense. The onlookers became elongated, fat around the middle, their grotesque heads bending inward toward the top of the frame like gargoyles.

And this was how they appeared in a national tabloid newspaper that Sunday.

, , , , ,

Phillip finished sellotaping the torn pages of a set of recently sequestered high school yearbooks and went outside to turn over the CLOSED sign, ready for business.

After half an hour spent writing notes to himself in a private journal, notes to remind him of tasks, aims and objectives, he heard the squeaking of rubber soles on floorboards and looked up to see Delia Chapman in her factory whites and gum boots walking toward the bookshelves.

She moved to browse among the shelves of limply bound books. She trailed her index finger across the fabric spines, feeling the many shapes of rain-contorted volumes. At the end of the row, she pulled out a dilapidated world atlas and only just managed to support it on her right arm as she carefully turned the wrinkled pages. Her eyes wandered randomly across the colored pages before she gently closed and replaced the book on the shelf. She was aware of being watched.

She had noticed the librarian's attentions ever since she'd come through the door. He had looked at her with such familiarity, she wondered if she might have seen him before. Perhaps it was just every librarian's duty to monitor all visitors and protect his stock of books.

In the center of the room she opened a file drawer, inserted her finger midway into the bank of age-spotted cards and idly studied the fading information. The tightly packed cards exerted a pressure on her finger, and when she withdrew it a fine puff of dust rose up. While the librarian's eyes were lowered she took the opportunity to run her fingernail down the length of the file in an arpeggio, and a cloud of paper dust formed and then dispersed. She repeated the action a couple more times, and stopped only when she realized she was being monitored. In the packing of offal, you never found textures like this. She liked this brittleness, the dry-attic atmosphere of this library, the preserved secrets only a puff away from disintegration. To work in such a swarm of decay must be exciting. It would be refreshing. It was the opposite of her own job, she thought: butchered hearts, almost indestructible, compared with books like autumn leaves; her animal junk versus these brittle treasures. She turned to ask for help.

Phillip addressed her before she could speak.

"Just what kind of book were you after?" He approached, wearing a strong cologne, and her memory awakened her to the possibility that she had smelled it before.

Without saying a word, he closed the file drawers, reimposing a stately order.

She looked into his face. His eyes were dark, like his hair, dark skin, in his late twenties, a nicely turned nose, clean-shaven, arguably handsome except for his ears which were out of scale, just on the big side. There was a tension she could read in his face, one not related at all to the question he had asked. With their bodies close, almost touching, he said, "I was wondering if you'd ever come in." Then she understood what this thing was in his face: It was the tension of someone begging to be recognized.

She decided to help him. "I never come in here. So why were you wondering that?"

"You returned a book."

"A book?"

"Yes."

"What book?"

"You returned a book. To the late returns box. The other day. Actually, three weeks ago. You don't remember?"

"Did I?"

"Do you need glasses?"

She was finding him difficult. "Why?" she asked.

"Your eyes are squinting."

"I've been working all night, that's all."

"I know. You work at the freezing works. Don't you remember me?"

"Why should I remember you?"

"We've met before."

"I'd remember you."

"But you don't."

"I might."

"Do you?"

"No."

"Are you going to show me how to use this or not?" Delia indicated the card files. A strange guy, this one, she thought. Full of obscure questions and something odder: no sense of humor. Other men would have attempted a joke by now, no matter how cheap. This librarian was almost rude. If he didn't want visitors, he shouldn't put a big sign in the window.

Phillip asked her for a title. She didn't know one. He asked for the author.

"I don't know that, either," she said.

He said it would be hard for him to help her further unless she could be more specific. What was the general subject which interested her?

Delia asked if he had any books remotely to do with the unexplainable.

With mounting nervous tension she watched him pull out one impressive drawer after another and flick vigorously through the files, raising a storm of dust. His ability to read the information on each card in a fraction of a second impressed her. She realized that to some degree he was showing off.

Several times he left the filing cabinet to go over to the shelves and look for a book, but each time he returned empty-handed.

Finally, he slammed all the drawers shut and turned to her. "Nothing. Sorry."

"Doesn't matter."

"The files are in a mess. I haven't sorted everything out yet, so I can't say for sure, but there doesn't seem to be anything, as such, on what you want."

"Doesn't matter." She was growing uncomfortable with his stare. He looked annoyed again. Perhaps the failure of the library to provide even one book on such a general topic was an embarrassment.

"Y'see, people around here usually want explanations most of the time," he said. "The books we've got here are pretty much fifty percent gardening, fifty percent war. But I could order something from Wellington."

"No."

She started to leave. He followed her.

"I looked up everything. I looked up 'Miracles.' Then I went to 'Supernatural,' but there was nothing. I'm sorry. 'Ghosts.' There was a play by Ibsen, but I can't find it on the shelf, either. There is a book called *Unsolved Crimes,* but I don't think that's what you want. Finally, I even looked up 'God' on a cross-reference. But there is only the Bible listed under him. And that's out on loan."

She stopped and looked at him. His ears weren't too bad, she supposed. "Where did you learn to do this?"

Without hesitation he told her how, during a two-year commission in the army, he had completed a diploma of librarianship.

"The army has a library?!"

"Oh, yeah."

"What sort of library does an army have?"

"Fifty percent war, and, ah . . . fifty percent gardening."

Delia smiled. He wasn't entirely weird. "Really?"

"Yes."

"So, why aren't you in the army still?"

He paused and then continued. "Court-martialed."

"Did you kill someone?"

"No. Is that what people are saying about me?"

"I don't know." She regretted her question. She was no good at jokes either, was disastrous at them.

"I lost my temper."

"What happened?"

"I threw someone across the canteen and knocked over fifteen gallons of boiling hot soup."

"That was all?"

"No. Then I started to hit his head against the floor. I had to be stopped."

"Why?"

"I had my reasons." His face clouded.

A mystery man, she thought.

Delia decided to ask him a question then, for reasons she couldn't quite place. She could think only that it had something to do with the smell of his cologne, which reminded her of a dental clinic.

"Do you believe in people from . . . from outer space . . . and stuff?"

He paused, remembering the sight of her in his headlights three weeks earlier. "Oh, I should have said. I looked up in the files under 'Alien' too."

"Why?"

"I've heard about you and this thing. People come into libraries and they talk."

"I thought that wasn't allowed? Talking."

They fixed each other with unwavering stares. She sensed his cynicism. "You don't believe in it, do you?" she ventured.

"In aliens? Who knows. Why not? It's an interesting hypothesis."

She liked the way he said hypothesis, at least. He was comfortable with big words, perfectly at home in them. She bet he came up with a hypothesis every five minutes.

"I can't believe you don't remember me, though," he said.

"I've got to go."

"I can order you a book, if you like?"

"Don't worry about it," said Delia, and walked to the door. She felt his eyes on her from behind.

"How about a drink sometime?" he called.

She stopped in the foyer and turned. "What?"

"I wondered if you want a drink sometime?"

She thought about it—a drink with a librarian, big words, jokes which died, odd questions, a dentist's smell, unwanted emotions—and then shook her head. Her gaze had fallen onto her hands, which she rotated as if inspecting them. A new idea had occurred to her, which brought her suddenly back toward him. She asked if she could wash her hands.

He pointed to the women's cloakroom, and watched as she walked squeakily across the floor. He listened for a very long time to the sounds of running water. And then, after ten minutes, she came out, nodded politely and left the library without another word.

Phillip felt he'd lost both a customer and a potential date.

. . . . .

Delia walked down the street pursued by half a dozen small children, one of whom wore a Space Invader T-shirt, skipping at the head of the sudden parade like a cheerleader. As the group passed, occasional front doors opened on the council flats and still more kids spilled out to join in, taking up chanting the theme from *Star Wars*. But this was even better than a movie, far superior to a distant Luke Skywalker and the corny practice of *letting the force be with you* in a galaxy *far far away*, because this was happening right here in Opunake. And as much as Delia shooed them away, the kids were undeterred, circling her, demanding confirmation, but scared to touch her. She was their neighborhood superhero! First had been the story itself, but now had come the hard evidence of a landing site: It was the fulfillment of years of doodlings and rocket-ship talk, of a lifetime of games played with Lego in the car, of conjured lunar landings on the lounge carpet, all conducted to a soundtrack of *wiishes* and *whooshes* and *whiirrs*. Here at last was the real thing, in Harrison Street.

At the town limits, the kids finally gave up their pursuit. Superheroes needed their rest after all. Superman needed to restore himself in the Ice Citadel; Batman had his mansion; let Delia then return to her sanctuary. The children watched her go, hoping to see something amazing, but soon realizing she preferred to walk away like a normal person. Quickly, they broke sticks, made antennae of them and turned back to town.

. . . . .

Deborah Kerr, Suzy Jackson, Yvonne McKay and Lucinda Evans—who had been allowed to join the group now that Delia had stopped socializing with them—tried to recall exactly what Delia had said. In their renewed lust for details Suzy Jackson said, "I don't believe it. Maybe she went out to Philpott's place herself? You reckon, or not?"

"Oh, yeah, and carried a dead cow in there herself?"

"This is brilliant," said Suzy, letting out air.

"I know, I know."

"This is the best."

"I know."

They were sitting in the park on the green bench under the statue of the unidentified soldier, their legendary meeting spot. They fell silent for a moment, speculating on how the most entertainment could be extracted from this development.

"Apparently Harvey is freaking out," said Deborah.

"So is everybody. Mum won't even let anyone talk about it around our place," Suzy added.

Additions to Delia's original story, including the embellishment of the group-sex incident with aliens, had done the rounds. Someone had spray painted on the outside wall of the rugby club rooms the slogan DELIA DOES A DOZEN. The only person who didn't think it was even vaguely funny was Delia.

Deborah had no sympathy. "Well, she started it. It's no fuckin' good getting upset now."

Everyone agreed. Suzy produced a pack of Horizon Mild.

"This is the best," repeated Yvonne McKay.

. . . . .

Half an hour before sunset, the mayor paid a visit to the reputed landing site in the company of the sergeant. By now the cow had been removed, so Watson walked into the center of the trampled patch to impersonate the animal for Sullivan's benefit.

"Get up, you fucking idiot," said the mayor, appalled to see the sergeant assume the proportions of a dead cow.

"You wanted to see."

"I've got an imagination."

The men stood in silence on the edge of the outrage.

The mayor had a question. "What do you reckon about the cow?"

"Don't know."

"Someone had to get it in here somehow."

"No way. A vehicle would have carved a road in here."

The mayor laughed and pointed. "What's that, then?" He indicated the new "road" leading in to the site—freshly churned mud marked with heavy tire tracks.

"That's how we got the cow out," the sergeant countered. "That's what I mean. Look at the mess we made just getting it out!"

The mayor's short nod conveyed an element of doubt.

"What is it?" asked the sergeant.

"You're sure that wasn't here before?"

Blood rushed to Watson's face. What kind of question was this?

"You sure you didn't miss seeing it?" the mayor asked.

"Yes!"

"How did it die? Throat cut? Did you see a bullet hole?"

"Crushed. Just crushed." Watson thought he'd better calm himself. "By the looks of it."

"Jesus," said the mayor, who wondered briefly if this could somehow be turned to his advantage as a tourist attraction, before discounting it. "There's always someone who thinks he's a comedian."

The sergeant agreed, familiar with the irrefutable logic that every group held together by alcohol had, in its midst, an individual who would always take it upon himself to provide crude entertainment. What resulted always required his presence.

"What are you gonna do?" asked the mayor, feeling he had no reason to become involved.

"Nothing. Pretty harmless stuff. The dead cow is the only worry, that's all. I'll be looking for whoever is responsible."

"Don't want this to get out, all the same."

The mayor's application of delicate pressure did not go unnoticed by the sergeant.

"No," he replied. "Of course not."

"I mean, out of the area. Don't want this sort of thing drawing attention away from our Aquatic Center. You know what journalists are like."

"Of course," agreed the sergeant.

Five

. . . .

THE ROAD TO BETHLEHEM

The journalist Vic Young drove a mud-caked vehicle into the concrete labyrinth of a multistoried basement car park with an urgency his superiors had not seen for some time. Playing in his head was a vague but interconnected group of concepts: the noon deadline, physical exhaustion, a history of poor relations with his fellow human beings, a history of pitiful relations with the opposite sex, a brewing midlife crisis, the failure of the sixties to deliver the promised utopia, and a pinch of professional excitement related to his latest story. He jumped on the brakes with a deafening screech. Unbelievably, some corporate dickhead had taken his parking space.

Where once he might have quelled his emotions and parked elsewhere, he now decided to shunt this enemy car backward and so teach its driver a sharp millennial lesson. The car park underpinned the *Sunday Enquirer* newspaper, his home office: He had his rights, and he would invoke them. This new Vic, quite unlike the old Vic Young from Features, Vic of Midweek fame,

Vic of clever axioms and inspired entendres, whose sudden loss
of good humor in the past year alone had severed most of the
lifelines to his past, seemed determined to reinvent himself as a
monster. Twenty years of casual indulgence had brought him to
this point, where pleasure was now merely repetitive and everything else meaningless and dull. This chronic professional and
personal coma now required him, like a masochist, to seek ever
more severe jolts of electrotherapy, if just to keep his wits alive,
and this car park situation would serve as his latest stimulant.

Coupling like beasts, the two fenders became locked in combat.
The engine of Young's car revved to its outer limits and his freely
rotating tires created such an amplified scream in the chambers
of the car park that it quickly drew a small crowd. He lifted his
foot from the accelerator only when the offending car was
shunted well clear. He switched off his engine and confronted
the small gallery, among whom, identifying himself quickly, was
the car's owner. Young rose from his vehicle, imperious, happy
to pursue the dispute verbally.

"You were in my space," offered Young with conviction, checking that his mini ponytail, the last vestige of a hippie past, of his
relaxed free-thinking freedom-loving casually copulating history,
had not fallen loose.

"Your space? What's your number?" barked the bald Asian
man, veins appearing on his neck.

"Twenty-five. Okay? See there? Twenty-five. Read it! My car
park, asshole."

"What deck?"

"Deck?" asked Young, his voice bleeding away.

"Deck! Deck!"

Young looked around. The sign said 2B. He was on the
wrong deck.

Abruptly, his mood switched from self-righteous bravado to
shame. "Oh," he said. "You're right. I'm not sure how this could
have happened. Let me move my car at once. No hard feelings,

eh? Dreadfully sorry about that." Young's now lugubrious voice
was that of his former self, as it had been on his first day of
employment: shallow, threatened, insincere. He returned to his
car, escaped his audience and offered them the squeak of his tires
as he made for lower decks.

He arrived in his boss's office without announcement, still
sweating hard and with his hand venting his shirt at the collar.
Fumbling with buttons, he fell into a chair in front of the editor,
who looked up and at once was taken by the startling enormity
of the cleft in his employee's nose.

Ray Hungerford was the claret-faced relieving editor who had
just been watching the afternoon fade in the window. Hungerford
had maintained what was to have been a short-term position for
five long years, and no replacement for him was in sight. His
tenure was like that of a sentry who had been sent out to stand
guard for a few minutes and await further orders, but whose commander had forgotten him so that five years later, the commander
killed and the war over, the sentry was still out there alone, gun
cocked and primed, fighting an imaginary one-man campaign.

"I'm back," Young sighed.

"I see that."

Young sat in the chair and next began tugging at his cuffs as
if he were trying to escape his clothes. "I've got something for
you," he announced. "It's utterly fucking brilliant. But first, did
you get my flood stories?"

"You spell like a five-year-old." Hungerford had just been reading Young's reports on the flooding in South Taranaki. "We
couldn't even decipher half of it. My granddaughter writes more
clearly than you."

"I wrote it in the car. The road was cut off by a river. Water
was coming in through the door. I'm lucky to be alive. Welcome
back, Vic. Thank you, Ray. It's nice to be here."

"What have you got?"

"In a minute. Banalities first. How are you?"

"I can't breathe. These high rises, five thousand windows, none open, not one. They know we'll jump. Now then . . ."

"Okay. Get ready." Young joined his hands in excitement.

"Can you please spare me the preamble?"

"Ready?"

"Go ahead."

, , , ,

The editor listened patiently to the report and then said, "You're kidding."

"I've got a photo."

"Where?"

"Right here." Young tapped his camera bag with a satisfied grin.

"But how did you—"

"I stopped for gas. Heard the story. Then followed a stream of traffic into the countryside."

Hungerford stared at his employee. Young began to nod his head, realizing his news was having its intended effect. "You see?"

Ray Hungerford rocked back in his chair. He was sixty-two years old, and bore such an uncommon resemblance to Spencer Tracy that people were often fondly disposed to him without quite knowing why. His interest, which had been stirred by Vic Young's initial description, now blossomed into a carnivorous appetite.

Young rose to his feet and adjusted his collar. "I need expenses and another car. The Granada isn't running well." He was clearly requesting use of the Rover, which was usually reserved for the personal use of the editor.

"Take the Honda."

"I don't want the Honda. I need four-wheel drive. You should see this area of the country. It's half submerged in mud."

The editor demanded to be called on the telephone every four hours, afraid that this could become an expensive ghost chase. Vic Young was already gone from the room, but his agreement to the last demand came to Hungerford from the hall.

Seated in silence once again, Hungerford sighed heavily, the bellows of his chest trying to alleviate the stuffy, artificial climate of the office. He leaned forward across the desk, switched on a small fan and directed it, with his forefinger, toward his face. He attempted to breathe freely for the first time, his lips slightly parted, his lonely tenure now a protracted struggle for air.

, , , ,

Vic Young slid into Opunake like an eel into a river. Only Phillip Sullivan noticed the ripple, as the green Rover rolled up the main street past the library. Phillip was high-glossing the edges of the new bulletin board in front of the library, an improvement of his own which he hoped would soon carry public notices and work-wanted cards, and generally enhance the library's function as the nexus of community life. When he looked up, Young's large mud-caked wagon crept past him. The stranger's face was visible through the wiper-made arches on the windshield. At such a speed, it would have been polite to give a friendly wave or a nod of the head, but none was given. And before Young pushed the sunglasses back onto his nose to drive on, the two men locked eyes with each other, oblivious to either the other's employment in the service of the printed word or, more important, their mutual interest in Delia Chapman. Though they would never speak a single word to each other as long as they both lived, the accident of their recurrent nonmeetings would be a feature of the next few weeks.

The cleft-nosed journalist took a room at the Sahara Desert Motor Inn. He was told that the difference between a motor inn and a motel was that the former had more car parks than rooms. Above the reception desk was a sign: NO RACKET. NO GUESTS. NO STEREOS.

Young made a favorable impression on the manager by concealing the purpose of his visit. He convinced her that he was a writer of articles for the ministry of agriculture and fisheries simply by sounding knowledgeable on the subject of seawater. Dirty seawater, he intoned, needed to be detected early because all life on the planet was reliant on our vast oceans. He noted with concern that she served fish on her cafeteria menu, and asked in an official tone if the fish were taken locally. She confirmed nervously that they were. He replied that this was just as well, and left her standing there, perplexed but relieved.

He was afforded the best room in the motor inn. It was situated as close as possible to the main building, which was desirable because it placed him farthest from the generator which raised an infernal din every six hours, sending the household beagles into a crazed ferment consistent with a dose of hydatids. He was allotted two car parks, under an awning, and was treated from then on like a dignitary. But no greater attention was paid than to the quality of the water served to him in his room in a cut-glass decanter with quartered lemons and a daily note consisting of the single word: "Compliments."

Shortly after his arrival he phoned his employer in a state of considerable excitement to say that the story had already improved dramatically. Refueling at the petrol station which Young had used the day before when passing through town, he had talked again to the pump jockey named Max, who told him that a young local girl was saying she had seen the spaceship, met with the visitors and had sex with them. Not with one, but with several. She had even made a report to the local cop. The editor's silence on the other end of the phone was all the encouragement he needed.

After having settled into his small, uncomfortable room, Young took a drive down to the freezing works. He sat in his green wagon eating foot-long licorice straps, waiting for a changeover in shift workers, hoping to identify the girl by the description expertly elicited from the manager of the Broadway Petrol Station. He looked for a reedy girl, trusting somehow that she would do something to identify herself. Perhaps she would be at the center of a gang, already famous, a coterie in her wake. But at the end of the shift he failed to find her, and he left without his snapshot.

. . . . .

The next morning, after a breakfast fit for a king, Vic Young bought film for his camera, avoiding all questions about his identity or intentions from the curious girl in the chemist shop, and walked across the main street to take a photograph of the noticeboard in front of the comically small library. Pinned to the new blue felt was a card offering "Gardening Services" and another "Taxidermy—Good Rates, All Animals and Pets Considered."

Inside the library, Phillip Sullivan was taping strips of cardboard to reinforce the spines of old books. Young nodded when he entered but did not speak as he moved toward the first shelf of books. He ran his eye along them in idle amusement. Phillip recognized him as the driver from the day before, and suspected that it was something other than an interest in literature which had brought him here.

Traipsing slowly along the shelves, Young's eye observed local histories, pioneer works and the dilapidated volumes of dated government almanacs. But it was his journalistic talent for stumbling upon unsought gold mines that made him stop in front of a pile of Opunake High School yearbooks. The journals were piled in sequence, dating back a hundred years, and as he picked up one journal after another he passed back in time. In less than ten minutes he found what he had not dared hope to find. In a small, aged photograph the pubescent Delia Chapman held a netball: a serious girl from what he could see, long dark hair, prettyish, somewhat apart from the others, either by accident or disposition, squinting, no more than twelve. She wore GS on her uniform, for goal-shoot, he presumed.

This picture allowed Vic Young to put a face to the name which had kept him from his laptop all through the previous night, failing to make a start on the story, waiting for inspiration, and disturbed from sleep by the distant generator.

Out of sight of the librarian, he was about to cough and covertly to tear the page from the annual when Phillip appeared like an avenging angel behind him. Young's thumb and forefinger froze, already applying tension to the desired page. Phillip had caught him in the throes of a familiar library felony—the excised leaf—but before either man could say a word the voice of the mayor broke up proceedings, saving Young's reputation.

"What the hell is this?!" Sullivan walked up to the front desk, brandishing a yellow slip. Phillip went to meet him. Young watched from a distance, still holding the yearbook.

"They were overdue," said Phillip. "I left you three reminder notices on the kitchen table."

"And you *bill* me?"

Phillip took the slip from his uncle and read the titles aloud. *Fishing the Tongariro, The Cross and the Swastika* and *Chile Under Pinochet*. He looked up at his uncle. "You've got them?"

"I don't know. You could have looked yourself. I'm putting a roof over your head!"

"I did look."

"Then why didn't you talk to me about it before you billed me?"

Phillip pointed out that he had sent out 485 such slips at the same time and didn't discriminate. Also, he added, he had tried to talk to him. "You told me not to bother you with it. You said you were busy. You said I had to take complete control."

"You call this *control*? No, I'll tell you what this is called. In the army, buster, this is called friendly fire. You're taking out your own fucking men here!" He had grabbed the yellow slip again and was waving it, wounded.

Phillip faced his uncle confidently. "I don't think so. It was applying one rule for everyone."

"This is bullshit! I'm speechless. I'm speechless!"

Vic Young had moved toward the door, holding up the yearbook.

"What do you want?" barked the mayor, turning upon him.

"I'd like to have this issued."

"What's stopping you? Give me the fucking book, then." The mayor had assumed complete authority; he rolled up his sleeves and took charge of the situation himself.

"But I'm not a member. I was wondering if I could borrow it for just the afternoon."

"What do you mean you're not a member? And what do you mean just the afternoon? Just the afternoon? What is that all about?"

Young showed the mayor the yearbook. The mayor, already the most hostile of librarians, was further puzzled. "What do you wanna read this fucking thing for, eh? This isn't for reading."

Young had been anticipating this moment. He'd felt all day that the cloak of his secrecy was threadbare. The stares of local people had steadily denuded him all morning. Still, the time was not yet auspicious for him to make plain his purpose.

"I'm interested in the history of the Opunake High School. I'm a journalist," Young said.

A decisive moment was at hand. The mayor and the librarian gave Young their full attention. A journalist? It became clear both were waiting for elaboration.

"Well, I, ah . . . I document old provincial-type institutions," Young replied, strategically ignoring the younger man, looking at the mayor, the key player.

At a loss as to how to respond in the capacity of librarian, Jim Sullivan merely smiled. "Old institutions, eh? I see." Then he rallied. "Well, you would need to produce some pretty convincing

ID before I could let you borrow something like that. That's irre-
placeable, that book."

The journalist nodded, the book a worthless weight in his
hands. He produced his press card from his trouser pocket.

The mayor studied it. "I see," he mumbled. "And what newspaper is this, then?"

"The *Enquirer. Sunday Enquirer.*"

"Oh, yeah, okay." The mayor reacted coolly, then turned to
look at Phillip, from whom he had just confiscated all responsibility, and said in a voice intended to sound as if the timely arrival
of the journalist had been expected, "Well, why didn't you say
so? Phillip, here, will help you with this request, won't you, Phil?
Good man. Good man."

, , , , ,

Some two acres of prime commercial land had been cleared in
preparation for the Opunake Aquatic Center, and it was with
tremendous pride that the mayor showed the site and its plans to
Vic Young.

There was to be a park area with fountains and statues hem-
ming an Olympic-sized swimming pool: Here, Sullivan proudly
indicated the flooded pool site, a filthy swamp. But the most startling feature would be the hydra-slide—a huge tubular plastic
pretzel, which would carry the thrill seeker down through a dozen
hellish twists and turns to expel him at the bottom into a small
plunge pool. It was hoped that the wake in the splash would make
spectators gasp. The mayor had already pledged to make the first
descent himself, and this publicity stunt would be the keynote of
the opening ceremony. At a cost of one and a half million dollars
he was committing his quiet rural taxpayers to a five-year program
of repayments. The object of this, as he explained to the journalist
while standing in the middle of the devastated land, was to beef
up the area's tourist potential and scotch the perception among

travelers that Opunake was a one-horse town. The journalist nodded with professional patience, boredom seeping into every cell of his body. "I see," he muttered woodenly from time to time.

The first preconstructed section of the Hydra-Slide, the loop-the-loop, was to arrive from Auckland that night by road. The mayor, imagining that the journalist had come to town expressly to observe this moment and had chosen not to mention it before now only as a professional courtesy, clapped Vic heartily on the back.

"I never believed that story about you being interested in old provincial institutions, not for a second."

Young closed his notebook, upon which he had written only three words—"loop the loop"—and asked, "So, what about this spaceship thing?"

The mayor was still surveying the estate while he absorbed the question. He didn't immediately turn to face the journalist. But when he did, his voice conveyed an aura of such gravity that it was clear his words were to be considered both his first and his last on the subject.

"Mr. Young, we don't know anything about that sort of thing around here."

Immediately, the mayor steered the conversation back to the safer shore of his other major achievements: angle parking in the main street, and a savage 50 percent cut in his own council staff in the last year. Even the lighthouse keeper, the mayor bragged, had been replaced by a silicon chip and now remained at the remote outpost in a humiliating supervisory capacity only.

VIRTUAL VIRGINS

Delia's cousin had been playing netball in the Saturday morning match, taking the position of center, and she was not feeling her best. She had consistently incurred the wrath of Harvey Watson, in his capacity as netball coach, who shouted at her from the waterlogged sideline of the court.

"Yvonne! Yvonne! Go forward! B3, B3! Oh, Jesus Christ!"

The girls were not moving well, often taking far more than the lawful two steps before throwing the ball onward. Suzy Jackson, fighting a hangover from an illicit night at the pub, beckoned blindly at midcourt for the ball. Deborah Kerr, too short for her opponent, was flummoxed. Watson was beside himself. His new moves, a series of vectors, dotted lines and arcs which had a poetic simplicity on paper, had no place in reality, and the game was in total disarray.

"Get it to, Delia! Get it to, Dee!"

Delia Chapman had just been substituted onto the court and ran to take up her position as goal-shoot near the hoop. Bruises were visible on her arms and legs. She received the ball within seconds and, almost without looking, tossed it toward the ring, a lob which fell through the net with a swish. Watson shouted with relief, "That's it now! Like that again! Come on now!" Delia was his secret weapon, his ace in the hole. She often gave him a sweet taste of victory: the feeling that for a moment he was a winner in this life. It was no wonder he favored her and held her in reserve.

With Delia's goal, the complexion of the game changed. Strategies which had been collapsing all morning suddenly flowed across the court, almost as Watson had imagined them all week over his pungent breakfasts, and by the final whistle, his voice hoarse from shouting, he was surrounded by his players in a triumphant rush.

He tried to embrace the team as if it were a single entity, throwing his arms around the huddle like a madman in love with a massive tree. The shrill screams of young women filled his ears. Their joyful kisses on his cheek were endless, and the aroma of sweat and damp cotton intoxicated this man for whom duty, honor, a pension and professional respect all played bridesmaids to sweet moments such as this.

They went to celebrate at the pub, where he bought Fanta for all the young women, a beer for himself, and sat, a picture of contentment, the envy of all the other men in the bar, a "lucky bastard," the Hugh Hefner of netball coaches.

Yvonne McKay felt sick after her very first mouthful. She was as white as a sheet, and as she tried to go to the bathroom to wet her face she fainted in the middle of the floor. Her knees buckled and her head narrowly missed the edge of a table as she fell.

Watson was called. Leaving his beer, he knelt over her, tapping her cheek. When her eyes opened, he said, "I think we'd better see the doc." Yvonne was given a send-off from the pub as if she were emigrating abroad. Anthems were sung from the car park, and arms waved good-bye in an emotional farewell magnified many times out of proportion by the victory.

At the doctor's office, Yvonne sat on the edge of the examination table, swinging her feet, feeling much better, and still wearing her hornet-yellow netball T-shirt with the logo of a cow. Watson waited outside, idly flicking through a *National Geographic.*

Dr. Jonathan Lim was a Chinese surgeon famed in Beijing's cardiothoracic scene for his small hands. Where other surgeons needed to crack ribs apart to insert their large hands into a chest cavity, Dr. Lim, as diminutive as a dancer, was able to slide himself up to his wrists between the ribs of a patient without needing to break a single bone, a feat which won him a thousand grateful admirers in three cities. Incriminating himself during the Tienanmen Square demonstrations for lending medical relief to students, he had forsaken China for the welcome obscurity of New Zealand where, because his credentials were not recognized, he was reduced to the status of GP.

He wanted to take a closer look at Yvonne. He was concerned about her color. She was pale, as well as unnaturally thin. Trained also in homeopathy and Chinese herbal remedies, Dr. Lim was puzzled at what he called "an imbalance in internal chemistry," and he started to question her about her menstrual cycle. Then he learned that Yvonne had not had a period for three months. Dr. Lim immediately conducted a pregnancy test.

Stammering, faint-hearted, sixteen-year-old Yvonne was soon told that she was pregnant. The doctor held up a positive result in front of her and she stared at it, then the doctor, and then burst into tears. When she spoke again, she insisted there had been a mistake.

"Why so?"

"Because," she answered hesitantly, as if she too were mystified, "I've never had sex with anybody."

Now she was scared. She asked him to do the test again. Right now. He must have mixed up her urine with somebody else's.

Dr. Lim asked for further clarification on this matter of her virginity. He was told in a quiet but resolute tone that, yes, she was a virgin, and so couldn't be pregnant. Even doctors are not prepared for some replies, and he said nothing.

Finally, the door to the office opened. Dr. Lim showed Yvonne McKay out and put her into the care of the coach. Watson left his magazine open at a page dealing with theoretical black holes in space, as if he hoped to resume his study at some later time.

"She should be fine now." The doctor smiled and held out a famous hand for Harvey Watson to shake.

In the patrol car, having decided against going back to the pub, Watson asked Yvonne why it had taken so long for the doctor to prescribe a few pills. Yvonne paused for a moment and then replied, enigmatically, that he had needed to wait for her to urinate.

, , , ,

Mrs. McKay opened the door for Yvonne, blowing her fingers to speed dry red nail polish. She was concerned at once, seeing Watson's hand on her daughter's shoulder.

Watson answered her questioning expression.

"I took her to see the doctor. Wasn't feeling too good, were you, Yvie?"

Yvonne shook her head.

"Fainted at the pub."

"What's wrong with you? What did the doctor say?"

But Yvonne could not withstand the question, and burst into tears, rushing past her mother, flying down the hall where her bedroom door slammed hard.

Watson shrugged.

"What's going on?" Mrs. McKay asked sharply.

Watson had no answer, except to say what Yvonne had told him—that the doctor had asked her for a urine sample.

In a second Mrs. McKay's eyes widened, a mother's mathematics solving the algebra of the situation in a second.

"Oh, please, no," she said. "Don't tell me."

. . . . .

In the controlled quiet of the living room that night, and between hysterical bouts of crying which drove her father into a marathon of pacing, Yvonne stuck with her insupportable story.

Mrs. McKay wanted to slap her. Mr. McKay said that wouldn't help anything. Perhaps they should phone up the priest. Perhaps the fear of God was what their daughter needed: Certainly talking to her was getting them nowhere. Yvonne refused to speak with a priest, and she slammed her bedroom door again.

"You'll talk with him if I say you will," Mrs. McKay called through the door.

"Leave me alone," came the reply.

The McKays laid down a rule of law. Yvonne would not be let out of the house until she surrendered the name of that "fucking little bastard" for whom she had dropped her knickers. It didn't matter how long it took; no one was going anywhere.

Yvonne was unrepentant. Yes, she admitted she was pregnant, but she was equally adamant she was a virgin. Not usually courageous, she showed a new strength in the face of her parents' rage. She was a girl who would not normally change the channel on the TV without first winning consent, but now, somehow, she seemed happy to be engaged in a full teenage revolt against not only her family but also her former nature.

Mrs. McKay suspected that her niece, Delia Chapman, might be linked to this. She knew about Delia's spaceman claim, and made an inevitable connection. She decided to call her brother Marty.

Two hours later, Marty and Delia Chapman were ushered into the living room by Mr. McKay. It was an emergency session, and the first time the family had been drawn together since the funeral. For the McKays, at least, this occasion was no less strained. Tea was served in an atmosphere of mortifying silence.

Yvonne sat curled in an armchair. Delia was on the couch beside her father, tea balanced on her knee. Mr. McKay, too angry to sit and unable to pace, stood at the window, and Mrs. McKay, to whom everybody but Yvonne looked for instructions on how best to proceed in the matter, sat rigidly on the front edge of the La-Z-Boy rocker, the chair tipping forward under her imperious weight.

"It just seems to me," said Mrs. McKay finally, "that Delia saw a spaceship, and now Yvonne is pregnant but can't remember who to, or so she says. Something is obviously going on. So what is it, you two?"

The three parents fixed the two girls with laser-beam stares.

"Are you in some kind of . . . some kind of cult or something?" she asked. "Is that it? A cult?"

Mrs. McKay had never used the word cult before; in saying it now, she shocked herself even further, and the situation seemed to worsen for everyone. Could the girls have fallen into a satanic circle of which they were unable to speak?

"Answer your mother," Mr. McKay told Yvonne, his alarm growing.

"No," mumbled Yvonne.

"Speak up, will ya!"

Delia intervened. "No. No, we're not."

"Well, it sounds like a *cult!*" Mrs. McKay accused, warming to the powerful new word. "If it's not a cult, what is it, then?"

Marty Chapman bumped his daughter with his knee. Her tea spilled into the saucer.

"There's nothing going on," Delia told the group.

Mrs. McKay turned to her, giving up hope of learning anything from her catatonic daughter. "So, you're telling me you don't know anything about Yvonne getting . . . pregnant?" The word stuck in her throat like a fish bone.

"No," Delia said.

"Nothing at all?" Mrs. McKay felt that her only chance was to get the stronger girl to talk.

"No. But, I wish I did," Delia said, looking at Yvonne, and just as puzzled as everyone else.

"I don't believe that, actually," said Mrs. McKay. "I think you two are in this together, and I'm going to get it out of you."

Marty Chapman had not said a word up to this point, so buried was his concern; his only contribution now was to bump his daughter's knee a second time.

"Okay," said Delia. "You can try, but there's nothing to tell."

"Well, she didn't get pregnant by herself!" shouted Mrs. McKay, finally losing her temper. She stood up, releasing the rocker, which banged violently against the wall.

"Well *I* didn't get her pregnant either!" Delia shouted back.

And nobody could argue with that.

During the exhausted silence which followed, Marty and Delia rose to go, feeling nothing more could be achieved right now. Marty gave brisk handshakes and pushed Delia out toward the door. He would stay in touch with his sister, he pledged, and would follow all this up with Delia at home.

At the door, Mrs. McKay spread herself across the door frame like a portcullis, announcing her home off-limits.

"And tell any of those other girls," she instructed Delia, "to keep away. Yvonne won't be going back to work at *that* place."

Delia nodded at her aunt, who looked tired. She wanted to say that this wasn't easy for anybody, but thought it wiser to stay silent. She noticed how closely the woman resembled her father in the instant before the door was slammed.

, , , ,

Within the diocese of the Catholic Church of New Zealand, Father James Richard O'Brien was, at forty-four years old, known to be an intemperate radical. A well-read scholar born in Timaru, he was ordained in Rome at the age of only twenty-three, considered to be the youngest age at which a man might accept the onerous mantle of "Father." For this reason, he was even granted an audience with the pope. O'Brien had expected a conversation, but the pontiff had merely knelt and prayed with him for forty-five seconds.

A high flyer, O'Brien had been "given" Opunake, for reasons he had never questioned, although his theological credentials would have found a greater calling in an urban environment such as Auckland, or perhaps in Wellington, among its turgid intellectuals.

The case of a pregnant girl comically claiming virginity should have excited him, awakened powers so long allowed to slumber in this backwater. But he did not look at all pleased.

At the end of the meeting, in which Yvonne was left alone with the priest in her parents' living room, she seemed even more distressed. She ran from the room as if fleeing an exorcist, and raced to her bedroom with such urgency that her parents wondered about the nature of the dialogue which had preceded the dash.

"I think we have to back off," the priest advised, looking as adversely affected by the encounter as Yvonne had. He was only just able to keep the emotion out of his voice.

The parents nodded, acceding to his advice, but not before asking him to violate the secrecy of the confessional.

"She wouldn't tell me anything," the priest said.

At the door, he gave his verdict. "My feeling would be, she's frightened. More pressure isn't going to do any good. I think the opposite is needed, actually. You should ignore her. Go on as normal, if you can. It won't be easy, but this much I know. That is the only way the truth will ever come out."

Out on the path, in private, Mrs. McKay raised the shadowy subject of a church-condoned abortion, which she understood to be possible in the case of a rape. Her voice was little more than a whisper as she compromised all her old beliefs.

Angered by the suggestion, Father O'Brien urged that the

pregnancy be considered a fait accompli by all parties. He would not sanction Mrs. McKay's desperate request, no matter how much pain the situation was causing.

"But you have no idea what we are going through," she told the curate, her voice draining of force.

"True. But the laws of the Church are infallible. Don't make the mistake of falling prey to the sin of vanity."

"Vanity?"

"A human life, Mrs. McKay, even a bastard's, is more important than a wedding."

Later the same day an agreement was formed that, for the sake of the expected baby, Yvonne would allow herself to be examined by Dr. Lim's nurse, a trained and respected midwife. Almost incidentally, a virginity test, a quick examination, might also be done to put paid to Yvonne's most disturbing claim. The choice of the nurse was a compromise. Mr. McKay wished for Dr. Lim to make the examination, but Yvonne refused: She wouldn't have his "funny hands" on her again. However, as the nurse was not paid for weekend calls, the McKays would be forced to wait two days for the five-minute gynecological examination.

The result of the examination confirmed the parents' belief: The hymen was not intact. Not expecting it to have been, not for one second, Mr. McKay's anger exploded. He raged through the rooms of his house over the waste of time and his duties that were piling up. He had found damp in an upstairs bedroom. He wanted to get to the root of it. Someone had screwed his daughter: Who was it? All else was hogwash.

Mrs. McKay convinced him to consider the absence of tissue between their daughter's legs a huge step forward. They agreed, in a weary embrace, to heed the priest's advice: to back off and let the truth come out in the fullness of time. Difficult as this might be, they could take some comfort from the antique idea that faith, if perfect, would eventually be rewarded.

. . . . .

Delia told the other girls in the packing room all about
Yvonne. Soon, a stream of visitors was marching off to Hennessey
Street, in flagrant disregard of Mrs. McKay's quarantine, to hear
the story for themselves. Last to visit was Delia.

Able to cajole her way indoors by disarming her aunt with
promises that she would be able to talk her cousin out of this
present stupidity, and by agreeing that Yvonne, who was prone
to imitation, was merely copying her, Delia knocked and slipped
into Yvonne's bedroom. Yvonne was lying on her back on an
unmade bed, only half-dressed and reading a magazine.

Delia pulled a large bottle of Scotch from her satchel, then put
a chair against the door to insure their privacy.

"You know what?" she said, loosening the cap. "If you keep
saying all this virgin stuff, they'll probably drag you away to some
mental home. That's what Dad wants to do to me."

Yvonne tried to smile, and Delia saw just how fragile her
cousin was. She softened her voice. "Who are you trying to protect, Yvie? Who is it? You've gotta quit all this and tell me."
Yvonne was a stone. "Okay, if you don't want to tell me who
made you preggers, you don't have to. But you're going to have
a baby. You've gotta think about the baby."

Yvonne was silent. "I'm not making it up," she said.

"Aren't you? You're really saying you don't remember who you
had sex with?"

"I didn't have sex."

"But your hymen—"

"I really wish everyone would stop talking about that. You know?
It doesn't mean anything anyway. I could have lost it anywhere."

Yvonne couldn't take this anymore. Tears were falling down
her face. To conceal them, she took the whiskey from Delia and
knocked back a slug. She screwed up her face as it scorched its
way down.

"What the hell's happening with everyone?" asked Delia. She reached over, took back the bottle and had a slug herself. "Listen Yvie, some people are saying that you reckon you maybe saw a spaceship too. That the same thing that happened to me happened to you. But with you, I dunno. Maybe they brainwashed you or something. Did you tell anyone that, Yvie? Did you?"

Yvonne shook her head, a definitive no, but then clouded the issue immediately by saying, "I can't remember."

"Then maybe you did, eh?"

"What about you, Dee? Did you really see a spaceman?"

Delia took a moment to respond. Perhaps she should have expected this question. "I saw someone out there. I saw something." She was so earnest that Yvonne dared not question her further. But Delia herself had a question. "Do I seem crazy? Tell me the truth." Her voice for the first time showed real fear, a real belief that something decidedly spooky was going on.

Yvonne considered for one second, then said, "No. And nor am I, Dee."

They stared at each other. Yvonne's obviously insane insistence on her immaculate conception was no stranger than Delia's own claim. And suddenly, there was nothing further to discuss. You didn't ask a blind man for directions.

Delia punched Yvonne affectionately on the arm, took back the whiskey and said she had better be going. Yvonne followed her to the door.

"I'm coming back to work tomorrow. Mum's gonna try and stop me, but I'll be back. I think."

"Take it easy, okay?"

Yvonne nodded her promise and Delia left her cousin there, alone in the room.

DELIA'S BLUE CROSS

All week Delia had been having trouble captaining her memories of the spacemen, and she was frightened by her growing amnesia. What had initially been so clear, so vivid whenever she summoned her memories of that night, became more translucent day by day, more vague and insubstantial. But to whom could she reveal this now, after all the trouble she'd caused?

Seated on top of Hughson's Hill in the morning light, beside the impotent long-range gun directed at a calm sea, she was prey to new bouts of dislocated thinking. She smoked a cigarette, but it did nothing to calm her nerves as new pictures invaded her head, contradicting older images of that controversial night. For example, she knew she hadn't run from her visitors at all. That much she knew. Everything had been very cordial. But now, in her head at least, she could envisage legs, her own legs perhaps, or perhaps not, flying through the grasses and ferns, being cut and scratched. How was it possible that she could be running?

She had not been afraid. How was it also possible to have two such conflicting memories of the same event? Yes, her legs had been cut the next morning, and scratched below the knee, as if she had run through heavy scrub, and there had also been a couple of bruises on her arms, but all of these, she knew, had been received in the netball game the week before. She was sure of this. So, was she falling prey to illusions, or was she just stark raving, as Deborah Kerr had called her?

She lit another cigarette, and thought about living everything twice: once happily, once not, with the ability to choose which one to remember, which to forget.

Once, but only once, had Delia allowed herself to think she had not seen a spaceship at all. She let herself imagine that she had run out to the edge of the highway. She briefly imagined the flashing image of human arms, of a car in the trees; of grunts, of force, the use of it against her. But then she became confused again and quickly dismissed the idea.

A retired Carmelite nun said that Delia Chapman was going to go to hell. Delia learned of this from Deborah during their smoko. Deborah had learned it from her eight-year-old sister. The nun, a substitute teacher, had told the class of eight-year-olds that Delia was bound for hell. She instructed that there was no excuse for painting a universe in which humanity and God had rivals. Everyone knew very well that after God created mankind he had broken the mold, and anyone who put other ideas into the minds of little children would either purgate in a fiery pit or drift in that arduous place which the catechisms still called limbo, for time immemorial.

Perhaps she did need help, thought Delia finally. She was beginning to see herself as her own enemy, and a carrier of a disease which infected others.

She put out her cigarette as it began to rain. She was not feeling well. It was amazing how quickly thoughts could make you sick.

, , , , ,

The next day Delia received a small green card in her letterbox, notifying her that her requested library book had arrived.

She looked thinner to Phillip when he saw her in the doorway of the library, but then it was the first time he had seen her in something other than a baggy white coat. He told her in a businesslike tone that a new book, one edited intelligently by Llewelyn Hart (New York, 1987), had just arrived and he thought it might interest her. He omitted to tell her that he had ordered it expressly.

The slender octavo-sized book dealt in phenomenology. In sixty-five pages, it contained not only astute investigations into unsolved mysteries of every kind as well as a welter of paradoxes of a spiritual nature, but also a number of documented sightings and firsthand reports of visits by interstellar entities, which might, he thought, even throw some light on the subject in which she had shown a small interest.

Delia hesitated to tell him that she had no interest whatsoever in that particular topic. Just because a person once saw an elephant in the zoo, it did not mean that, from then on, they were elephant fanatics. She opened the book and looked through its first pages. She tried to look pleased.

The book was typical of its genre, he said. Photographic evidence and artists' impressions detailed the experiences of ordinary-looking people, each one swearing to have been snatched without warning from their lives and altered forever. She was unable to match his excitement.

He read to her from the cover.

From farms and suburbs, during lunch breaks or school picnics, while arguing with their partners, or going out to feed a dog, walking from a sister's house down the street or vacuuming the bottom of a swimming pool, these decidedly normal people had all done nothing more than look up at the right moment. In that instant their former lives had ended, for they had seen a chariot of the Gods.

Delia thought Phillip was a bit weird. But he was gentle. She felt he might even be trusted. She turned the pages slowly as Phillip explained the photographs. His calming voice drifted over her shoulder.

"You don't have to read it to me," she interrupted.

He nodded. "I noticed that you returned a copy of *Teach Yourself to Read*. I could, you know . . . help you, if you want."

"And you're pretty smart, are you? Smart enough to teach me something?"

"I don't know."

"Look, I can read, okay? I read every day. I read everything. So don't go spreading things around like I can't read."

She opened the book and began to read perfectly. After a few sentences she closed it with a clap, and announced, "The learn-to-read book was for my father, if you want to know. My mother was trying to teach him. Didn't work. That's all."

"I'm sorry. You just hadn't visited the library much."

"What are you, Sherlock Holmes?"

"Only once. To wash your hands."

"To look for a book! Anyway, you haven't got any books in it, except war ones. Why would I come in here?"

Phillip shrugged. His job wasn't easy. He explained he was doing all he could, and that he had ordered 250 indispensable classics from Wellington which were due any day. "But you know what? Do you want to know *why* most of the books on the shelves are war books? Because the majority are still out there in people's houses."

"And aren't those all war books too?"

"No. They are not."

"What sort of books are they, then?"

After a pause, Phillip confessed a truth known only to him and perhaps to his long-departed predecessor. "Mainly romance." He held his look on Delia. "Only a few regular borrowers get out the war ones, mainly the shopkeepers. But the most common books we have on file, apart from gardening, and the ones which have stayed out there in people's houses all these years, are romance. A few people like war, but the overwhelming majority . . . they prefer romantic fantasies." Delia made no response. "The same thing was true in the army," recalled Phillip.

She noticed for the first time that his nose was crooked.

"I know," he said, reading her thoughts. He touched it as if he could adjust the jut of bone near the bridge. "It wasn't set right. I got it during a fight in the army."

Delia wanted to know more. "Why did you join the army?"

"Because of my father. Well . . . my stepfather. He was in the army."

Delia had found another topic. "What about your real father?"

"I never met him."

"Why did you never meet him?"

While it rained outside, Phillip told her how his biological father, reportedly a good-looking Maori man, had contributed his genetic donation in 1967 and then disappeared. The last anyone had heard he was a taxi driver in Palmerston North with a preference for night shifts.

"You could ride the taxis and find him," she said. "Sit in the backseats of taxis and ask questions until you found him. You wouldn't even need to identify yourself. You could talk to the man who is your father, and he'd never know."

"I don't want to do that."

"Why not?"

"Fuck him!"

She understood the sentiment. They shared problem fathers.

Phillip changed the subject. "So what about you, and all this stuff?" He tapped the book in her hands.

Delia anticipated his next question. "The ones I saw were different."

"Did you see their faces?" He sounded sincere.

"Yes."

"Did you really?"

"Yes."

"Tell me about them."

"Do you believe me?"

After a moment, "Yes."

. . . . .

She had seen a spaceman. Well, that wasn't quite true. She saw ten of them. They were standing in a pool of light. They talked for about two minutes. Then they took her on their vessel. They had silver suits and stainless-steel boots. The vessel was ultra-modern and entirely impressive.

Light, this was the first impression. A figure moving toward her through a pool of light. Who expected that, when you took a walk because you couldn't sleep, you'd be approached by a figure, the epitome of a man, graceful, perfectly built, calm, his skin in the moon glow as white as milk, strange-looking, attractive even. A beautiful body, she had to admit, stunning, even though the head was over-large, which was her only criticism of the visitor, and the face was more beautiful than she had ever seen before. Actually, she couldn't really see the face all that well, but strangely this didn't matter. She felt his warmth immediately, and his huge intelligence—yes, she felt his intelligence too, even if he didn't say a word. And when he reached his hand out toward her and suggested she follow him toward the light, what could she do? She followed. The girls had called Delia a slut. But if they had seen him themselves . . . Deborah Kerr would have been all over him like a rash!

Phillip laughed at her joke. Then he looked at her long and earnestly, and she became uncomfortable under his steady gaze. She said she had better be going, but first she made another lengthy visit to the ladies' toilet, a ritual Phillip was growing accustomed to.

When she was gone, Phillip had to replace the hand soap, which had dwindled to a wafer. Strange girl, he thought.

, , , ,

Outside the library, Delia shielded her eyes against the morning light. The rain had stopped temporarily and people were jumping the flooded gutters, shaking water off umbrellas and trying to start waterlogged cars.

Gilbert Haines, from nowhere, surprised Delia with a gift. It had taken the mechanic three weeks to find the courage to follow his employer's advice.

Flowers were for moments of shared significance, the mechanic had reasoned, and chocolates would perhaps be important later, but right now he needed to surprise her with the full weight of his personality. Developing the idea given to him by Max, he reasoned that a gift had to communicate what words could not, and his choice of a hothouse pineapple specially wrapped in blue plastic with a ribbon was a courageous proclamation of his feelings.

Delia stopped in front of him, looked down at the outrageous gift and asked, "What the hell is that?"

He thrust the fruit at her again with offended pride. He had even put on a clean shirt and combed his hair for the occasion.

"Take it."

The gift was suddenly exposed as a grievous mistake, and it turned from a treasure into a calamity in his hands, an act of transubstantiation which took less than a second.

"No. I don't want it."

His blackened and ugly fingers encircled the contemptible pineapple, and he had no choice eventually but to lower it. Rejected and unable to look into Delia's face, he was gripped by a self-hatred which imposed a new authority over him. He was struck mute.

"But thanks, Gilbert," she said, and walked around him.

The pineapple crashed to the ground beside him. He watched her, besotted and miserable, as she walked away.

, , , , ,

Delia stopped at the bench under the unidentified soldier and opened the library book at the chapter headed "Unsolved." She flicked through it and found a picture of an alien, one of the common renderings as adult in size but with the head and hands of a five-month-old fetus. Though the picture didn't correlate at all with her own experiences, it was the closest thing she had to a record of her encounter. She studied it with care and then set the book aside, turning over the corner of the page to mark the spot for the future.

She wondered whether perhaps she needed a hobby. Her mother had believed strongly in the therapeutic value of hobbies and had amassed a large collection of wind chimes which had hung on the veranda during the last months of her life. Although the sound of the chimes was pleasing, the immense rustling of glass pipes, brass bells and copper tubes with every breath of wind cast such an unsettling spell over the rest of the house that the family stopped functioning correctly. A sharp fall in Delia's grades at school coincided with unusual stock losses as a result of Marty leaving open farm gates which he usually closed, so that both father and daughter were left with the conviction that the chimes were a jinx. It was to end this necromancy that, late one night during a wind storm, Marty tore down the chimes and took them in a box to his implement shed forever. His wife did not contest their removal, and Delia was relieved to see them go, but it was a gruesome fact that within two weeks of the rejection of her last hobby, Christine Mona Chapman was found on the banks of the creek with a trail of poisonous green foam oozing from the corner of her mouth.

Perhaps, like her mother, Delia needed to be saved by a

hobby—a normal hobby, however; one with a rigidly popular following. And as she had recently learned, there was no more popular hobby than romance.

She walked home slowly, stopping at a chemist on the way for one essential product.

. . . . .

The ghost of Delia's mother had not shown itself for several weeks. Marty Chapman, until recently persecuted by visions, now felt the reverse fear of being abandoned. Speaking into the void, he accused his deceased wife of ingratitude. The only thing worse than possession by familiar demons, he observed, was the sudden loss of them.

"Where have you been? You know I've been waiting for you all morning?" he called at the open door, which banged in the wind.

He waited in his armchair, pushed his eyeglasses up onto his forehead and looked across the room at the figure suddenly in the doorway. "Well? What have you got to say for yourself?"

Several seconds passed before he was answered.

"You know where I've been. It's Saturday."

"You're not working today," Chapman grunted.

Delia came in and sat on the end of the couch, as far from him as possible while remaining in the same room. He raised the newspaper to resume reading. He looked at a picture of a local small-aircraft accident under the headline FIVE DEAD, CHILD SURVIVES, then glanced back to check on his daughter. There was no one on the couch. Chapman returned to the newspaper, looking to see if he knew any of the people who had died.

The noise of the fridge door being opened came through to the living room, then the clink of milk bottles, a glass banging down onto a tabletop.

"Delia?!"

No answer came, and he rose with his newspaper and followed her into the kitchen. Delia was making a hot drink, stirring the chocolate.

"Delia? Did you hear me?"

She looked up.

"No more netball for now. Not until all this trouble you've started dies down," he announced. "You can blame yourself." It was the last threat he had.

Delia made no response.

"Spaceships . . ." Marty shook his head, still unable to explain what had induced his daughter to talk to the police. "You told Harvey Watson . . . told him . . . with all the problems this family has had . . . you told him that!"

Delia stirred her drink. She heard the same thing every day, a tireless routine of questions she had long since stopped answering. Silence, she'd realized, was more helpful.

"You want to ruin me? Is that it? Punish me for something?"

The crystals of chocolate would soon dissolve.

"Then what are you trying to do? You're trying to punish me, for . . . what?"

She walked away from him. The discussion was over.

When she pushed open the door, he didn't just feel that Delia was leaving one room in favor of another; Marty felt with all the clarity of experience that she was leaving his life, just as every woman he had been doomed to love had left him.

He stood in the kitchen and heard her feet on the stairs, and for a second mistook them for those of his wife. He called "Christine!" But no answer came.

, , , , ,

The ten-dollar pregnancy kit came in a long blue packet. Although certain to have set tongues wagging, Delia had no choice but to make a public purchase. She was ten days late. She was never late.

Locked in her bathroom, her knickers down around her ankles as she sat on the cold toilet seat, she opened the pack. A small plastic cup needed to be filled with urine. She got up and ran the taps as inspiration. Eventually she was able to produce a sample. A strip of litmus paper had to be in contact with the urine sample for three minutes. On the lid of the plastic vial was an indicator, a small but profound blue minus sign. In the event of pregnancy—and diagrams on the instructions indicated this—a vertical line would emerge to transect that line, turning the minus into a plus.

Delia sat on the toilet seat, hardly able to make herself look down at the lid of the vial, her heart beating as fast as a bird's, her future hanging on the appearance or not of a simple line segment. She was going to hell. The old nun would have been right. She would have to pay. She was being singled out by God. A minute had gone by; a full minute in which she didn't know whether to cry or to flush the vial down the toilet.

She glanced down and saw with great relief that there had been no change. No vertical line had come to complete the cross on which she would be crucified.

She prayed that two minutes, two more little minutes, would go by, and that fate would leave her miserable life alone. She waited, breathless. She could hear her father downstairs. Doors were being slammed. He was contrite. These were noises intended for her to hear, gratuitous slammings. He wanted her to forgive him for his faults, understand the difficulties he had in raising a young woman alone. Well, he didn't know the half of it.

As two minutes expired, tears formed in her eyes and her body began to shake. She was looking down at the indicator in her frozen hand, and now she couldn't take her eyes off it. Her grip was so tight she might break it.

"Shit. Oh, shit, no."

There it was. Appearing. Materializing. A faint blue line. She rubbed her thumb across it, hoping it might rub off. A vertical crossbar. Delia tried to wish it away, but it grew stronger, adopting a life of its own.

"Oh, God. Oh, God. Oh, no. Oh, God."

Delia's thumb couldn't rub it away or slow down its appearance. She'd stopped breathing, and was becoming as blue as the mark on the vial. Finally, she dropped it onto the toilet floor. It rolled slowly across the linoleum and away from her two immobile feet. It came to rest only when it reached the middle of the room.

She had received her cross.

In the shower she scrubbed her skin so intensely that the soap bar broke apart into small pieces. Leaving the water running, she climbed out, tore open another bar from the vanity and returned to the shower, still trembling. With the second wash, her mood finally began to calm. The water ran over her freely, and the strong smell of herbal soap cleared her head just enough for her to contemplate her fate.

Delia Chapman was going to hell.

Eight

. . . .

SATAN'S CONCUBINE

Lucinda Evans, pariah and witch, spider breeder and stealer of domestic cats, Lucinda the overweight and ubiquitously pierced wearer of gothic wardrobes, was among the first to get hold of the Sunday paper, and see that Delia Chapman's picture was on the front page.

She took it to the packing room before the 8:30 A.M. shift, and waited there, dressed in her hygienics, reading the article for a third time until the other girls arrived. Beside the photo of a very young Delia Chapman was a shot of the landing site.

Lucinda's very presence, ahead of schedule and not her characteristic ten minutes late, was sign enough that something had happened.

"Take a look at this," she said, flaunting the paper, unable to conceal a tincture of jealousy, as the conveyor belts came to life.

Six other would-be front-page starlets gathered around the tabloid.

"Je-sus," said Suzy Jackson.

"She's bloody famous now!" chanted Deborah Kerr, green with envy.

The chatter rose to deafening proportions. And that was when Delia walked in and glided through the middle of the convention with all the detachment of an excised heart.

The girls rushed after her. What had happened? Had she given an interview? Who was in town? Journalists, or what? Why had she given the newspaper an old yearbook photo? Did she realize she was a fuckin' national celebrity now? *National!* They bet the papers had paid her a ton of money—how much, how much, how much?

In the face of this barrage, with the weight of sixteen hands on her shoulders, Delia maintained a sedated, almost glazed expression. She didn't know anything about it, she said. This was the complete truth.

"I don't know where they got any of that. I haven't talked to anyone."

She thought about telling them, right then, that she was pregnant, but realized how freakish this sounded, and how impossible it was for even her to digest, let alone everyone else. Pregnant! If they were excited now, just think how they'd be if they knew she was now going to have a baby: It would start a riot, people would be killed in the stampede, her own life definitely would be in danger.

But Delia's denial was instantly taken as confirmation that she had given a major interview. You only denied what was true. Furthermore, each girl assumed that a large sum of money had changed hands. If you were famous you *had* to act like Delia was acting now: disavow all rumors, stay aloof and pretend that all the attention was a nuisance. This was obvious.

A climate of jealousy was, however, inevitable. Lucinda Evans had wanted to be famous ever since she'd first punctured herself with nose studs, but her hard-earned notoriety didn't even remotely compare with Delia's fame. And as for Deborah Kerr, she didn't share her name with a screen legend for nothing: Deborah was filled like a Christmas stocking with unlived aspirations! Suzy Jackson, to name another, was one of nine children and could already see herself buried alive up to her asymmetrical ears in drudgery and recipes and mewling babies, in washing on the line and tea at 5:30. Nothing less than a time machine would be required to change Suzy's fate, so her envy need not be estimated. All the girls knew, as soon as they saw the photo in the paper, that Delia Chapman had won herself a free ride on a time machine.

At least the lucky cow could show a bit of excitement.

. . . . .

By the time Vic Young's photo of the landing site appeared in the Sunday paper, the entire matter had been officially dismissed by most people in Opunake as a very bad joke. Ironically, though, it was this photo, capturing the most solemn assembly of citizens in one place since a natural-gas explosion from an underground lagoon ended the region's hopes for a gas industry, which lent historic importance to the hoax and made it appear that the town officially endorsed the idea of life from other worlds.

What had so excited the newspaper's editor was this apparent warranty, and what gave the story its sensational legs was the riddle of how the cow could be conveyed to the barley field imperceptibly and had its ribs crushed. It made good reading to hear local "experts" like the chairman of the borough works department speculate that it would have required a massive operation to move the cow, and yet there were no signs. The dirt track, softened by rains, bore infinite hoof marks and the usual tire ruts, but no major access had been carved into the barley, as Daphne Philpott had testified.

And so the cow slowly became the fulcrum upon which counter-opinions wildly teetered; but it was also a tiny hole in the cynic's logic through which a river of fanciful tabloid speculation could pour. The vandal argument was dismissed, and no single solution sufficed; only the spaceship scenario fully satisfied all the conditions. It was not surprising, then, that the dead animal, which had at first seemed a secondary detail, should become the crux of the entire incident—a mascot for the absurd, and also its first victim. Eventually, and day by day, the aroma of the animal's death began to endow the saga with the irrefutable ring of authenticity.

But Vic Young was not happy. In the days following the release of his first and most profane article, a professional heaviness had overwhelmed him. He was agitated and he didn't understand why. It was his style, on any assignment, to retreat to his room after the most cursory round of interviews and, armed with the barest facts, complete his articles in one sitting. And yet the bin in his cramped motel room was overflowing with rejected printouts. Pinned to the wall above his desk was the front-page photo of Delia Chapman, which he had torn from the yearbook, photocopied and sent to Auckland. He had spent many hours looking up at her fresh face from a distance of a few centimeters. He admitted he'd had passing sexual obsessions with very young women before, but he could not believe he was developing feelings for this young girl on the basis of a pubescent snapshot. Several times he took the photo down, but always reinstated it when the loneliness of the room became unbearable.

In truth, he was also feeling guilty. His article, as it had appeared in the Sunday-morning newspaper, did not bear the least resemblance to the much more complimentary study he had submitted. It had been sensationalized by the editor, without consultation, and every humanizing detail had been omitted. Delia Chapman was described as a screwball, and Opunake as a desperate backwater hopelessly trying to impose itself on the modern world. This had been his worst fear while writing his report. Young had actually chosen his words very carefully, trying to make them unalterable, but the editor had been vicious with his pen and had eradicated all of his celebrations of the high school girl, whom he continued to portray as an innocent twelve-year-old.

Young rated himself a serious journalist even now, after years of slippage, and aspects of this story stirred his dormant sense of vocation. In prose that was perhaps too ornate, but by his own estimation occasionally glorious, he had drawn Delia Chapman as a victim of some hideous catastrophe, a misunderstood beacon of provincial despair. He had hoped to discover an approach to this material worthy of his former skills and to remain true to the emergency in this girl's life. He was not simply a hack and now saw an opportunity to prove this to himself again. Yet no matter how much he tried to elevate his material, he feared that his words could be rendered comic: COW—WEIGHT OF SEVEN MEN—CRUSHED BY CRAFT?; LOCAL GIRL—NIGHT OF SEX WITH STUDS FROM SPACE. This was his problem, the fatal flaw in his job, and the seed of his guilt. When he read his own article and discovered the degree to which he'd been rewritten, his guilt fused with impotence and paved the way for a writer's block quite unlike anything he had experienced before.

Throughout a night of fruitless turmoil, the face of Delia Chapman looked down on him with the placidity of a saint.

, , , , ,

On the following Monday morning, Vic Young again drove to the gates of the freezing works. In an effort to explain himself to the victim of the bastardized article, he took a copy of his original, to prove to her the extent to which he had been edited.

He was in time for a morning shift change, and stood at the gates amid a cavalcade of women in white, hoping to make his apologies in person. If he could explain that his article had been rendered meaningless by a barbarian, and point out that what had appeared in the paper was no reflection of his true feelings, perhaps he could put the issue behind him at last. Besides, he was also desperate to meet Delia face-to-face, to feed his rampant curiosity, and to update the photograph which now hung permanently in the gallery of his skull.

Despite offering twenty dollars to anyone who would talk with him, he was unable even to catch sight of the woman at the center of both his problems and his passions.

He remained in the courtyard of the factory ten minutes after the last worker had gone inside. Then a lone figure appeared in the distance, coming toward him—a young woman, a little on the heavy side, but at least with a ready smile, which made a change. This time when he said hello, he was not ignored. On the contrary, this woman said she was thrilled to meet a journalist, introduced herself with her wicked and peculiarly attractive gypsy smile, and told him that it was in her charts that they should meet. Vic Young blinked twice and offered to buy Lucinda Evans a coffee. She accepted at once, discarding her job as if it were a wrapper on a chocolate bar.

In the cafeteria, the journalist listened intently.

Lucinda Evans wished to be officially added to the growing list of witnesses. She too had seen a UFO and its occupants. She was willing to go on record with a full account of an abduction: a two-hour visit to the flying saucer, her willing consent to being examined and her participation in verbal exchanges on "a kind of wavelength." She confirmed that the creatures were "about as tall as you . . . but had bigger heads." Young had to dissuade her from drawing a likeness of the crew commander on a napkin.

"What's the matter?" she asked.

"Nothing. It doesn't matter. Keep going."

"Aren't you going to take notes?"

"I'm not sure yet."

"Have you got a camera?"

"In my car."

"When do you want to take my picture? Now, or later?"

Young scrutinized Lucinda, and sensed that to proceed down this road amounted to pulling a pin on a hand grenade.

"Are you sure all this happened to you?" he asked cautiously.

"Yes."

"When?"

"Two weeks ago."

"What happened?"

She blinked. She'd gone over this, she thought. "I told you."

"Tell me again."

"Haven't you got a tape recorder or something? You don't seem too hot at remembering stuff."

"I've got a good memory. What happened?"

"Exactly the same as Dee."

"Delia Chapman?"

"Right. Y'know, aliens, heat waves . . . everything."

"Mmm. And did they . . . ?"

Lucinda now knew exactly what he meant.

"Yes. All of them," she said.

"All of them? So . . . did you try and resist them?"

"Course not. There were heaps of them. Y'see, they put you in a kind of a trance . . . with their hands, kind of. They've got these eyes in the palms of their hands. And they sort of go like this . . ."

She demonstrated, clenching and unclenching her fists in a palm-flashing rhythm.

"Right," said Young, nodding. "Right. Go on."

"Oh! And there's something else." She dropped her voice, confidentially. He stared at her as she leaned toward him. "I'm pregnant too."

"Pregnant?"

"Yeah." Lucinda waited for him to write down the crucial word, glancing at the pad until he eventually did so.

"I see," he said, unimpressed. "Go on."

Nine

A BLESSED TRINITY

The night sky, once a banal canopy to the farming mind and purely a source of undependable weather, was now attaining a whole new status in Opunake. In the White Hart Hotel there was suddenly talk of "the firmament." "The heavens" had been heard at weekly Bingo play-off, "celestial orbs" in a queue at the dole office, and a farmer buying fertilizer at the local cooperative received a stinging rebuke from Sergeant Watson for using the expression "the ether": "Who fuckin' knows what's going on out there in the ether, anyway?"

In the past four weeks, a thousand cattle a day were routinely sent through Borthwick's Freezing Works. The farming season had shifted into top gear with little surprise. But at night, when the stars emerged, a new potential descended from above.

The fame of Delia Chapman, Yvonne McKay and Lucinda Evans spread beyond their respective neighborhoods as new articles appeared each Sunday. Unstamped and hand-delivered letters from readers began to arrive in their letterboxes, sometimes one a day, sometimes three or four. Yvonne's were intercepted by her mother and were thrown unread into the rubbish. Delia also threw hers out before her father could see them, knowing full well the effect an invasion of envelopes would have on him. Lucinda, however, virtually papered her living room with these anonymous pledges of support. In this way, it became clear that the imaginations of a smattering of locals were stimulated as never before. It was as if a new age with all its unknown technologies and promise had arrived in Opunake in one starry night, exploding the drowsy calm of their humdrum lives.

And other mysteries came with this new age. The general store owners had noticed, for example, a sharp and unaccountable increase in the sale of flashlights and batteries. Only sometime later was it discovered that not all of Opunake's young women were in their beds at night where they belonged. Creeping out of doors, lonely and bored, homework or housework abandoned, flashlights pointed upward, who could blame them for the odd hopeful communiqué? On and off went their lights, pointed toward the heavens, on–off–on in a haphazard and illiterate code, beams just strong enough to reach the letterbox and yet optimistically pointed at Mars.

With this new age, ushered in by a triumvirate of so-called virgins, came new demands: Everybody had simply to be more amazing, it seemed. Only in this way would fame follow, should that be your wish—and it widely was. If you really sought to be a media star like any of the trio from Borthwick's, it appeared that you needed to become more sensational in every way, just as they had. This was their talent and it was received in some quarters as a challenge, a new benchmark of achievement: To win entry to the new age you had at least to match this triumph of excess. The reward was that if you succeeded then you too could be officially reported on a Sunday morning, in small black letters on flimsy newsprint, to be in league with a superior intelligence, be dizzy with insights and exhausted by visions. Envy was prolific.

The most envious of onlookers were Deborah Kerr and Suzy Jackson, who watched stunned and speechless as the three publicized pregnancies moved into their second months. A fabulous ship had departed the dock without them, had drawn up the gangway at their feet, leaving them abandoned, marooned, their group ruined. They dubbed their former friends "the three witches," and, in a day, reduced all their workplace dealings with them to turned heads, snubs, overloud use of the word slut, and acts of locker-room sabotage. One era had ended. A wilder one had begun.

, , , , ,

The body was human but the head in silhouette was unearthly. It appeared in the main street of Opunake on a night when the streets were empty. Unexpected headlights forced it to slip into the shadows until the car had passed. Then the figure reappeared elsewhere. . . .

Three streets away, in her room on the third floor of the state housing block on Harrison Street, Deborah Kerr climbed into bed and turned her light off.

Immediately the front door opened and shiny, heavy, silver boots climbed the six flights toward her flat. The boots were almost too big for each step, and the toe on each made small clipped noises as it climbed. On the top floor, the intruder had not the slightest trouble either with the lock on the main door or, a minute later, with the front door to Deborah's flat—number 16A—located at the other end of the hallway. The figure, now walking on carpet, made for her bedroom with an almost clairvoyant knowledge of where she could be found.

Deborah was dozing, her mind clearing away last thoughts before sleep, content with her decision to drop out of school in the best family tradition, leave home to live in a flat, and take up a permanent position at the factory conveyor belt at the end of summer when her friends would return to school.

Her flatmates were asleep. She sighed and shifted. Her window was open on a pleasant breeze which fanned the curtain. She did not open her eyes as a silver glove turned the knob on her bedroom door.

The figure stood unseen in the doorway, a rare silhouette, then moved forward and stood over her bed. For some moments it studied the sleeping, subdued and undefined form protected only by a sheet.

Deborah Kerr opened her eyes. She heard its breath at the foot of her bed. She lifted her head and made out a shape standing over her, but she did not scream. She seemed to be waiting for a word, for an announcement.

The creature said that it had come for sex.

She didn't hear this properly, and so asked the creature to repeat it.

"I have come. For sex."

"Bobby? Is that you?" she asked.

"No," the creature said.

"Your voice is all muffled."

There was no response.

Deborah switched on the light.

"Take off that ridiculous mask and get out of here."

A plastic mask from a joke shop. A human hand rising to shield it from the light. Clothes spray painted silver with auto paint. A silver ski jacket.

"How did you get in?"

"Robyn gave me a key." Bobby slumped on the end of her bed, holding his mask in one hand and scratching his head with the other. He was too depressed to look at her. "I want us to get back together."

"What?"

"I want to go out with you again."

"Not in a million light-years," she replied. "Now get out."

Bobby left, closing the door. Deborah listened to his heavy

boots on the stairs until the front door closed. She switched off her lamp, annoyed by how all this was getting out of control, and tried again to sleep.

. . . . .

Harvey Watson read a tabloid headline aloud: SPACEMEN SCORE HAT TRICK!—SAUCY NIGHTS ON SAUCER.

"So what's going on?" asked the mayor after a thoughtful moment, his back to the sergeant, his hands clasped behind him as he looked out the police station window.

"I don't know," answered Watson.

"Well, somebody has been having sex with these girls."

The mayor's annoyance had less to do with the case and more to do with the fact that it was distracting him from the main business of jump-starting the town's economy.

"What are we going to do about it?"

The sergeant knew that what Sullivan actually meant was, What are *you* going to do about it?

"I don't know," Watson replied. And he didn't. He wasn't even sure whether this was truly a police matter. No crime had been reported, and it had not yet become the cause of any public disturbance.

The mayor decided to be more precise. Two of the pregnant girls were in Watson's netball team. Wasn't this unusual? Surely Watson, as their coach, must know something.

"I hope you're not saying I know anything about how they got pregnant," objected Watson.

"Let's just say," the mayor fired back, fueling emotion in the hope of learning something new, "that we mustn't rule anything or anyone out." It was a time for taking shots in the dark. You never knew what you might hit.

The sergeant's eyes were livid. "Would you care to say that again?"

The mayor had gone too far. He realized it in time. But he

was not practiced at backing down. He held his look for a courageous few seconds, then waved his hand dismissively. This was as close to capitulation as he would come.

"Okay, come on, Harvey . . ." he said. "Forget it. No one thinks you're connected with that. Well, we all know you couldn't be."

"Good," said Watson, temporarily content with that answer, then upon further consideration adding, "What do you mean . . . 'couldn't be'?" A note of alarm had entered his voice.

"Well," said the mayor, staring at his friend, searching for the most diplomatic phrasing. "We all know you've had the old nip." And with scissor-fingers—snip-snip—he cut the air in an insensitive evocation of Watson's mutilation.

The knowledge that his top-secret operation had never really been the secret he'd imagined dried his mouth and gave Watson the painful taste of his wife's treachery.

The mayor saw the sergeant blush. "So, we have no doubts about your involvement whatsoever, Harvey. Actually, I couldn't think of a more perfect alibi!"

Sullivan laughed in an attempt to rescue the situation, but he did so alone. The sergeant saw behind him only a year of prattling mouths and unkind remarks, long months of satire of which he'd been blissfully unaware, a broken promise. He was remembering that he had agreed to his wife's wish that he be unmanned only on her absolute pledge that she would die before telling a soul: He had his pride and his reputation, after all. But now, and for the rest of his days, he would be condemned to a purgatory where, when anyone laughed out of context, he would think they were doing so in reference to his disenfranchised loins.

"I'm seeing all three girls in about an hour," the mayor said, "as a favor to the McKays. They want me to talk some sense into them. I just thought you might be able to tell me something I don't know. That's all."

But Harvey had risen and was already headed out of the room.

"Harvey?!" the mayor called, trying to summon Watson back, but to no avail.

. . . . .

The mayor, when he was anxious, had a way of tugging his collar and walking on the tips of his toes as if about to break into a run. After he had returned to his office and taken an urgent phone call, he added to this list the kicking of furniture, slamming of doors and bellowing at his secretary to type up letters which he had not yet dictated.

In his appointment book was the single note: a meeting that afternoon with Yvonne McKay, Lucinda Evans and Delia Chapman. But this was not the cause of his rage.

He asked his secretary to phone a number. He would take the call in his office. Mrs. Markham nodded, not wanting to tax him further, aware of the exact reason for his panic. She had been with him when he had received the devastating news that Borthwick's Freezing Works was to shed eight hundred jobs within the next six months in a restructuring plan which would introduce automation and industrial robotics to the area. This number represented 75 percent of Opunake's work force. The mayor had kept mumbling "Dear God" and "They've killed us" into the telephone receiver, and the secretary had had to brew extrastrong coffee to return his grip on reason.

Now his shouts came through the walls, forcing Mrs. Markham at her desk to play the radio. But the managing director of the freezing works could not be reached at this time. The mayor slammed down the phone and summoned the three young girls who were already waiting, pale at the thought that the commotion was related to them.

"Leave us alone," said the mayor to his secretary. The girls looked back at the woman as if she were their protector and lifeline, and her exit seemed to lend a more austere chill to the occasion.

"How you all doing? All right?" He waved a hand in the direction of a red chesterfield, urging them to sit.

The girls nodded. It was the first time any of them had been in the mayor's office, and it was imposing.

"Now, let's get this straight," the mayor said, needing to get directly to the point, a riot already raging in his head. "Which one of you is Delia?"

Delia raised her hand coyly.

Sullivan referred to his notes. He had agreed to this meeting as a personal favor to the McKays, who were old family friends. They believed the weight of office might bring something to bear that had so far been lacking. He would make this quick.

"Okay. The father of your baby is . . . is not from here, is he?"

Delia, after a pause, nodded.

"From space," interjected Lucinda Evans.

"From space," repeated the mayor. "Yes, that is what I meant. Okay. And now who is Lucinda?"

"Same," said Lucinda, speeding up the process. "Space."

"You say the same thing, then?"

"Yes. I do."

"All right. Now that means you're Yvonne." He had not seen her for many years.

"Yes," said Yvonne softly, looking extremely pale.

"And are you 'space,' or not?"

"I don't know."

"You don't know."

"I don't think so."

"You don't think so."

Lucinda and Delia looked at Yvonne.

"Maybe I am," Yvonne said, conferring looks.

"You are . . . what?"

"Space."

"A second ago you didn't know. Now you're saying that you think the father of your baby may be from space."

"Yes. I don't know." Yvonne was starting to get agitated. "I think so. Maybe."

Delia put her hand on Yvonne's arm to quiet her. "She doesn't know."

The mayor regarded the girls with as much tolerance as he could marshal. "Okay, so that's two absolutely positive and one 'don't know.' Now, then. What shall we do now?"

The girls were confused.

"Eh? What shall we do now? You tell me."

Silence.

"You see," said the mayor, "I see it as my job to talk you out of all this."

The girls returned his gaze with equal concentration.

"For your own sakes, because you're part of our community. You're part of the family that is this small town, as, in many ways, we are like a family. What we do affects those around us. Do you agree with me?" His voice had become louder.

The girls nodded. They had been reduced to frightened schoolgirls.

"And so, I want you to look at the facts. I want you to do something very difficult in this life. And that is to accept something that makes us uncomfortable. I want you to accept a fact, even though it may complicate your lives. And that fact is . . . there are no such things as spacemen. Not in this life. We might want there to be. I agree with you, it may be a nice thought, that there is other intelligent life out there, it's interesting, it's exciting, but . . . *but,* from what we know—and people have been looking at this, studying it since the pyramids—from what we know . . . it seems as though we are in fact on our tod here, so to speak. And I think that as adults we have to start to accept these kinds of facts. Do you follow me?"

The girls nodded again.

"Okay." The mayor paused. "I'm going to ask you again. I'm going to ask you all again. And I want you to be courageous. You're all friends, aren't you?"

They nodded again.

"Well, I want you to consider me as your friend too. And I want you to trust me. Now then, Delia. This started with you. I would like to hear from you, first. And remember that the others here are influenced by you. So you have a responsibility. Not only to them. But to their families, who are having a very hard time because of this. As are the rest of us. Because like I said, it affects everyone."

"What do you want me to say?"

"The father of your baby is not from space, is he?"

"I don't know."

"I want you to say it. Be clear."

"I don't know how it happened."

"That's right."

"It just happened."

"What happened?"

"I don't know."

"What happened, Delia? Come on."

"I was running, running through the bush."

"And what did you see?"

"SPACEMEN!" interjected Lucinda, angry at the route this was taking.

Yvonne McKay had gone into shock. Her mouth hung slightly open; she was rigid in her chair and had stopped exhibiting signs of life.

"Be quiet, Lucinda!" howled the mayor. The meeting was breaking up. *"Delia?"*

"I don't know what to tell you," Delia said, emotion leaking into her voice now. "If you don't believe in what happened, then, it's not up to me to talk you out of it, and I'm not gonna deny my child the truth of what happened just to make everyone's life easier."

"You seriously believe in spacemen, then," said the mayor.

"I didn't. Until I saw one." Delia was becoming upset.

"You believe in spacemen."

"Obviously. We're carrying their babies," said Lucinda. She turned to Delia and whispered, "He's trying to brainwash us."

"You're out of your minds." The mayor's patience was exhausted.

"What about Area Fifty-one?" Lucinda was on the offensive now.

"Be quiet!" Sullivan bellowed.

"Area Fifty-one. It's a secret air base in the Arizona desert in America. They've got five flying saucers, which crashed, locked in a hangar, and they're keeping them from the public in exchange for technological secrets . . ."

"Be quiet!"

". . . and up till 1965 they had an alien there, alive, a prisoner of the U.S. Air Force."

"Get out. Get out! The three of you."

"And even *Time* magazine said there's evidence now of organic life on Mars."

The mayor was buzzing his secretary furiously.

The trinity rose, Delia and Lucinda supporting Yvonne. The mayor herded them toward the door and wanted to lock it against all human beings, phantoms, betrayals, acts of God and managing directors. Opunake was going to hell in a wheelbarrow and it was happening with such abandon that he felt powerless to stop it.

In the hallway, where the girls gathered after the conference, Delia asked, "They had an alien in Arizona that they kept alive?"

"Yeah," said Lucinda. "As long as they could, until it died of the flu."

WAR AND ROMANCE

Marty Chapman called for widespread abortions. One he could insist upon, another possibly influence, but a third, he admitted, was beyond both his control and concern.

From the moment he had first learned of Delia's pregnancy, suffering the double ignominy of having to read about it in a newspaper like a stranger, he had violently insisted that Delia go to New Plymouth at the first opportunity and have it done quickly and secretly. He had also taken the added initiative of driving over to his sister's house to encourage the McKays to think similarly. That would make an end to this business.

Delia found her father sitting on a backyard bench in the orange twilight between two rain-filled watering cans. From the look on his face she knew immediately that he had a weighty speech to deliver. She was not surprised when it took the form of an ultimatum. Either she agreed to his demands at once, he told her, or she would no longer be welcome in his house. He had waited long enough and knew that she was developing ideas

of keeping the baby. He had worked hard to build up a fine inher-
itance for her, a lucrative farm which would one day be hers. He'd
be damned if he was going to let it fall into the hands of a bastard
heir. He had not labored his whole life for that.

She stood silently and listened to it all. He had contacted the
family-planning clinic in New Plymouth, but they had refused
to enter into further discussion until they could see Delia. It
was possible for a termination to take place before the twelfth
week of pregnancy. Delia calmly announced that she was already eleven weeks gone and that the last thing on earth she
would do was kill her growing child. She placed her hand over
her belly.

Marty's anger erupted. Two hours of silent meditation over
tactics and subtle ploys evaporated. But as he raised his arm to
hit her, he was struck motionless. He froze, finding mercy within
him, his hand arrested in midair. Delia saw that in protecting her
unborn child, she in turn was suddenly protected: The baby was
her unborn savior.

She left him there, frozen like a statue in the garden, and
rushed indoors, suppressing tears.

, , , ,

After an evening meal, Phillip Sullivan returned to the library.
Near the park he came to a fork in the path and chose the one
which led past the Statue of the Unidentified Soldier, under
which sat Suzy Jackson and Deborah Kerr, smoking and reading
the most recent *Sunday Enquirer.*

The girls fell silent as the librarian approached, and stared at
him menacingly.

"Not bad, is he?" whispered Suzy.

"Hands off," muttered Deborah. Suzy chuckled.

"Hello," said Deborah loudly, flirty as ever.

"Hi," answered Phillip, blushing at once. He allowed himself
only the most fleeting glance and a brief smile, but didn't break

his stride. This small evidence of nervousness was enough to produce an uproar which accompanied him to the end of the street.

"There's your spaceman, I reckon," said Deborah.

Suzy Jackson nodded in agreement.

"I heard he was in prison for violence."

"Really? I heard he was in the army."

"That's not what I heard."

"Isn't he the mayor's nephew or something?"

"Nice bum, anyway."

When Phillip arrived at the library, where he now preferred to
spend even his leisure hours, he was startled to find Delia sitting
against the locked door in the shadows, waiting for him like a
ghost. She rose, smiled shakily, hiding her panic, breathing hard
as if she had just run to meet him. He tried to smile back, surprised to find her there, and in a voice already being lowered to
suit the library's inner atmosphere, asked if she wanted to come
inside.

"There was just . . . a few books . . . I wanted to look up. And
I just noticed that you're open late quite a lot," she said. "That's
all. I sometimes go for a walk."

"Not exactly open," he replied quickly. "I close at five, really.
But come in."

He went straight to his desk, lowered his head and paid no
attention to Delia as she stood in the empty and tranquil library.
She looked around her. There already seemed to be a great many
more books than on her previous visit. Many shelves were now
tightly packed, and she guessed that it was the lost romances,
now found, of which Phillip had spoken which were the reason
behind the transformation. Phillip's quiet industry as he worked
filling out cards, and the serenity of the empty library quietly
swelling with these cheap tales of love, brought a first gust of
peace into a life which had otherwise been disintegrating. She
discreetly watched him work, and found it absorbing, telling her-

self that it was his dedication which attracted her, his clarity and his belief in order. She didn't credit herself with feeling an attraction at the sight of his articulate hands moving with great concentration, although she did find small favor in their hygiene. His neck was long and fluted with veins, his arms a polished teak. He was a good librarian, she guessed, because he imposed strict rules on noise levels, creating the reverent ambience of a church.

Phillip got up and began shifting books onto a shelf from a nearby trolley. Delia did her best to respect the SILENCE sign on the wall as she finally approached him.

"He can't hit me anymore, at least that's something," she whispered.

Phillip's quick placement of books on the shelves showed seemingly clairvoyant knowledge of where the books belonged. When he did not react, she decided to be bolder, raising her voice further.

"I think he may be going crazy now. My father. My father may be."

"Why do you say that?" he answered, returning to the trolley for another book.

"Because he's started to put up my mother's wind chimes again." This stopped him. She continued calmly. "Out on the porch. Put up the first one last night. I asked him why. He said . . . my mother told him to do it."

He nodded, puzzled. "What are you gonna do?" he asked.

"I dunno." She inclined her head, flicking him a look. "He wants me to have an abortion."

Again Phillip nodded.

"But I'm not going to," she added casually, giving him no clues.

"You're not going to," he parroted. "No." It was neither an agreement nor a criticism.

"He's going to kick me out, but I don't care," Delia said with increasing emotion, seeking a clearer response.

Again he only nodded, and for the first time a look of dismay crossed her face. Two huge opportunities for him to offer advice had passed by without a single comment. He was a total weirdo, as she'd first thought, a bookworm, a hermit. Yet she was drawn back to him because it was exactly these qualities which distinguished him from the packs of other local young men she knew and whom she despised. How could she find herself interested in someone like this: a brick wall?

But it was not Phillip's place to offer advice, or at least not until she directly asked him for it. Bursting with questions, he disciplined himself. He believed there to be an unspoken agreement between them that neither would pry into the other's life unless they were invited to do so, and at this point he was not at all certain whether such an invitation had been given. So he remained silent.

He returned quietly to work and Delia, devastated by his failure, was left to contemplate her situation alone. He pushed the trolley of books toward a new shelf.

"You're an intellectual, aren't you?" It sounded like an insult.

"Not really," he said.

"I reckon you are."

"It depends how you define an intellectual."

"How do you define one, then?"

He did not stop replacing books to answer. "An intellectual is someone who can keep a world of contradictions alive in his head."

He was so matter-of-fact that she instantly took this to be the last truth on the matter, and pondered the term "world of contradictions" for some time.

"Why do you like reading?"

"Reading? It helps me develop a coherent philosophy of life. That's all." He was so casual, and spoke with so little forethought, that Delia did not find any of this pretentious. In fact, it was fun: It was like pressing a button on a computer and receiving a well-composed answer.

"Oh," she said.

"Do you know what I mean by that?"

"Sorta."

"I think it's important for everyone to have a philosophy for living, and one that they can clearly articulate. One, at least."

Delia didn't have one, not a single one. It was terrible. She tried to come up with something. She couldn't.

"How many have you got?" she asked. "Philosophies."

"One or two."

"What are some of them, then?"

He stared at her, and she judged by his look that this was the first time anyone had put him on the spot like this. "Go on, tell me," she asked.

"Okay. You sure you want to know?"

"What are you waiting for, stupid?"

"Okay. Well, we can probably start with Heidegger, if that's all right?" He took a deep breath, filled his arms with books, and went to replace them, one by one, on the shelves, almost turning his back on her.

"Fine," she said.

"Well, generally regarded as the founder of Existentialism, he argued against an ordered metaphysical universe, suggesting that we each create our own being which is specific to ourselves, and I like that, I like it a lot, but at the same time I'm also drawn the other way toward the Romantic and I suppose the Rousseauesque school, which advocates that we are not special at all, that we are a force of nature, like a tree, hence the term 'human nature,' and that therefore we should view ourselves more as an undifferenti-ated force, like in a painting by Picasso or in the music of Rach-maninoff, where the individual is almost swallowed up in the surroundings, because it seems to me that this makes death more palatable and much less of a cataclysmic transition. So I respect where Kierkegaard is coming from, Husserl's positive individual-ism, William Blake's line that a separate universe is contained in every grain of sand, but I also think we ought to celebrate the empirical truth that there is nothing so specific about us as to prevent us from being reconstituted tomorrow as a drop of rain, or as a glint of light on the surface of a lake."

Delia nodded.

"You know what I mean?"

She nodded again. As best she could, she was trying to do what she thought she ought to be doing just then: keeping a world of contradictions alive in her head. She wasn't doing too well. All she could think about was that she hadn't a single philosophy of her own. It was embarrassing.

"Wow," she said. "But have you got any of your own?"

"What?"

"Those are other people's philosophies. Have you got any of your own?"

Phillip smiled. "Only one. It's important to read. That's my philosophy."

Delia nodded. She understood what was needed. Something simple to grasp. Then she could be like Phillip, and let one philosophy carry her right through her life. Look at him: a librarian; first came the philosophy and then flowed direction, purpose, a job. "Wow," she said again.

She was alone in the world. She would have to come up with her own. She didn't need anybody's help. She never had.

He noticed her picking up her jacket. "Right. Are you going?"

"Mmm."

Phillip couldn't tell if she was annoyed or not, and he was grateful that he had not bombarded her with unnecessary questions or advice.

"Good night," he said softly.

"Good night," she replied. She walked away without looking at him, vowing never to return until she had a philosophy she could call her own.

. . . . .

Alone in the library later that night, Phillip opened a relatively
new medical almanac. In his private journal he copied down word
for word an entire paragraph:

Diagnostic criteria for Obsessive Compulsive Neurosis.
  Sub-heading: *Washing fixation.*
Essential features: *Recurrent obsessions or compulsions sufficiently
  severe to cause marked distress, be time consuming, or signifi-
  cantly interfere with the person's normal routine, or usual social
  activities, or relationships with others.*
  Age of onset: *Usually begins in adolescence or early adulthood.*
Symptoms: *In extreme cases, it may show itself in a belief that the
  world itself is unhygienic and needs to be redressed. A "washer"
  may therefore believe that his fixation is a realistic defense
  against invasionary agents such as germs or other invisible and
  hostile contaminants.*
Impairment: *May become the major life activity.*

Where once the journal had been a diary, a repository for
lists and daily appointments, it had now found new purpose.
Phillip began to record his thoughts, and foremost in these
was Delia.

. . . . .

The next day, when a violent wave of morning sickness made
it impossible for Delia to continue work on the morning shift,
she pleaded for time off and walked slowly home, a route which
took her once again past the library.

Phillip waved to her through the window when he saw her out
on the grass, delighted that their meeting the previous night had
destroyed nothing. Quickly he joined her, hanging a BACK IN FIVE

MINUTES sign on the door: The library was not so popular that it couldn't operate like a small business.

They walked together through the town, neither one mentioning their discussion of the previous night. Delia was wan and smiled with difficulty, a mood Phillip tried to redeem.

"I could, if you like, tell you all sorts of weird things about some of these people around here, just from working in the library."

"Like what?"

"You see that old guy there?"

She turned her head to where a familiar figure in a tweed jacket was just then crossing the road. "I know him," she said. "Peter Entwistle. He's chairman of the Lions club. He bought some farm equipment off Dad, and one of his daughters plays netball with me. What about him?"

"Cuts out the topless pictures from *National Geographic* and the sex scenes from all the books he borrows. He's very neat, uses a razor blade close to the spine. One day he cut too deep, because the book fell apart on me. I then checked back through other copies, and the missing pages were all about intercourse."

Delia marveled at his detective work. She hadn't appreciated that a quiet job like his had this other dimension to it.

Phillip was pointing somewhere else. "And you see that woman over there, with her husband?"

"Yes. I know her." Jane Peterson, a local woman in her mid-forties.

"An affair! With an eighteen-year-old farmhand. Still going on."

"How do you know that? I mean, all the details? How do you know he's eighteen?"

Phillip smiled, amused by her enthusiasm and pleased he had revived her. "Well, books have a lot of other uses, apart from being read."

"Do they? What uses?"

"People often use them as a way of slipping messages to each other, for one thing. Sometimes the messages are left in the book. Well, that woman left a letter in the back of a Jackie Collins novel. I checked her boyfriend's name and age on our records. He's a library member too."

"You're joking! The letter, you read it then?"

"They have a system. She and the farmhand, they meet in a shearing shed. It happens while her husband raises the temperature in . . . is he a potter or something? They have a furnace."

"Glass blower."

"I presume he can't leave the furnace or something, once he starts it up, so she and her lover have two hours. I had to read the letter because it may have been historical."

Delia watched Mrs. Peterson with new eyes. She was window-shopping, and had paused in the doorway of a shop as if she couldn't decide.

"You want another one?" asked Phillip. "Don't look at him, he's coming this way."

One of the Haley boys was walking toward them reading a comic. Delia watched him as he came close, passing them, glancing up to look at them, before looking down again.

"What about him?" she asked.

"Guns. Fanatical. He uses the new photocopier, brings in these magazines, leaves the master on the machine."

"I do that!" shouted Delia, sensing the truth of it, amazed at how we shed evidence of our secrets like scales.

"Everybody forgets the master. Anyway, military-style weapons, information mailing lists, that sort of stuff. He's planning an arsenal."

"His mother is a lay minister at the church."

"I know," said Phillip resolutely.

She looked at him, bursting with new-found admiration. "What else? What else?" She was excited now, thrilled at the invisibility of her community. "Some more about sex. Who else? Who else is sleeping around?" Her voice dropped to a whisper.

"Well," he said, thinking. "One woman, I don't know her name, because the book was issued on someone else's card, came in. She was very attractive. Well, she is currently sleeping with two guys at the same time."

"You can't know that! How can you?"

He smiled. "I know."

"You found a letter?"

Phillip shook his head. It was not that obvious. "People read books in bed. That's where they usually slip up. They leave evidence—little clues about their most private secrets."

"Like what?"

"Pubic hairs."

"You found a . . . a pubic hair?" Delia thought he was joking.

"She's blond, and she left a pubic hair in the pages. But I also found a brown hair and a black one in the same book! That's extremely rare. To find three."

"Well," said Delia, thinking hard, not yet completely convinced, "they could be from three different borrowers." She was pleased with her own thoroughness.

"No. I don't think so. They were on the same page."

Delia was stunned. The same page! God, it was amazing what could be discovered in books! All roads seemed to lead to the library, and he had just shown her the map for the first time.

"So, don't worry," Phillip told her. "The same people who talk about you are actually just pleased that the spotlight isn't on them."

"I know that." Delia believed him.

"They're all looking at us because they don't want to look under their own beds."

"What's under there?"

"All sorts of nasty things," he said, realizing she had not appreciated this last metaphor. "And most probably . . . a few old library books too."

Delia laughed loudly for the first time in months.

When it was time for Phillip to return to work, she walked back to the library with him. And when he anticipated her desire to be asked inside, to work beside him as usual, she acted as usual, as if the invitation had taken her by surprise and that coming in would mean turning down a dozen other invitations. This familiar tango of manners and concealment of the fact that Delia was about to become homeless in her own town lent the moment a warm feeling of complicity.

The afternoon had almost gone and her predicament became more critical with every passing minute. Finally she had no option but to ask a large favor. She summoned the courage and tried to sound casual.

"The back room. I wonder if I could put a mattress down in there. Just for a few nights?"

The back room was for the storage of old books, mops and boxes. She explained nervously that she couldn't go home anymore. There was no one left on whom she could rely. Her friends had all abandoned her. She needed somewhere to stay—but only for a few days, until she could leave town.

"You can't just run away with nowhere to go. You have to think of the baby."

She told him that's exactly what she was doing: She had to escape her father to save her unborn child.

Phillip saw an opportunity to help, and took it.

"Look, my uncle has offered me a house that the council owns. I want you to take it. You're gonna need somewhere stable once the baby comes."

He magically produced a set of keys from his pocket and held them up.

She stared at them. "What about you?"

"I've bought the trailer from my uncle. He never used it. It had no tires. If you don't mind, I'll park it on your back lawn. If you don't mind sharing the electricity with me."

"A council house?"

Phillip carried another book over to the stack and left the set of keys provocatively on the trolley. She rose and looked at them.

"I even got the power switched on yesterday," he said. He sat down beside her, holding the last novel from the trolley.

Her hand rested absentmindedly on her belly. "Having this inside me makes me feel special."

He nodded. She seemed impossibly fragile, barely capable of being a mother.

"It's the first time in my life I've felt like that," she said.

Phillip understood. And he saw not only that she was worn out by all this, but also that she might be on the verge of changing her story. Her next word, in fact, could begin a full confession.

She looked at him. "It doesn't matter where it came from, does it?"

"Yeah, I think it does."

To stop herself from crying, she took the novel from Phillip's hands, but her tactic failed when she cradled it like a baby and started to cry, clutching *War and Peace* to her breast.

He formulated his next words slowly and carefully. "Say I'm the father," he almost whispered.

Delia looked at him through her tears, stunned by the suggestion. "What?"

"Say I'm the father."

She stared at him. "Get out of it. I hardly know you."

"I know, but this isn't exactly an ideal situation for you, is it? It'd be better for you than anything else." He allowed himself a stupid gesture, pointing a finger upward in the direction of deep space. It was a mistake.

"You're not the father," she said accusingly.

"I know. I know that. But the real father isn't around, is he? If you're really gonna have a baby . . . then you've eventually gotta think about the kid. And all kids need a father."

She continued to stare at him.

He spoke quickly now, trying to bolster his case. "People already treat me like I'm from outer space. So, why not say it's me?"

It was a gentlemanly offer, a package deal: a home, a child at play on a rug, friends over for pasta, a serene life, house insurance, blue water in the toilet. . . .

"I've got to go," she declared.

"Delia! I don't think you can go on saying a *spaceman*'s the father."

She turned and faced him, incredulous. "Who said I was going to?"

A wave of relief broke over him. He smiled. "Aren't you?"

She regarded him with new suspicion. "And you can keep your mouth shut too."

Phillip was confused.

"You don't believe me, do you?" she asked.

"You want to know the truth?"

She nodded, but was of two minds, not wanting to let her sanctuary become yet another place of conflict.

Phillip saw his first opportunity to speak his mind. He had already decided to be direct. How could he believe her? There was no proof, he said, and there was unlikely to be any. It was one thing to see a spaceship; people needed to be shaken up from time to time, it was good; but it was another to go on saying that the baby's father wasn't a local man when it would mean that her innocent baby would arrive in an atmosphere of hostility and ridicule. Was it fair to the child?

"It's a bit late to worry about that," she said.

"Who's to say it's not going to adopt a human form, anyway," Phillip hypothesized, careful not to contradict her but keen to show the weakness in her story. "Then there's only your word for it. And if it does look normal, then wouldn't it be better to play down the fatherhood thing, and spare your kid the added trouble? Imagine if your parents had told everyone your real father was . . . a bat or a monkey. I mean, life is hard enough as it is."

Delia was stunned. She had never considered that her baby would be anything other than normal. Even at the beginning she had never visualized a huge head on a small wiry body; now she realized she hadn't actually thought through the full implications of her story. He was right! If the baby looked normal, then, yes, it definitely deserved a chance at a normal life.

She had fallen silent, so Phillip proceeded. "So, why not say I'm the father? If later it wants proof of its identity, then you can just pull out a flashlight, go out on the lawn and try and get through." He mimed a beam pointing skyward, and unfortunately smiled.

Outside the library again, Delia tried to breathe deeply. The offer had thrown her into confusion and remorse, but she could not suppress an unexpected sense of joy and relief. It was disappointingly short-lived.

Gilbert Haines chose this moment to hurry across the street and touch Delia's arm, making her drop *War and Peace* in the mud.

"I'm sorry," he said, and then, to impress her, added, "You can wipe the mud off on me."

He scooped up the book and turned his back to clean it, knowing how his mechanic's hands always repulsed women. He looked ill with love.

"What is it?" Delia asked him, hoping it wasn't another ridiculous gift of fruit and wishing he would go away.

Gilbert wasn't sure, but he smiled. "How come . . . how come you're spending so much time in there?" He offered the book back to her. Fattened by a rain of hammer clouts, the black pulverized digits were disgusting exhibits. He flung his hands behind him, realizing his terrible mistake. He was unworthy—but perhaps, just perhaps, her desperate situation made them more equal. He was sweating, knowing he must speak up before this shining opportunity passed forever.

Delia watched the ugly beads form and fall down his face.

"What do you want, Gilbert?" She lifted hair from her eyes, impatiently putting her weight on one hip.

He took a nervous breath, savoring her every movement, made drunk by her unreachable beauty. "We have to be . . . to be together." He tapped himself on the chest, indicating that he was the second party. "You and me. Together. It just makes sense."

"Don't tell me," Delia said. "You want to be the father."

Gilbert was suddenly relieved, a supplementary speech no longer necessary. "Yeah," he smiled, showing her unkempt teeth. "I do."

"Oh, Gilbert." Only pity and condescension showed in her words.

He knew all was lost. He still disgusted her, and would always disgust her.

"No," he protested. "You don't understand." He took a breath. "Don't you see?" He tapped himself on the chest. "It's me. It's me. I'm the baby's father."

Delia started to walk off. She had no patience with all these pretenders to fatherhood. She thought men were supposed to flee at the very mention of pregnancy, not form a queue.

He ran around her and jammed himself in her path.

"Look . . . it's true. You don't remember who the father is, everyone says. So you made up the spaceman story. But it's me."

"You're drunk."

"Doesn't matter. The baby is mine."

Delia put him straight. "Don't be stupid, Gilbert. I would never have slept with you. Okay?"

But Gilbert was unreachable by logic. "You slept with me. You enjoyed it. You just don't remember."

"In your dreams."

"But it doesn't matter if you don't remember, just take my word for it. The baby is mine. So we've got to talk about what we're going to do now. We've got to make plans."

He was assuming the role of a mature collaborator in passion, ready to face his responsibilities, and Delia's look of hatred went unobserved. He was trying to grab her again when Phillip arrived. Gilbert's hands immediately became fists.

Phillip instructed Gilbert to leave Delia alone.

"No," said Gilbert, his back to his chosen fiancée. "This is between family."

"It is not!" Delia glanced at Phillip, quick to reassure him that the idea of family with Gilbert was abhorrent.

Gilbert faced Phillip. "You keep out of this. She's carrying my child. I've got a right . . ."

Delia stepped forward then, ending the dispute. "Don't be stupid, Gilbert. You might as well know."

"Know what?"

"That . . . that Phillip's the father."

And before another word could be spoken, Phillip sealed the announcement by placing his arm around Delia's shoulders in a gesture of paternal responsibility.

. . . . .

In the morning light, No. 9 Harrison Street was not Buckingham Palace, but for a building designed for emergency housing it was not without features.

"It's yours if you want it."

Delia Chapman's problems, in that moment, seemed to be over.

The ground-floor unit, one in a block of six battered flats and across a quadrangle from Deborah Kerr's, had a cheerful garden in front, bounded by a fence. A straight cement path led up to its front door. The white clapboard walls were still bright enough under the pantiled roof three floors above. It had potential. Delia agreed to take it; she was not at all put off by the smashed windows.

But even as Phillip and Delia stood there, the curtains at neighboring windows drew aside and antique faces peered out,

witnesses to the moment, recognizing them. Nearby, the clipping
of a hedge stopped, the shears suddenly abandoned. They were
being watched as if something marvelous was supposed to occur.
But it was only Delia Chapman moving in.

, , , , ,

She packed her belongings that afternoon at her father's house.
If she had not been pregnant she would have stayed and dealt
with the tangled circumstances of being a Chapman. It would
have been her duty then, and the legacy left by her mother. But
the baby had changed all that, and Delia packed her clothes and
ornaments as if she were being commanded by her unborn child
to do so. She would save her baby by obeying it.

Three bags cannot hold very much of what has been gathered
over sixteen years, but when Delia packed and then dragged three
cases through the front door she did not feel she had left behind
a single meaningful item.

Phillip's car came into the drive. There was no sign of her
father anywhere, and he loaded her bags into the trunk.

Later that day Delia was left alone to walk through the empty
rooms of her new home, and she found pleasure in its dilapidation. It was a relief to be away from her father, his madness, his
parallel shoes, his salt and pepper shakers centered on the table,
his ironed handkerchiefs, his turned-back sheets, his timetables
and rules. Here in her new house she saw his antithesis, a house
crammed with rot and disorder, a house with no rules, sagging
with chaos and decay. She breathed easily.

Torn drapes were pinned by thumbtacks over the windows in
the living room. A livid smell came from the bathroom. The vis-
cous fluid from the fridge had leaked out into a puddle on the
kitchen floor. The bedroom with its burnt-orange wallpaper sent
a shiver up her spine. Undeterred, she planned a home. A couch
here, a table there. The peeling silver on a full-length mirror
flaked each side of a vertical crack, but she found she could view

herself evenly if she stood either to the left or to the extreme right, and she decided to keep it.

She started to clean, but put on two layers of rubber gloves before she touched anything. Three hours later Phillip returned with a used table, two chairs, numerous boxes of cooking utensils, old crockery, war-era knickknacks, a veteran armchair, and a single bed tied onto a trailer: his contribution to his newly adopted family.

"We should get it inside now," she said.

On the front gate a large cardboard sign had appeared, on which was scrawled: ALIEN GANG-BANGER GO HOME. The authors could not be seen. Phillip tore it down and threw it over the nearest fence, where it lay on the grass in two incoherent pieces: ALIEN GANG and BANGER GO HOME. No curtains parted now, and no one stood in their gardens. It was a declaration of war.

Inside, Phillip and Delia stowed the furniture. During their breaks they drank beer in the living room, sitting in a canyon of boxes. She did not remove her gloves.

"She wasn't mad. Even though everyone said she was," she explained. "What's 'mad' mean, anyway? Not much in a place like this."

Phillip had renewed the subject of Delia's mother. If suicide was Delia's companion, then he'd better understand it.

"She just didn't want to join the local Rotary Club, that's all, and they cut her off. She got lonely. Then she started her collections. That's when we should have known."

"Collections?"

She told him in greater detail about the wind chimes, about how they had started as a hobby, but how when they grew in number they ceased to be pleasant and became as unwelcome as bats hanging from the ceiling; and then she told him how they finally had to be put away, and all that happened as a result: the creek, the events at the creek. To console her, Phillip told her that Nietzsche believed that everything that happens, even accidents, is deliberate, and so every chance encounter is an appointment, every death a suicide. With a small nod of gratitude, or perhaps frustration, Delia recounted the events which culminated in her father, acting under instruction, bringing the chimes out again.

He changed the subject and tentatively asked whether she'd had boyfriends.

Delia shook her head slowly. "My father would have killed me . . . and them. . . . Anyway, I'm not interested in boys around here."

They sipped their beer. Then she told him she never wanted to get married. In reply, he cited Harry Houdini, the great escape artist.

"What are you talking about?" she asked.

"Well, it's just that he let himself be chained up and had the keys thrown away. It was a nice trick, but it killed him."

After a moment's consideration, she nodded. She supposed that this was how librarians talked, referring to obscure things they'd read to explain their feelings. Then, after another long silence in which they could feel the other's breath on their faces, they felt silently and abruptly compelled to kiss: their first, it was cautious and clumsy, dry lips touching, wildly off target but ardent; and Phillip smelled the unmistakable aroma of cleaning products and Delia his strong cologne which reminded her once again of being at the dentist: A jolt of memory catapulted her back to their first meeting, remembered in greater detail than ever before. Delia began to sneeze.

"What is it?"

"Whatever you put on," she said, and touched his chin with her yellow rubber glove.

He wiped his face as she wiped her nose on her sleeve. And he asked her a question which had intrigued him for three months.

"There's something I've always wanted to know. The very first morning I started work at the library, before it was even open, you dropped in a book. How did you know the library would reopen?"

"Because you *told* me. When you gave me a ride, the night we first met."

"How do you know I did?"

"Because I remember."

"Oh. You remember. I didn't think you remembered anything."

"Of course I do." Delia smiled at him.

Phillip didn't force the matter by reminding her of her initial failure to recognize him all those months ago. "Our meeting was . . . was real, Delia. But your other one that night, was that real too?"

She didn't answer. And interpreting her silence as an invitation to continue, he asked the crucial question.

"Can you tell me what really happened before I found you on the highway?"

She stared at him, betrayed.

"Delia, I'm trying to help," he said. "I just—"

She cut him off. "I think you should go now." She raised her voice. "Go on! Piss off!"

Phillip wanted to explain, but she wasn't listening anymore. She got up, pulled him to his feet and pushed him toward the door. Her voice was charged with emotion and accusation. She had thought he was different, but she was wrong and obviously he was just like all the rest—or, at least, he had become like all the rest: contaminated, infected, needing to be thrown out.

He stood out on the cement path in front of her new house, and then was blocked from her sight by the slamming front door.

Inside, her eyes shifted focus from the rejected object of love to three brass locks on the door, which she quickly bolted. No one would enter now. And to insure it, she pushed boxes up against the door, barricading herself inside. Then she turned off the hall light. She would build a fortress around her from now on, and whenever she went out she would even disguise herself, so that she couldn't be recognized or be contaminated by anyone again.

Phillip was knocking on the front door, his knuckles becoming raw, but she ignored the sound of his fists. Cowering inside, she was too shaken to speak. She stood amid the labyrinth of unpacked boxes until she heard the sound of his car driving away. Then she went into the bedroom, the only uncluttered space, where the full-length mirror caught her in cracked reflection. She lifted her T-shirt to expose her skin, and with her hand on her belly she remembered that she was not alone.

Behind the wheel of his car, driving fast, Phillip scolded himself for his monumental error in judgment, particularly after so long and painstaking a courtship. In the end, he had been unable to contain his true feelings. They had escaped at the first opportunity and had surprised even him. He had probed too deeply, and she had closed around a pearl of truth like an oyster. He saw no way to prize it free.

Devastated, he turned a corner and vanished.

Eleven

. . . .

PHILOSOPHY

"I can't go back there," Vic Young told his employer, unhappy with the very suggestion that he go back to Opunake.

"You'll go," Ray Hungerford said, not lifting his head from the latest installment of the Young articles as he spoke. "I mean, I love this. And it keeps getting better."

Vic Young sat in front of him picking dirt from under his fingernails with a paper clip in an act of purification. He had just returned to Auckland to take up other reporting duties, magnanimously delivering the last of his Opunake articles by hand. He believed that this was an end to it.

"I'm going to send you back down there," Hungerford mumbled, quickly turning a page.

"What for?"

"Because there's much more to be had out of this story yet, that's why. It's great. In fact, this is only just *starting* to get good."

"I don't see it that way."

"You don't *see* it? Well you *should*." The editor reached forward, took a red pencil from a mug and struck a redundant phrase from Young's copy.

"I've covered the story. It's over. They're gonna have these babies, these girls; they're gonna have them and they're not gonna be aliens, and the whole thing'll be over with. It's finished."

"Yeah, but . . ."

"But what?" His fingernails were now almost free of Taranaki soil.

"What if they have these babies, and they're . . . green, Vic?" The editor's tone was excited and not at all ironic.

"Come again?"

"Green, I said. What if they're green, Vic? With big eyes and long skinny arms, for example. Tell me."

Young was confused now. "What do you mean?"

"That's the story, you see. That's it right there. The 'what if' factor."

"The 'what-if' factor?"

"Exactly. That's the story I want you to go up there and bring back to me."

"They're not gonna be green, Ray." He didn't know how to say it more plainly. "Okay?"

"How do we know that, though? What if, for argument's sake, they are?"

"Green? Fine. Sure. All right. Then you go down there! Look, these are three innocent kids, that's all! Nice kids. They're hardly out of school. It's a prank. And I've given you six stories on it. It's over." He raised his voice but managed to control himself.

"Here's my point, Vic," Ray proceeded. "And I'm surprised I have to point this out to you. What if these kids aren't just making up stories? What if"—and he formed inverted commas with his fingers in the air—"what if these babies they're gonna have aren't like anything else we've ever seen before? And what if we're about to be delivered ET on a plate?"

Young sighed deeply. What could he do to end all this? He did not forget that he had started it.

"Are you listening to me, Vic?"

"Yeah, I'm listening."

"I'm saying . . . what are people's reactions to that possibility? That's the story. What's the official view on the possibility? Let's talk to a scientist. Find out what the scientific position is. There's a story. 'Doctors to Study Diapers for Clues.' What will the government policy be on dealing with offspring spawned by alien contact? Could an interstellar baby boom constitute a threat to national security? *Any* response'd be pure gold for us. Imagine if we provoked a comment from the governor-general. He might try to laugh it off, but three Taranaki girls with . . . synchronized pregnancies, no confirmed fathers, we could force him to answer! Money couldn't *buy* the words he'd utter, Vic. Imagine luring the government into taking an official position on this. See my point now?"

"I think so. Yes. You want me to chase . . . nothing."

"Yes. I do, Vic. I do. Because *nothing* sells like nothing." Ray gave a self-satisfied laugh. "Anyway, I think you see my point now. Before these girls deliver, yes, okay, completely normal and likely very healthy babies, we can make a killing here."

Young's brows furrowed. He sat mutely in the empyrean glow of his employer's excitement, listening with mounting disgust and cumulative guilt, waiting to ask one question, and one question only.

"Ray . . . ?"

"You see what I mean?"

"Yes. Yes, I do. Ray . . . ?"

"Mmm?" The editor had spun into his own orbit, adrift.

"What about these kids?"

"What kids?"

"These three girls, Ray."

"What do you mean?"

"Have you thought whether any of this is fair to these girls?"

"What are you talking about? They *want* the publicity. Obviously. Why else are they doing this?"

"That's where I think you're wrong. They don't want the publicity at all. They're scared. Well, two of them are, at least. You don't understand. They're scared shitless by all this. They're nice girls. They're just three simple country girls . . . who . . ."—he had begun the sentence and couldn't now avoid finishing it—"who just happened to meet . . ."

"Spacemen?"

It was not the word Young was searching for, and seeing his employer's eyes fill with renewed light he regretted his unfinished sentence. He had inadvertently provided the man with yet another opportunity for corrupting his words.

"I'm resigning."

"Nonsense." Ray Hungerford laughed with confidence.

"Use someone else. I've had it."

"You can hang on to the Rover. You'll need four-wheel drive."

"What about the closure story?"

"What closure story?"

"Of their freezing works in Opunake. 'Death of a Town.'" It was the conciliatory offer of a man in a leaking canoe.

"So what? Fuck that! Everyone else is doing that. In *this* story, *we* lead. Now get back out there. There's a good man. Be a pit bull. Sic 'em!"

, , , , ,

Monday came and the long-awaited books from Wellington arrived in thirty-five identical brown boxes. They were carried into the library by two removal men, who finally thrust under Phillip's nose a huge manifest, upon which was listed each book title: a weltering array of classics.

When the truck was gone Phillip stood and looked at the heavily potent boxes. No pirate surveying his contraband could have been more pleased with his treasure. It seemed inconceivable that such a motherlode could be delivered in one shipment.

In the reclusive peace of the library he excitedly cut the tape on the first box. The flaps crested open toward him. Inside lay the great works, side by side, the mighty tomes, squeezed to capacity. He prized out the first ones, modern reprints of the finest masterpieces, and joyfully stacked them on the floor ready for processing. The aroma of printer's ink was still strong, and the crisp new pages tempted him to fan through each book with his thumb before he set it aside: With each, a puff of air kissed his face. Everything he had requested for the education of Opunake's farmers was here, his annual budget spent in one consignment. All of them, from the Greek and Latin authors through to a faultless twenty-eight-volume *Encyclopaedia Britannica* with its companion set of *Great Books of the Western World,* were seminal works, containing, *in reductio,* many of the most persistent thoughts ever to have occupied the human mind. When he had finished stacking them on the floor he stood back and saw that he had built around him a circle of waist-high towers, a city of ideas, its diameter reaching from one side of the library to the other.

It would be his job, and his great pleasure in these first weeks of autumn, to card and catalog each one.

Phillip had other reasons to be excited that morning. His new resolve was to dedicate himself, in his spare time, to the full and unflinching mystery of Delia's predicament. He was determined to uncover the truth of her situation, if only to feel some indirect contact with the young woman he had grown to care for, above all else. He reasoned that if he could decode her fantasy and become a sleuth, he could also win her back.

With this single ambition in mind, he had called himself to action and decided to confine himself exclusively to the library until he had solved the riddle. His basic conviction was that all secrets had their solution in a library. This idea could be supported by simple algebra. He reasoned that if all lives conformed to Henry James's six or seven prototypical human stories, and if one allowed for all their possible permutations, then a familiarity with the contents of even the most humble library, which contained thousands of human scenarios, should supply the reader with an overwhelming surfeit of data upon which to predicate a solution to any riddle. To solve Delia's mystery, therefore, he could dispense with the outside world altogether and pursue instead a completely abstract literary route.

Already he knew much about the secret life of many of the town's citizens through pure observation and logical deduction, so he did not anticipate a difficult task. Confidence brimming, he opened his personal journal in which to record his findings.

He defined his project with the heading, "A Psycho-Philosophical Enquiry," a title which, although general, would constantly remind him of his original goal, for it was easy to become waylaid in the tunnels of philosophy. Keeping his initial research broad until the process became more clear to him, but with the view that it should at least pertain to current events in Opunake, then finally to Delia herself, he consulted the principal philosophers, hoping to move from the general to the particular like a microscope focusing upon its subject.

When the first opportunity came for him to display the BACK IN FIVE MINUTES sign on the door, he drew a volume from the virgin pile of *Great Books of the Western World* still sitting on the floor. He opened it at random, to be confronted at once by the steadying voice of Plato. He considered this as good a place as any to learn about Delia. At this early stage he read mostly for amusement, as a warm-up for what he anticipated would come later, so to help him order his thoughts he copied the occasional line into his journal. Five minutes passed like a second.

As the day passed, an ever-increasing and curious flow of visitors kept him from his studies, each one bending to inspect the cerebral books on the floor but moving quickly to the restored

selections of pulp romances and Nazi-obsessed potboilers in uniform lines on the shelves. It was with some relief that he showed
the last guest out and locked the door. He was exhausted. But
with his best energies gone he was still determined to burn the
midnight oil. He selected another volume, this time Witt-
genstein's *Tractatus Logica-Philosophicus.* Finding no clues on his
subject there, he leapfrogged into a superficial reading of Hegel's
Selbtsbestimmung. Finally, he was in his element. He soaked up
the first pages, and precisely because he understood almost nothing of what he read, every word was imbued with tremendous
power. Only odd words and phrases leaped out at him, but when
he thought they were relevant, even in the remotest sense, he
wrote them down studiously; lofty, impenetrable, archaic phrases,
sometimes comprehensible only on an intuitive level. He copied
them into his personal notebook with an air of growing monasti-
cism. He had not consciously turned his back on modern writers,
but no serious thinker wishes to owe anything to his contempo-
raries. And so he leaped into the past. And the volumes grew
around him.

Twelve

INVASIONS

Delia had almost entirely closed ranks and excluded everyone from the sealed hemisphere of No. 9 Harrison Street, so she was reluctant to answer the first knock on her front door. It interrupted a marathon week of vacuuming and disinfecting, days in which she had continued her shifts at the freezing works but had hardly spoken to anyone at all.

Her visitor was a dissolute Vic Young.

She wondered if the man was hurt, he looked so timeworn and sorry for himself. His clothes were rumpled and he hadn't shaven in days; his long hair was unwashed and gathered only loosely at the back in a festering and graying ponytail.

"I'm Vic Young. Excuse me."

Delia eyed him cautiously. He was filthy. She had to be careful who she talked to. "Do I know you?"

"I dunno, yes, maybe. Well, not really, but I know you."

"What?"

"I shouldn't be here."

"I think you've got the wrong address," she said.

"No, this is the right address."

Young was shocked by her appearance, horrified that she looked much older than he'd expected. Quickly he realized his mistake, that the girl fixed in his mind was based on a four-year-old photograph: He had been in love with a nonexistent child. He felt nothing for this woman in front of him, nothing at all; she was a stranger, an impostor.

"What is it?" she asked. "I'm busy."

"I'm a journalist. I've been writing the articles."

"Yes."

"Could we . . . talk?"

"No."

"I understand. I do." He spoke softly.

"No," she said.

"Believe me."

"What do you want?"

"Just . . . a couple of minutes."

"No."

"Please." When and how did he learn to be so greasy, he wondered. Jobs took you over. Finally you just became your job. Greasy.

"Leave me alone," she said, narrowing her eyes. "Haven't you done enough?"

Vic Young lowered his gaze and caught a glimpse of her large belly before she closed the door on him.

He was shocked. So this was where she was living. Alone. Probably given the boot by her father. Ostracized by everyone, as well. Hiding from all the talk in a depressing flat. He felt responsible for the whole situation. How wrong his employer was—that these girls were bathing in the publicity and loving it. The truth was that every one of his stories stuck in a new knife: This girl was writhing in pain while Hungerford laughed all the way to the bank. He wanted to leave, in shame, but decided to knock again.

"What!" Delia said, losing her temper as she opened the door. "I'll phone the police."

"I have some good news." Vic really wanted to tell her how his stories had been corrupted, their intentions skewed, but instead he simply said, "We'd be prepared to pay."

Delia was curious. "For what?"

He gave the message he'd been sent to deliver, adding that of course she could refuse, and he'd quite understand it. He might refuse too if the roles were reversed. But this didn't change the fact that he had been authorized to offer her a complimentary flight in a helicopter.

She stared at him.

Transport to Auckland, a checkup at the maternity hospital, a specialist consultation and return transportation, all to be paid for by his newspaper. With a weary look in his eyes which discredited every word, he quoted his superior: " 'Let's get a look at the child early. For its own safety as much as anything else.' " He paused. "That's what I've been told to tell you."

Delia paled at the suggestion. She looked at the wretched character in front of her, a dissolute figure who had arrived with a lunatic's offer. A helicopter to Auckland? Were they serious?

"It's no joke," he added. "Believe me. And when the time comes, the newspaper will pay for all maternity costs, in exchange for . . ."—he had to finish, now that he had begun—". . . for exclusive rights. That sort of thing."

Before he could begin to make his personal apology for having dragged her name and story through the mire of his newspaper, she cut him off.

Door and locks were bolted against him.

He waited on the step for a moment, oddly content, happy that at least he'd given her the opportunity to insult him.

. . . . .

Within the hour there was another knock on the door. It would be the same man, or another journalist, Delia decided. She peeped through the curtain but saw only local children running away down the street, giggling in fits of mischief, tripping over each other. When she opened the door she saw a small doll lying on the step. It had buttons for eyes of differing size and color. She picked it up: a stuffed doll with a cute human body, but its head, crudely stitched on, was ugly, misshapen: It was the head of an alien, a monster's head.

The street was empty. She knew she was being watched from a distance. She held the doll tenderly and took it inside, her emergent maternal instincts aroused, even by this ugly effigy. In her bedroom she laid it on her single bed.

, , , ,

Half an hour later a third visitor arrived to disturb her cleaning. "Hello," the priest said coyly. "I hope I'm not interrupting anything." He had with him a cheap framed painting of a Hawaiian hula dancer and a box of aluminum cooking pots. "A couple of things for you from the St. Vincent de Paul."

Delia blinked. What on earth was going on here?

"Would you mind if I came inside for a second?"

She stared at the curate and his presents, then ushered him into the living room, thinking that priests had automatic right of entry.

Father O'Brien did not look much better than the journalist, and possessed a similar air of entropy. He appeared to have lost much of his hair. Everyone around Delia seemed to be suffering, and she couldn't pretend to understand why.

She excused the state of the house, and explained that she had no shelves yet and so had not unpacked much. The priest set aside his gifts, sat on a chair in the cluttered living room where a large box served as a perch for his elbow, and amid an arsenal of empty disinfectant bottles immediately invoked the formal atmosphere of the confessional.

"Before I speak, I want you to tell me if there's anything on your mind."

"Listen, Father, there's nothing I want to say."

"You're sure?"

Unlike Anglican ministers, Catholic priests were duty-bound to wear their collars in public and Delia noticed the unavoidable rash on the priest's neck. Dark bags also underscored his eyes. "Well then, let me speak," the exhausted man continued.

Delia just wanted to get on with her cleaning.

"I'll come to the point, Delia." And like the journalist before him, the priest came to the point. "If we accept for a moment that the child is of unusual parentage, it will still be important that it be offered a reasonable explanation as to who the father is. Agreed?"

"Okay," said Delia. "I know you're humoring me."

"Humoring you?"

"Isn't that the word? You don't really think my baby could be of 'unusual' . . . what did you say? . . . 'parentage.' You're just saying that."

"No, I'm not. If you promise to keep an open mind, then I will too."

"You can't do that though," she protested.

The priest could not argue. On this matter he wasn't truly open. For all his talk about open-mindedness, he had as narrow a vision of the playing field as anyone else.

She continued. "You all talk about having open minds, but if someone like me, who is no weirder than anyone else around here, tells you they saw something that you don't believe in, then your minds close up like that." She clicked her fingers.

"You're right," he admitted. "I don't have an open mind."

"Well, then, why should I?"

The logic was irrefutable and the priest paused to consider a way around the impasse. "I was humoring you, you're right."

"Then there's nothing to talk about, is there?"

"Perhaps not. Perhaps not." He was quiet for a minute, then he asked with sincere curiosity, "How is the baby doing, Delia?"

"All right, I think."

"How many months is it?"

"Twelve weeks."

"Have you picked names for it yet?"

"Not yet."

"Been to a doctor? Had a checkup?"

"No."

"Don't you think you should?"

She nodded, then shrugged.

They sat in silence. The priest felt unusually irrelevant. His own mysticism was as untenable as hers. Where, after all, was the evidence that his God existed?

"Wanted to get a baby carriage for you, but they're like hens' teeth down at St. Vincents," he said. "I'll keep trying, though, if you want."

"Okay."

"Do you believe in God at all?" he asked gently. "Probably don't."

"No," said Delia without hesitation.

"He appears to people sometimes, through the Holy Spirit. Would you like to see something like that?"

She shrugged. "I suppose so."

"So would I. I mean, more often." The priest sounded wistful.

"Why do you believe in God?" asked Delia.

The priest spoke without thinking. "I'm not sure." He turned to her, their roles almost reversed. "I suppose he revealed himself to me, and I felt his love reaching out to me."

"What was that like?"

"Profound."

He looked at her. It suddenly sounded to him an extremely flimsy cosmology. In the first flush of his ministry, high on God, discussions like this would have thrilled him. Why did they now leave him so depressed? All this endless *believing:* Where was it all going? Too often the priest wanted to tear off his tunic, drop all this talk of God and simply help someone—just that, help someone in a practical way. What was he doing visiting this sweet girl and morosely lecturing her on the Holy Spirit when all she probably needed was a hundred dollars or a good night out? What did he—a man riddled with theological doubts, who was frankly unable to remember even the last time he cracked a joke—what did he have left that he believed in?

He eventually returned to the subject of his visit. Paraphrasing an obscure theme from one his own sermons, he asked Delia to try replacing for a moment the word *spaceman* with the word *God,* and see how it felt.

"After all, it's about who we look to for answers, isn't it? Isn't that all?"

And if she could do this, just for a moment, and see how in this television age, one had virtually become a substitute for the other, then she and her friends, with their extraordinary conceptions, were simply reinventing the nativity story.

"To make contact with God, or in this case a spaceman, you have simply imagined that you are having his child."

He understood this impulse to believe, if that was what it was, but three unborn children had to be considered. His tone changed.

"I've had a phone call, Delia. That's really why I'm here. An informal phone call with an old friend of mine at Social Welfare in New Plymouth. She confessed to me, off the record, that there is a little bit of concern about the future well-being of your baby once it is born. I'm going to be completely frank with you. I'm a little bit worried about what I was told. The Social Welfare have a lot of power, Delia. And if they feel that a child is . . . well, if they weren't perfectly satisfied that you'd stopped believing in this . . . this alien thing, then . . . then, I think you can guess their reaction." Anticipating the impact of his next words he paused. "They could actually take the baby away from you. As horrible as that sounds. They have the power to do that. If they have a concern that you may not be, shall we say, in a fit state of mind to be responsible for your baby right now, then they have an awesome amount of power."

Delia stared at him, and the priest, reading this as incomprehension, put it all in a single sentence. "It could mean that they come and take the baby away from you if you don't have a change of heart."

"When?"

"Soon after it's born. I've seen it happen within hours."

"No."

"They can come into the maternity ward. It sounds cruel. It is cruel. But there is a very conservative guiding principle and I'm just afraid that something like this could happen. This baby of yours will need its mother, I'm sure of that. And I want to help you, to see what, together, we can do."

"It's no one else's business but mine."

"I know that."

"No one's business at all except mine!" She was losing her temper.

"Now, calm down, Delia. We're going to see what we can do."

She sat back down on the chair and tried to catch her breath. Her hands unconsciously fell to her tummy.

The priest continued. "Now, I've already talked with Yvonne several times. I'm working with her and her mother. And we're at the point now where Yvonne is pretty certain that she can remember something of the events leading up to her pregnancy, and she is on the verge of telling her family, when she has the courage. She has told her mother that she didn't see a spaceship after all, and she is going to tell us who the father actually is." The priest's look of exhaustion indicated to what degree he'd been instrumental in this revelation.

"I know she never saw a spaceship," Delia said. "She never said she did."

"Of course this doesn't necessarily have any bearing on your experiences. I admire you for sticking to your guns. And I can assure you that you still have the full support of Lucinda Evans. I talked with her yesterday, and she is . . . well, the only word is stubborn. However—"

"I'm keeping my baby. They can't force me."

"But they can. Unfortunately they can. They have powers to break in a door. Most mothers resist having their babies taken away from them, and this is why the department has the powers it does. Delia, listen to me, now." He leaned forward, to emphasize the point. "I've worked with women who have never seen their babies again. They have been kept from learning their whereabouts. They lose their kids. For God's sake, this is something we have to avoid. I want to see this baby growing up in this house. Don't you?"

Delia was utterly shaken. The front door should never have been opened today. That was her mistake. And she wouldn't let it again.

"Will you let me help you, Delia?"

"Mmm?"

"Will you let me help you?"

Reluctantly she nodded.

"We'll do what we can, then. But you have to do one thing for me. You have to keep an open mind. Even if I can't. Please, Delia, if only for the baby's sake, think about the baby."

On this valedictory note Delia showed the priest to the door. He stopped at the threshold, nodded, then slipped into the darkness, his black shoes clipping down the path.

After sitting a while with her head in her hands, she climbed into the shower, where she was plunged again into a stream of involuntary images, that meaningless newsreel which flashed into her head more and more in recent days. Sometimes an odor or a noise triggered it, and she would see a car, its door opening . . . and legs running through bush . . . someone's running legs, arms hurting from a blow, and lacerated calves. All unexplained, the pictures lit the back of her skull and faded a few seconds later. These were bad moments for Delia, moments of shadow and fear, and in the middle of them she believed that she was going nuts or, remembering the more expert term directed at her mother, drifting into insanity. But washing helped. Soap was good: right under the nails, where the dirt collected, and behind the ears, where it hid.

Under the cascading water, her thoughts were exploded by a crash from her living room. She dashed from the shower in a towel, almost slipping on the cold linoleum, to find an avalanche of broken glass covering the floor. A rock lay on the carpet, the window smashed. She opened the front door, and her scream carried down the street. "Go away! Just go away!" But there was no sign of her harassers, and after a few moments, having pro-voked only more unwanted notoriety among her neighbors, she went back inside and laboriously picked glass out of the carpet, particle by particle, carefully wrapping the bigger pieces in news-paper so that rubbish collectors would not lacerate their hands. She taped pieces of cardboard from her packing boxes over the smashed window, to keep out the cold mountain air. Finally, when she was tired of crying, she climbed into bed and tried to seal out the world. A single streetlamp, however, kept her awake through a curtainless window.

Thirteen

INVESTIGATIONS

The morning whistle sounded at the factory, a whistle which had become a countdown to the works' temporary closure, which the nonunion workforce had been unable to derail and against which Opunake had no defense. Soon a billboard would appear over the main gate to warn TRESPASSERS WILL BE PROSECUTED, and the shrill sound of that whistle, which had formerly been an annoyance to everyone, would seem the nostalgic wail of extinction itself.

Delia rose, brushed her matted hair, and remembered all the sour events of the day before. She tied her cotton hygiene mask behind her neck as she did every morning, but this time drew it up over her face.

She walked to her gate and down the street and, indifferent to the stares of onlookers, wore it all the way to work.

To Delia, wearing the hygiene mask in public seemed as normal a precaution as looking right and left before crossing the road, or as logical as washing her hands before eating. Everything and everybody could infect you with their evil diseases, their hatred and jealousy and their filth. Even the air could no longer be trusted. A mask was only sensible.

She entered the funereal packing room and sat down ready for work. The other girls were already gossiping.

"She wore it all the way here!"

"Did she?"

"I saw her. Walked through town with it on."

"Bullshit!"

"Did! Like one of those Muslims!"

"Wonder how much she got for that last article?" Suzy pondered, looking up at Delia ahead of her in the assembly line.

Deborah always had an answer to every question, and if she didn't know, she promptly invented one. "I heard she got five grand. Lucinda Evans too."

"Bullshit! Evans got that too?"

"Bobby said."

"How did Bobby hear?"

"He talked to the journalist over at the motor inn. Met him in the restaurant one day."

"Five grand?! Both of them? Fuckin' hell . . ."

"Shrewd at least, isn't she."

"Shrewd all right. That's just gonna be the start of it too. They'll make a bundle out of this."

"Bitches." Then, after a pause, "Ya think we oughta root a spaceman too?" Suzy laughed.

"I'd root the whole crew if it'd get me out of this place."

"Better than eight bucks an hour."

"No," said Deborah, "it only has to be better than the dole."

It was possible to pick up, wrap, tray, and box 120 hearts an hour. There was no incentive to do better than that.

"Hey, Bobby saw Delia with the librarian again. Out on the highway in his car!"

"He's shagging her while she's preggers?"

"Definitely! She told Gilbert Haines that the librarian's the father, by the way."

"I know. You think he did all three of them?"

"Doubt it. Doubt he'd go for skinny old birdbrain McKay. Hers is probably one of those hysterical pregnancies, Melanie reckons."

"You mean, like . . . ?"

"Yeah, one big bubble of air's gonna come out. Whoosh!"

"And as for fatso Evans, it could be anyone's. She's a slut. That's if she's pregnant at all. At least the other two are showing something. But Evans is so fat, you couldn't tell anyway. Baby or a big meal makes no difference. She hasn't stopped smoking either, I noticed. The cow."

Suzy was giggling and missed her share of hearts. It was the way Deborah had said cow. The backlog drew a complaint from the girl behind her.

It was generally agreed by the group that the librarian could take most of the blame for the scandalization of their former friends.

"Something should be done about him," said Deborah, less angry that he had so far escaped retribution than by his apparent lack of sexual interest in her.

"Definitely," agreed Suzy. "Cut his knackers off." She seized a cow heart and strangulated it. Juice flowed graphically through her rubberized fingers.

Deborah and Suzy had decided that they would go on the dole the day the packing room closed, when they would be replaced by robots. Deborah would move in with her old boyfriend Bobby, to whom she was giving a second chance, since the librarian had faded from view. Suzy wanted to do pretty much whatever Deborah did, and so, to effect a perfect symmetry, she was already scouting for a man of her own—one as compatible with Bobby as possible so all four could double-date, and who would move in with her after the bare minimum of preliminaries. Their lives would then be organized forever, or at least until they were thirty.

. . . . .

When the last visitor left the ever more popular library at six o'clock, Phillip locked the door and immersed himself so deeply in his private investigations that he could barely force himself to leave his desk at the end of the night.

This was the hour when he seemed to do his best detective work, alone with his books, as secluded by his profession as a monk. This was when he was able to indulge himself, and best imagine that the whole universe was a library and vice versa, since a library in its purest sense, like that attempted in Alexandria, was the potential repository of all knowledge, containing every idea enunciated as well as its refutation, every question posed, every mystery decoded, every significant deed recorded. And in the center of this pantheon, *ab aeterno,* cataloging and indexing it all, both lending and reclaiming, was the Librarian, analogous to a God.

Just in the last day Phillip had uncovered an array of clues which had a bearing on present events. With a very clear sense of their pertinence to Opunake in general, and to Delia in particular, he sat at his desk and took the unusual step of copying into his journal Latinisms from Lucretius's *De Rerum Natura: Whatever by its changing exceeds its frontiers, breaks out of its limitations. By so doing it brings immediate death to itself.* Clearly, this was relevant to Delia: With her vision of spacemen she had exceeded her own limits and invited the destruction of her former self. Perhaps this death was her only problem: She was in mourning for a loss she had not wished to bring about.

Intoxicated by the process of discovery, and by the conviction that he was making some kind of progress, Phillip began to feel his search linked to the destiny of civilization itself. With the flick of a page he met Nietzsche's view. Everything which happens to us, from the moment we are born until we die, has been preordained. Phillip thought he could have written the German's ideas himself, so perfectly did they clarify his current thinking. He was fated to have come to Opunake, destined to receive these ideas. Not crediting the authors, Phillip jotted in his journal, word for word, the observations on the cultural flattening of life in the industrial era, the erosion of memory, of history, and even of Time itself, all things which Phillip saw happening around him. He even added a pretentious thought of his own, one related to Opunake and his floating presence there: *We step into the future, but with our suitcases empty of everything.* Nietzsche foresaw this teleology, demanding a new kind of man in response: a Superman. Not since the dawn of the epochs of Islam and Christianity, Nietzsche wrote and so Phillip also wrote, did we so desperately require a new kind of human being.

As the hours of his lovesickness passed, Phillip's selection of quotations became less and less scrupulous, bound together only by a personal logic. A mental ghost train carried him through unanticipated twists and turns. He became hot and sweaty. Was he running a fever? He had hoped to come to a better understanding of Delia and her situation through a process of textual detective work, but instead his scope had become so wide and so incredibly vague that now there was almost nothing which did not deserve entry into his journal!

When he raised his head after a particularly intense stint of old-fashioned scrivening, one which had lasted hours and left his body shaky and poisoned by an overdose of ideas, he reviewed what he had written and was shocked to see before him three dozen closely written pages of mostly meaningless drivel.

This moment of clarity was a lucky escape, and he saw his journal for what it was: nothing but a tragic attempt to distract himself from Delia's dilemma with a rash of esoteric plagiarisms.

. . . . .

Deep in her deepest thoughts, in territories of shadows and half shadow, Delia ate lunch alone in the factory cafeteria and then returned early to complete her shift. At the final whistle, she walked back to her new home, once again in purdah, comforted by the cloth mask, her pace almost ceremonial. She looked at every familiar tree and building and landmark with affection, possessed of a sense that she was walking this route for the last time.

She opened the front door of her flat and found in the action a pleasurable sensation: the click of the new lock, the precise feel of the key, the yielding of the door opening exclusively for her. She went inside to wash and change into freshly clean clothes.

The first part of the evening was spent, as usual, in further cleaning the immaculate flat, but later events were unheralded. The reports of what took place that night were sketchy, as they came from fellow residents of Harrison Street, who, because of their antipathy, could be deemed biased at best, and treacherous at worst.

"She didn't have any clothes on," testified an overexcited young girl in a streetside report to the sergeant. By then, a small crowd had gathered around Delia's front door. Sergeant Watson was endeavoring to disperse people and maintain order.

The neighbors, some in their nightclothes, insisted that the sergeant finally do something about the young woman who was so upsetting the communal peace. Apparently, Delia had appeared half-naked at her letterbox, raving psychotically, seemingly possessed, only a towel wrapped round her, screaming obscenities for all the world to hear. It was admitted that someone had released a string of firecrackers on her doorstep just prior to the incident, but in no way did this justify her tirade.

The crowd made way for Phillip, whose late arrival could be blamed on a circuitous skein of informants. The sergeant stopped him at the step. "You can't go in. The doctor's in there."

"What happened?"

"She just snapped. She went crazy. I don't know."

"What do you mean, crazy?"

"Just relax, okay? Relax."

"I want to go in," Phillip said, hoping for sympathy, his eyes red-rimmed with scholastic fatigue.

The look in the sergeant's eyes made it clear he'd been stretched to breaking point by this last half hour of his career. "No one's going in there and that's final. Okay?"

By the time the doctor emerged twenty minutes later, the sergeant had largely succeeded in clearing the area. A few diehard ambulance chasers watched from their doors across the court-yard, and only Phillip had been permitted to wait outside Delia's flat.

"I've given her a sedative," Dr. Lim said in his soft voice, which had always been a natural sedative. "It wouldn't be a bad idea if someone stayed with her overnight. Is there anyone?"

Phillip volunteered before Watson could speak. "Okay. What should I do?" he asked.

The doctor instructed him on the critical importance of doing nothing at all. "Let her sleep. She'll sleep eight hours or so. Just check on her from time to time. She'll be fine."

Dr. Lim walked down the path followed by the sergeant, and Phillip used his own key to open the back door.

"How is she?" the sergeant asked in a clandestine voice once he and Dr. Lim were alone.

"I think proper treatment wouldn't be premature. Some sort of arrangements should be made tomorrow."

Sergeant Watson understood and was shocked.

"But it's not my field."

Watson nodded. Nor was it his.

"There's a good hospital in Auckland now," Dr. Lim continued.

"You mean . . . ?"

"It's a psychiatric hospital, yes."

The sergeant nodded, feeling a stab in his heart. The word *psychiatric* was one of the most menacing in the English language; it was like broken glass, fingernails dragging across a blackboard. The sergeant thought of Delia and visualized Victorian funny farms, dayrooms filled with dribbling dullards, psychotic screams in the night, padded cells overseen by obese wardens: all images from the movies.

"Are you sure that's absolutely necessary?" Watson asked.

"I don't know. Again, it's not my field. But when I examined her she seemed deluded, disturbed, and didn't seem to recognize me at all. I really think a specialist is called for."

With a violent sense of failure Watson watched the doctor drive away. He felt this failure as a policeman and as the mentor he considered himself to be.

Sedated, eerily immobile, Delia slept on her bed. Phillip peeked into the bedroom to check that she was comfortable. Carefully he closed the door.

In the living room he sank into the single armchair, put his feet up on boxes and fell into a sleep as deep as the one which had been artificially induced in Delia.

When he awoke it was daylight. Magpies were singing in the eucalyptus tree as he unfolded himself from his makeshift bed, a curled cripple. Even the most customary movements sent shooting pains into his numb legs. It took him several minutes to feel stable on his feet.

His clothes were crumpled. He would need to go home and change them before going to work. But the idea of having some coffee first appealed to him. The kitchen was pristine and well stocked: Everything was meticulously clean. He switched on the kettle, located instant coffee and, while waiting for the water to boil, went in to check on Delia. She was not in her bed.

He called for her several times but there was no sign of her, either in the bathroom or outside in the small backyard. He ran through the remaining rooms, calling her name. Her clothes were undisturbed in their bedroom drawers, and her coat still sat on a chair. She was gone, vanished without preparation!

He thought to chase her on foot, but this was pointless. He didn't know her well enough to anticipate her escape plans. Perhaps she had defied her sedatives and gone for a small walk, just a matter of a few blocks. He should drive around and look for her, comb the streets, conquer his crazy but sudden fear that he would never see her again. He was being ridiculous. His ominous hunches were unfounded. Any minute he would see her walking up the street. He would wait by his car for her, to greet and console her.

He barely remembered his own jacket before leaving Delia's flat. As he picked it up, his wallet fell onto the floor, already open, the zippers undone, empty of cash.

The theft alarmed him more than anything. One stole money for a journey, and one stole a substantial amount of money for an odyssey. Phillip had had enough cash in his wallet for someone to virtually emigrate: He had never trusted banks to safeguard his money, and kept a lifesavings in his pocket. He rushed to his car. She couldn't have gone far. Not on foot, in a half-drugged sleepwalk.

Despite his reservations, he got in the car and conducted a grid-patterned search of such military thoroughness that after an hour he was certain she was not to be found on any of the town's streets.

"I woke up, she was gone," Phillip told the sergeant when he finally drew up at the station, defeated and panic-stricken. "I went into her room: nothing. I'm going back out now and look again."

Watson advised the pale librarian that this was a police matter now. If, however, he received any information about Delia, then he should remember he was duty-bound to report it.

"Where do you think she could have gone?" Phillip asked.

"My guess?" replied the sergeant, with unconsidered irony. "Thin air."

. . . . .

Later that morning Harvey Watson placed a missing persons alert on Delia. But his initially vigorous inquiry had petered out into a second-rate phone campaign, yielding only the unsurprising news that Delia had not gone to work.

Vic Young entered the station. "Get out of here," the sergeant warned sharply, acting busy for the journalist's benefit.

"That's no way to speak to a respected member of the press."

"Okay. Piss off!" Watson lifted the phone receiver, shouldering it at his ear.

Young watched the officer run his index finger down a column of numbers in a phone book.

"Any word?"

"Do you really think I'd tell you that?"

Young shrugged. "Rightio. I'll say you're reluctant to comment at this stage." He pulled out a notebook and made a pretense of jotting down the phantom reply. "Oh, and bad luck about your four-game losing streak. Netball."

"I'd really like to know where you get your information from. That's the only thing about you that interests me." The sergeant lied. More than once he had officially considered whether this man with the motive for creating news, an abundance of opportunity and a suspicious presence at crucial moments could be at the heart of the troubles.

Young turned to leave. "I actually just called to see if there was anything I could do to help. She's a nice girl. If anything happened to her, I'd hold myself responsible."

Watson did not look up to see that the journalist's exhausted state validated this declaration of concern. His finger had fixed on a single irrelevant number which he proceeded to dial irrationally, partly to demonstrate that he was too busy to pass time with a visitor. Mercifully, he heard the engaged signal.

"The day I need your help they can shoot me, all right?"

"I should just keep anything I hear to myself, then?"

The sergeant's eyes glanced up for the first time. "What have you heard?" He disconnected the line, still holding the receiver to his ear.

"Nothing, I'm sorry to say."

"I can arrest you for withholding information."

"If I hear anything I'll let you know. How's that?" Young's tone was defiant.

"Where are you going now?" the sergeant asked, struck by the painful notion that his own line of inquiry was being superseded.

"Actually, I'm going back to bed. To try to get some sleep."

Young left as abruptly as he had appeared.

Watson sat in the chair, the dial tone droning in his ear. He replaced the receiver, rose, collected his jacket on the way out of the office and walked quickly to his car.

As he headed for the Chapman property, he tuned the police radio to an open channel to listen for reports. After several minutes of static came a call out in New Plymouth, a holdup at knifepoint in a sauna parlor: real violence, a brawl in motion, urgent reinforcements required. Adrenaline pumped inside Harvey Watson's professional heart as he responded vicariously to the distant emergency. He reached for his revolver under the seat, his passions fed by an irrelevancy. When he arrived at the Chapman house he was already in his own personal state of alert.

"She's gone missing," he told Marty Chapman loudly enough to inform a crowd, his energy dissipating, however, when he received from the farmer a long look of boredom and disgust.

Chapman returned to his repairs of a rusty plowshare in a shed near the house. "She can do what she wants. She's no daughter of mine."

"That's no way to talk, Marty," Watson reproached, trying to regain some of his initial excitement. "The doc's worried about her. He thinks she may need some kind of help. I think she's in a bad way. So if you've got her inside, maybe you'd better tell me now. You haven't got her in there, have you, Marty?"

Marty gave no reaction, finally convincing the sergeant that he would need a search warrant to take this any further.

Watson left the shed unanswered and stunned by this corruption of fatherhood. As he walked back to his car the sound of more than two dozen wind chimes carried from the porch, an orchestra of clanging xylophonic rattles which, in their discord, made him wonder how anyone within earshot could remain sane for more than a second. He drove away, his nerves already undermined.

As the car jolted down the unpaved track, he hoped he would not have to return very soon with an arrest warrant for Marty Chapman. In his rearview mirror he searched the reflected house for some sign of Delia. Had Marty dispatched her somewhere, to be with family or friends? This was a traditional solution, but it was unlikely for an isolationist like Marty.

Badly needing another burst of adrenaline, Harvey tuned the radio for an update on the sauna parlor emergency. He always responded to the core of his being to such calls to arms, to their affirmation that justice was bigger than injustice, that doing good was the business of professionals and evil the domain of amateurs. From this he derived a palpable feeling of vocation—one he hoped would sustain him in the difficult times which lay ahead.

F o u r t e e n

. . . .

REVELATIONS

Vic Young went into his room at the Sahara Desert Motor Inn. The large outline of his clandestine lover stirred in an unmade bed. Her head appeared at the foot end. Her face was startled, but became relaxed again when she saw Young's silhouette. "It's you," she mumbled sleepily, and then withdrew back into the sheets as he removed his trousers.

The constant and irritated bark of a sick dog outside accompanied the journalist's return to a state of nudity. He sucked in his stomach to free his belt. "Whose is that fucking dog?" He quickly shed his shirt, his undershirt and his tight black underpants to reveal a skeletal frame with arms so thin they looked barely capable of supporting him in the missionary position for more than a minute, and yet not once had they failed to hold him above this woman throughout a punishing three-week sexual regimen.

The young woman answered him murkily from under the covers. "Dunno," she said. "It's been like that for three days. Don't think they feed it, it's all skin and bone, poor thing."

He took off his socks and moved nakedly toward her.

He placed his wallet on the bedside table, among festoons of jewelry and crystals, potpourri and bric-a-brac, and climbed into a bed flanked at its head by plastic lamps in the shape of princess swans. He lay back, hoping to breathe freely.

"There's no ventilation at all in here," he complained. "It's like a crypt."

His lover swung her insatiable body around to align with his, and he felt the sensation of her fleshy thigh riding up his bony leg.

"So?" Lucinda Evans asked. "What's happening about Delia?"

"Nobody knows anything."

She nodded thoughtfully. "I told you. It's what I said—"

"I don't want to hear that now," he interrupted, severing her latest theory that Delia had been snatched by supersensible beings.

"Everyone says she's gone crazy."

"Everyone says a lot of things," said Young, leaning on his elbows.

"Sshhh," she said, kissing his chest lightly.

He looked down at her and saw her nostril studded with a shining stone. He allowed her kisses to calm him. Eventually, she climbed on top of him, and he surrendered to her explanations.

"They came back for her," said Lucinda, as she moved. "I'm telling you. They want their kid." Her unpinned hair completely obscured her face, and when he looked up he saw only a black shape from which a voice came. "It's obvious. They didn't come for sex. They came to spawn."

"What about you, then?" moaned Vic Young, buried beneath her. "Why didn't they take you too?" This was an insensitive remark, and it caused her to cease her undulations.

"Because I'm happening slower, aren't I?" she said.

"Oh, that's right, I forgot."

"I don't want to talk with you about it. And remember your promise. Remember?"

"I remember," he said, impatient only to continue. "I haven't told anyone. So don't worry. Just keep moving."

"Not until you promise."

"As far as anyone knows, your pregnancy is just as advanced as the others, okay? Now, either keep moving or let's forget about it and go to sleep."

The dog began another chorus of barking as she resumed her rocking motions, and Young dreamed he was a passenger on an ocean liner. He let his mind drift; and Lucinda dreamed she was a passenger too, but on another sort of vessel altogether, being conveyed at light speed, just like Delia Chapman, in majestic transit, a precious trophy bound for a distant star.

The "delay" in Lucinda's pregnancy was scientifically exceptional. And "delay" was the best word for it. Because although she had conceived, by her own reports, at roughly the same time as Delia, a curious thing had happened. Recent test results, the first tests she had confidentially agreed to, confirmed that while she was indeed pregnant, just as she'd claimed, thereby proving all of her detractors wrong, she was lagging four months behind her friends in her baby's development.

A very simple explanation, but one denied by Lucinda, was that she had been impregnated only within the last month in a desperate attempt to fulfill her destiny, and that the father of the child was none other than the disheartened journalist who at that moment fought for air beneath her. The dates of their first thrashing rendezvous in the aphrodisiacal atmosphere of a breaking story were consistent with this theory. However, Lucinda had other explanations.

Her first meeting with the journalist had been a fragile affair. It had not been easy for her to reveal the intimacies of her soul to a stranger. But it was clear to her, when looking into his eyes, that an unutterable connection existed, one which would require their combined strengths to resist. Such a struggle never took place.

The initial stages of the affair needed to be conducted in secret, and the small room at the Sahara Desert Motor Inn became the location for these repeated failures of willpower. Because Young did not believe that Lucinda was pregnant at all, he saw no impediment to a sexual relationship, and in the early stages he was happy to participate in her elaborate charade in the hope that it might distract him from his own wrecked career, his faded dreams and bankrupt future. That he was slowly building a prison of recriminations for himself was lost in the lunar madness of their carnality.

Lucinda, for her part, was unaware of the journalist's deep skepticism, and whenever she discussed the strange and glorious transformations taking place within her, she interpreted the strange look in his eyes as sympathy. Confident that she had at last found a soul mate, she revealed to him her deepest fears for the first time: She wasn't sure of the implications of this baby on both of them, or why she had been chosen in the first place. Once she believed that he had been so moved by her confession that he'd cried. She kissed him gently as he sat on the edge of the bed, his head buried in his hands.

In this climate a strange symbiosis began, both wanting something that was not to be found in the other; she, a fully accepting lover with whom she could confide her deepest and most bizarre hopes and dreams, and he, a filter through which he could screen out his own polluted past. And although both were destined to be unsatisfied, and even sensed this, both were still happy, in their desperate states, to take a chance on the other.

Their talks waxed affectionate as those first days passed. He was clearly vulnerable, and Lucinda lavished upon him her superficial gifts of healing. And Young saw a new side to this girl as well—one which he, like everyone else, had failed to notice: that Lucinda possessed enough shamelessness to cure not only him but a hundred towns just like this one.

Now, after three months, she *was* pregnant, and he had perfect

reason to believe the child was his. One night's oversight after a
drinking binge was responsible. The alcohol had made him reckless, and eschewing the rubber, he had blissfully sought salvation
and a moment's amnesia. When the pregnancy test, which he this
time insisted upon, came back positive, and when she refused to
show the slightest surprise, he did not correct her fantasies which
had become so much a foundation of their union, but merely bit
his tongue, swallowed his knowledge and commenced a paternal
vigil on the adipose folds of her swelling stomach. If he was going
to be a father, then he would start to act like one.

Lucinda was breathless with respect for this man so eager to
treat a bastard child as if it were his own. It was the stuff of which
timeless love affairs were made.

, , , , ,

In an unusual dream, Phillip and Delia met in the parallel aisles
of his library. A thin phalanx of books separated them, but by
removing a novel by Flaubert from a middle shelf he was able to
glimpse a portion of her, a surprising rectangle of naked belly.
An essay by Goethe withdrawn from lower down revealed a nude
oblong of pink thigh; and so he became bold, choosing with some
consideration a very large book at chest level by Hardy. Faster
and faster he pulled the classics, undressing her geometrically,
and when he came to her face, clearing the last books, there was
no head: She was decapitated. He gasped, and awoke in a sweat.
He had fallen asleep over the backlog of new books forgotten in
the heat of his research.

He was disturbed by a sharp knock on the door.

Father O'Brien looked remote behind a cigarette, which he
extinguished as he talked. He apologized for the late visit but had
seen the light on and wondered if an exception could be made to
the visiting hours. With his sparse hair disheveled and his collar
loosened in uncustomary disorder, the priest said he understood
the need for rules, but he had learned that a copy of the complete

works of Saint Thomas Aquinas had been obtained from Wellington, and he felt in need of drawing a note or two from the *Summa
Theologica* for his Sunday sermon. No one, the curate said, had
interpolated the essence of holiness like the cell-bound Italian
master.

Magnanimously, knowing it would mean further delaying a
late-night car search for Delia, Phillip showed the priest to a chair
and took down the relevant volume from the *Great Books of the
Western World*.

Father O'Brien looked for his road map to sainthood and knew
where to search. He fell on the text almost in prostration, de-
vouring pages at once as if satisfying a long-repressed hunger.

Phillip went outside and watched over the main street, showing
the priest the respect for privacy which both their professions
demanded. When he went back inside he found the curate crying,
dabbing his cheeks quickly with a handkerchief.

Phillip presumed that a passage from one of the lectures had
shaken him. Perhaps, in comparison with the life of Aquinas, the
priest felt he had fallen short of his ambitions. Phillip had only
the librarian-general with whom to compare himself professionally. The priest had the example of saints.

Father O'Brien got up to go, leaving the book open on the
table in his haste. He came toward Phillip at the counter.

"Thanks a lot," he said. "Very worthwhile. Very. And I . . . um . . .
I want you to know that I appreciate what you have done here."

"It's nothing," said Phillip. "You can stay longer if you want
to. I don't mind."

"No, I didn't mean your letting me in. I mean, what you've
done with the library. Tremendous. A great gift."

Surprised at the first sign of gratitude expressed to him in Opunake, Phillip blushed.

"I mean it," said the priest. "I know how this place was. It
wasn't fit for cows." He walked to the door and stopped, his eyes

brimming with tears. "You're more like a priest than I am," he said.

Phillip watched the cleric shuffle away down the street, reminded how lost in this society even our supposed shepherds can be. He crossed to the table where the priest had been reading, and his eye fell on the open page. He was puzzled to see that instead of a study of sainthood, Father O'Brien had been reading a contemplation on mortal sin and moral weakness: The page was marked by a fresh tear.

He picked up the book and read the dampened passage: *The renunciation of one's sexuality led one down a path of sublimations, naturally resulting more and more in an increased interest in the young.* Such *renuncios,* he read, often became our priests, teachers, masters. They acquired the character of father to everyone's children, and their role was that of *paideia,* in the Greek sense.

He read the passage twice and gave this last word special attention. He consulted the new *Concise Oxford* for a definition but found no entry for it. However, patching together the Greek roots of several similar words he loosely translated *paideia* as "father . . . of children," and he wondered about the significance of the passage. Convinced it could be important, he decided to copy it into his abandoned journal.

, , , ,

Delia fled Opunake with one thought: escape. The level of interference had left her no choice. She was fleeing to save herself and her baby. Anger had made her feel like traversing the world, but she had settled for New Plymouth only forty kilometers away.

Within hours she had found a cheap private hotel whose dilapidation lent it an air of quaint Victorian charm. She had no idea that the hotel was in fact brimful of misfits. Over the reception desk hung the cautionary sign, NO FRIENDS. NO FOOD. NO CARRY-ON.

"What sort of rooms do you have?" Delia asked from the doorstep.

"Well, that depends how much you want to pay," the landlady of the Belgravia answered. "We have a number of rooms available right now at varying prices. We have one with a sink and walk-in wardrobe but no toilet. Or you can have a toilet but no sink. Or a sink and a toilet but no wardrobe. Or all three." Then she added, "Or none. Because we've got one room with nothing in it at all. Just a bed. If you want that. I don't know."

Delia chose the room with the toilet. She had no need of a wardrobe, having only a single change of clothes with her.

She learned that the landlady, a widow, had purchased the hotel on a whim with her late husband's life insurance. Originally hoping to attract European backpackers, the woman had weakened at a request from the Social Welfare department to accept a mentally fragile young man on a long-term contract. That was three years ago and now her entire guest list consisted of neurotics who would be homeless but for her.

Delia saw most of them on her first guided tour of the hotel: a clinically mad old woman knitting; a retard committing the solecism of mopping his own shoes; an old gentleman in a Morris chair nodding placidly in the afternoon light with his colostomy bag displayed on the outside of his shirt. In the dining room two men in their forties, twins with identical crew cuts, played checkers at the table in mirrored reflection of each other. And on the first landing an unbalanced woman tried to unlock her door with a hairbrush. The landlady gently removed the brush from her arthritic grasp and showed the poor soul that the door was not, in fact, locked at all.

Delia told her landlady that if it was all right, she hoped to stay several weeks.

"I just take the money. You have to organize your own life," the woman replied stoically.

The window in Delia's room had a small view of Mount Taranaki, only a slightly different aspect from that from her childhood window. Still, she was happy to imagine that she had indeed traveled right around the world and had approached the mountain from the other side.

, , , , ,

On her third day in New Plymouth, during one of her interminable strolls, Delia had noticed the sign.

Lost? Confused? Lonely? Depressed?
Come in. Talk to one of our FREE counselors.
Crisis Support Services.

Feeling that all four descriptions fit her, she had walked into the building, taken a number and sat on a bench in a waiting room of polished mahogany. A session was just being concluded behind the glass-paneled door, and the overheard tones were deep and confessional. She guessed that another lost, confused, lonely, depressed person like herself, one among the millions, was ready to talk to a total stranger in the hope of getting help and direction. She knew Phillip would say they needed to find a philosophy, one which they could "clearly articulate," and they would be fine. She had been trying to think of one almost continuously since he had advocated the need for it, but she was no further ahead. Her brain was empty of those kinds of things, and so she had become fodder for social services like this.

When her turn came, she rose and entered a small interview room, which was empty but for two chairs, a desk and a solitary rubber plant.

"My name is Delia Chapman."

"Please come in. Take a seat."

She sat shaking in the chair opposite a counselor who hid a thick handbook entitled *Clinical Psychiatry,* lest it break the air of informality.

Wearing the name tag "Angela," the woman had claret cheeks and the bust of a seasoned wet nurse. "I'm running a little late," she said, with a smile of infinite pleasantness. "First, I'm not a professional. I'm a volunteer, dear. You do understand that?"

Delia nodded.

"Good. Well, then, is there anything you want to talk about?" She inclined her head. "Anything in particular?"

"I think there might be something wrong with me. I do strange things and I see pictures in my head, like dreams, only I'm awake." Delia had prepared this speech and she delivered it without blinking.

The woman smiled nervously, then asked, with a nod at Delia's stomach. "How many weeks, dear?"

"Not sure. About five months, I think."

"How lovely," the woman replied. "I have five children of my own. Your first?" Delia nodded.

"And the father, is he . . . ?"

Delia didn't want to talk about the father: "I don't know him."

Angela's brows crossed. "You don't know who the father is? I'm not sure I understand."

"I thought I did, but now I'm not sure anymore. That's what I mean."

The counselor nodded.

"I never exactly had proper sex with him, anyway," she added. "I'm still a virgin. At least I think I am."

"Oh, I see." The counselor's voice projected calm.

"Yes," said Delia, hoping that she had been so precise she would not have to explain another thing.

The woman became thoughtful as she shaped her next question. "Well, Delia, you know it's impossible to be pregnant if you haven't had sex, unless you've been artificially inseminated, or"— and here she hesitated—"or you're the Virgin Mary."

Delia stared at her.

"Do you think either of those is a possibility?" The counselor sounded sincere.

"Course not."

"Okay. So you're not sure who the father is. Could this be because . . . there are several men who could be the father?"

Delia shut her eyes in horror and shook her head violently.

"Do you sleep with a lot of men?"

"No! None."

"Just one?"

"No. None." Delia had stopped looking at the woman; it was too difficult to look her in the face and say what she wanted to say. She wove her fingers into agonizing knots in her lap. "There is a guy who was going to say that he's the father, just for appearances, but it's not true. Nobody knows who the real father is because . . . because . . . well, I did know, but now I'm not sure anymore."

"This is where you lose me, dear," the counselor announced, frowning and rapidly losing objectivity. "You may need to talk with someone more experienced. I'm only part-time." There was a silence while Angela gathered herself. "You say you're a virgin, but you're pregnant, and there's someone who was going to be a stand-in-father sort of thing but he's not the real father. Is that right?"

"Yes," said Delia, sympathizing with the counselor's confusion.

"Are you religious at all? Very religious?"

Delia frowned. "No."

"Just a thought." She seemed disappointed. "Okay, now let me summarize what we have. The real father part. You say you once knew who he was, but now you don't? Is that right?"

"I'm not sure that I'm right in the head."

"Do you want to say anything more about that?"

"I keep getting . . . sometimes it's like . . . someone else's memories come into my head. They don't seem like they're mine. I want you to tell me if I'm going nuts. That's why I'm here."

The counselor leaned forward. "My dear, I'm not here to tell you if you're nuts or not, as you say. I'm here for one reason . . . to listen to you, and to offer advice if you want it. That's all."

Delia looked down again and finally said, "Could you please offer some, then."

The counselor had not made a single note on the pad in front of her, and now she pushed it aside, implying that there would be no need for notes from now on, that a test had been set and Delia had passed it.

"Do your family know about the baby?"

"My father does. My mum's dead."

"Does he care about the baby?"

"He wanted me to have an abortion. To kill it."

"Then I think we should contact someone who is prepared to take some of the stress off you. Because none of this is good for the baby."

Delia nodded.

"Is there anyone?"

"No."

"Nobody at all?"

Delia began to feel restless, impatient. "I just want you to tell me if I'm going a bit mental, that's all."

"No," the counselor said. "No. I don't think so."

"How can you tell?"

"Because mental people don't ask that question."

"Thank you," said Delia. "So, who do you think the father of the baby is, then?"

"Come back and see me tomorrow. Will you do that? We'll talk about that tomorrow. Here's my card."

Delia nodded and took the card.

"I think we made some progress. Don't you?"

Delia smiled, looked into the face glowing with amateur concern and left the room.

She dropped the card into the first rubbish bin on the street.

If she had spent twenty minutes walking in a small circle she could not have felt more detached from that word: progress.

, , , ,

Since Delia's disappearance three days earlier, Phillip had been paralyzed with worry and guilt, in that order. He worried that he had not done enough to find her, then felt guilty when he decided he had not. He distracted himself with a frenetic burst of productivity in cataloging all the new books, an overdue task since he had wasted so much time studying instead of filing them.

Exhausted this day, after hours of meticulous work, a file drawer slipped from his hand and crashed to the ground, spraying cards in a brilliant fan across the floor. He swore and bent to pick them up, trying to preserve their precious order, when his eye stopped on one card thrown clear from the rest. He noticed at once that it detailed a glaring nonreturn. He studied the date and returned to his desk, annoyed that his campaign to reclaim the library's old titles was now suddenly incomplete. Flicking through the membership files, he found the card upon which the patron's borrowing record over a small lifetime was itemized, and it revealed a history of faded violations, many still outstanding. As he read them, a sudden spark of intuition ignited in Phillip's detective mind.

He moved to the shelves again to check on the other books listed on the membership card. Perhaps the missing volumes had been returned but not recorded. But when he stopped at the relevant section of "Games and Hobbies" and looked carefully, his index finger gliding along rows, he was stopped time and time again by interruptions in the code sequence. Four books were missing.

He left the library immediately. As he locked the door behind him, he sensed that not only had he uncovered the first significant clue to a complex mystery but that he had found it hidden among his books after all.

, , , , ,

Phillip knocked but the back door was open. He stepped into the decrepit odor of cat's urine and turpentine and waited in the center of the room for a sign of life. The sound of a TV came from a nearby room. The kitchen was full of unwashed crockery, the sink surrounded by grease-stained towels, and there were huge bottles of industrial-strength hand soap in place of the traditional washing detergent on the bench.

Gilbert Haines was waking from a familiar pornographic dream which always gave him a restive sleep: In the dream he'd been at liberty to choose among several nude females who had presented themselves to him without the least effort on his part and without a word, each flattered when he showed them the slightest interest. He emerged from this fantasy world with a start, to find that he was being observed.

"I've come for the overdue books," said the librarian.

Gilbert was trying to open his eyes and focus on the figure standing above him. "What?"

"Overdue books. Four of them. I let myself in. Your door was open."

The impatient look in Phillip's face as he waited for Gilbert to rise from his bed showed a rage out of keeping with the banality of reclaiming library books.

"What are you doing in here?" Gilbert asked, but not as aggressively as he might have. He looked almost sedate, as if he thought a snap of his fingers could vanquish this visitor and resummon his imaginary concubines.

"I think you know."

"No. Tell me."

Phillip found it hard to say his next words.

"You're the father, aren't you?"

There was a deliberate pause, calculated to provoke. Gilbert shifted on the bed, finding a more relaxed position for the larger discussions which were now inevitable.

"Big deal," Gilbert said. "Took you long enough. How did you find out?"

Phillip's heart stopped. He scrutinized the timid and grease-clogged creature in front of him and ignored the question. He tried instead to visualize the skinny mechanic beside Delia, viewing him in her embrace, but he could see only a violation on Gilbert's part, and a rape.

"You're the father?"

"I just told you, Sherlock Holmes."

"Tell me again." Phillip wanted a categorical admission.

"I just said so, didn't I?"

"You're admitting it then? You're admitting it?"

"She finally told you, did she? Well it's about time. I've been trying to tell everybody for the last two months! 'Cept nobody'd believe me 'cause they all wanted to think it was you. . . . Can you believe that? They thought it was you." Gilbert smiled. "Every time I tried to tell anybody it was me they just bought me another beer and told me to shut up. Funny, eh?"

Gilbert looked genuinely relieved to have found an ear at last prepared to believe him, and he was more than happy to talk.

"You raped her?"

"Eh?"

"She had bruises."

"I did . . . I didn't!"

"You've got some overdue library books."

"Eh?"

"I know what happened."

"What are you talking about?"

"You forced her."

"What?"

"Didn't you?"

"No. Listen. No. I wouldn't do that. I couldn't, anyway. She's probably stronger than me. I love her, okay? I would never do that. I didn't have to."

"I know what happened."

"She was into it, I'm telling you. She actually came on to me, if you wanna know the truth. I couldn't believe it either. I couldn't be*lieve* it. Delia Chapman was coming on to *me*. I thought I'd died and gone straight up there to heaven or something!"

This slowed Phillip down but didn't distract him. He had worked out his own version of events while on the way to this house, based on the evidence he had. What was true was that Gilbert was not in the least bit threatening: Some people were larger than life; Gilbert was actually far smaller. He was a fly. A nuisance. But not at all a physical threat to anyone.

Phillip admitted all this in a second but still held the boy guilty. Being pathetic was no excuse when a horrible crime had been perpetrated. His blood was ready to boil, and Gilbert's marsh-mallow gaze would not subdue it.

"I don't care if you don't believe me, anyway," Gilbert continued. "Delia knows the truth."

"Tell me what happened." Phillip could not look at the mechanic, fearing he would lose control if he did, and so stared out of the window at the dormant volcano. There was no eruption; no earthquake threatened to swallow him up, but as he listened to Gilbert's twisted account of a freakish night of consensual sex with Delia in a car, he felt the ground disappear from beneath him. Gilbert even used the misnomer "affair" to describe a union which had lasted only one night but which had been so passionate that Gilbert was not at all surprised that a child had sprung from it.

"So, of course the kid's mine," Gilbert said. "I had sex with her. I'm her spaceman."

With one hand he smoothed his messy head of roosters' tails

which stuck flat with their own grease. "And she liked it." Gilbert chose this moment to smile, revealing stained and crooked teeth.

Phillip leaned forward. His strategy was to goad the mechanic into a full account of that night, no matter how painful it was to listen to. "How did you do it?"

"What do you mean?"

"How did you get her to go all the way? Come on. How?"

"We're old friends, that's all. We started to talk. Then she started to get hot. She really seduced *me*, actually."

"She got hot?"

"Yeah."

Phillip felt a rush of blood to his head. "Really?"

"Yeah. And I thought we were just friends."

"You didn't . . . you didn't do anything else to her?"

"Like what?" Gilbert grinned lecherously, and Phillip sensed his strategy was soon to be rewarded.

Phillip reached into his pocket and pulled out the four relevant file cards. "You signed for them ten years ago."

"I don't know what you're talking about," Gilbert said, a better defense beyond him. "What are those, anyway?"

"These four books." Phillip held the cards higher in the air.

"What books? I haven't got any of your bloody books. Look, it's time you got out of here, anyway. So . . . get out."

Phillip's eyes flicked toward the bedside table. The four books were there, prominent in a tower of reading material otherwise composed of dog-eared hot-rod periodicals. He did not need to take his eyes off the mechanic for the books' unspoken titles to resonate in the air between them.

"So?" Gilbert said, small now as the advantage of surprise moved to Phillip.

"Are you gonna tell me what happened now? Or not?"

"But . . . I . . . ah . . . I already told you."

"Tell me again."

Gilbert was suddenly pale, his former good humor shattered. To his right lay the books, which he could not disappear as he might wish, with just a click of his amateur fingers. *Introduction to Hypnosis. A Layman's Guide to Magic. Mesmerizing and Hypnotizing. The Magic of Hypnosis.*

Gilbert stood, exposed. "She enjoyed it," he repeated lamely and then started to giggle, unable to withstand the intense scrutiny of the librarian. In a fit of activity he grabbed the first of the titles and hurled it at Phillip. The covers opened midair, and the *Introduction to Hypnosis* flapped like a bird before thudding into the wall left of Phillip's averted head. "Okay. Now get out of here. I told you what happened. Get out!" His face was crimson as he threw a second book and then a third. The fourth book broke a glass on top of the television. Gilbert was suddenly screaming, a madman.

The last incontrovertible piece of Delia's jigsaw had fallen into place, and Phillip was on the mechanic in a second, pinning him to the ground. After a brief struggle and an exchange of punches, Phillip began to hit the younger man's head against the floor repeatedly, oblivious to the repercussions, until he felt jelly under each blow. Gilbert became motionless and his mouth hung garishly open. He looked dead.

Phillip stood up and looked at the halo of blood forming behind the mechanic's head. Ghosts of his violent past whispered to him to run immediately. He turned and vaulted from the house, leaving Gilbert Haines bleeding and half-murdered in the corner of the lounge as the TV played a commercial at low volume.

, , , , ,

Gilbert groaned, a low rumble from his position on his back on the carpet, numb and semiconscious. In his mind deranged fantasies were now free to merge at will with elements of true recollection in a chaotic theater of hallucinations.

He could see a bag of chips.

A bag of chips. Dropped in the dark. Delia out walking, bending over to pick them up. And Gilbert arriving in his station wagon. Gilbert, an unlikely rescuer of Delia and her chips, and yet, in his delirium, her savior.

"Whaddaya doing out here this time of night?" he asked.

"Could ask you the same thing."

"You want me to drive you home?"

She looked down the river road. "No," she said.

"I think it's finally gonna rain. A real storm," he told her.

He opened the door. Delia reluctantly got into his car. How long had Gilbert awaited this moment? There they were, the two of them, in the dark, on the river road near the highway, a decade of his fantasies within tantalizing reach.

He started with a card trick.

He knew that years of solid practice would someday yield dividends. He turned on the light in the cab and took out a new pack of cards from his top pocket: His cards on a Friday night were always new. He asked Delia if she wanted to see a trick; he had a simple one. She nodded. He placed an ace on the top of the pack in his hand, and asked her to keep an eye fixed on this card as he cut the deck beneath it.

She stopped him. She had already seen what he'd done.

"I haven't done anything yet," he protested.

"I saw you slip the ace inside your . . . your jacket there." She pointed, irritated, disappointed that Gilbert had failed to create a moment full of wonder.

"No, the ace is still on top."

"It's in your jacket."

Gilbert looked at her flatly, devastated for an instant. "All right, I'll show you another one. Hold on." He returned the ace from his pocket to the pack and began again in earnest. She told him this was his last chance.

This time a card chosen by Delia, then returned to the pack, fell prematurely between them on the seat, ruining the reveal. With beads of sweat erupting on his forehead, he explained that the finale was meant to have culminated in him reaching into her bag of hot chips and triumphantly drawing out the memorized card. It was no consolation.

"How long have you been practicing that stuff?" she said, her patience gone.

"Not long."

She looked at him. His colorless eyes were remote behind his freckled face. How dreadful it must be to be Gilbert Haines.

"You should give it up," she suggested. It was the only helpful thing she could think of.

"But they usually work out."

"Try something else. You haven't got the fingers."

Gilbert sensed the loss of his audience, the dimming of his charms, and in desperation decided to reveal his trump card: to unlock a secret door and prove he was no mere grease monkey. She seemed curious for the first time. Hypnosis? Was he joking? Could he really hypnotize people, put them in a trance, make them unconscious? Did he really have a success rate of 75 percent?

"How did you learn to do it?"

"Books. TV programs. Stuff like that."

"You can learn that from a book?"

"I saw a live show. Saw this guy do it."

Gilbert described a trip to New Plymouth when he was thirteen to see Olivier Samuels, a visiting international hypnotist, who could make someone eat a raw onion without flinching as if it were an apple.

He told her that this had been the climactic act in the show, but here he lied by omission. What he decided not to mention was that a finale had been added by the hypnotist to redress a new complacency with the onion act. People wanted more, expected something new. So Samuels announced that in full view of the public and by just clicking his fingers he would induce a girl to kiss a bony boy she'd never met before. But more than that: He would make her *want* to do this, make the girl actually *desire* the boy! The audience, Gilbert among them, moved onto the edge of their seats, stimulated by the thought that a great human aversion such as the repulsion of ugliness could be overridden; they waited, hearts in mouths, breath bated, pin-drop silent, happy to declare him a genius if he could pull off such a stunt, or a charlatan if he couldn't.

The girl was taken under, with a simple side-to-side movement of Samuels's finger, and a seed of desire was planted in her head with a basic command before she was reawakened. The girl knew nothing as laughter circulated around the auditorium. She smiled and shifted her weight on stage, awaiting a trick. The public, however, was bursting with the knowledge that the beautiful girl was an unwitting time bomb, liable to explode with passion at the click of the master's fingers. And it was at this moment that Gilbert resolved to become a magician, to possess such a power, because, of course, the young girl, at the snap of the magician's fingers, lavished the bony boy with kisses of quite virulent passion, and then, some said, she even had to be stopped from removing her clothes afterward in the foyer of the theater, so powerful had been the spell.

But Gilbert told Delia none of this.

"A whole onion? I don't believe that."

"I can prove it."

"How?"

"I'll show you."

"Go on, then."

"All right, I'll do it on you, then."

"You're not doing it on me. Do it on yourself."

"Don't be stupid."

"Go on!"

"Look, you want me to show ya, or don't ya?"

She paused to consider. "All right, then. Try if you like. But I bet you can't."

Gilbert started to wave his forefinger in front of her eyes. He lowered his voice, began to whisper and implied that she would soon grow weary. And then, miraculously, her eyes slowly closed.

"Now then, you have to do as I say."

But Delia opened her eyes and said it hadn't worked. She was only closing her eyes because he'd told her to, she said. She was probably one of the unsuccessful 25 percent.

"You're not concentrating," Gilbert said accusingly.

She agreed to try one more time.

He again waved his finger. Her eyes grew heavy at his continual suggestion, slowly closing like flowers, but it took so long that Gilbert's waving finger grew numb. In her final silence he feared asking her if she'd fallen under his control. But when at last he did inquire, she didn't reply, and her eyes remained tightly closed. He thought she was fooling him again, because he'd never successfully taken anybody under before, not into a full trance anyway, although several people had previously gone to sleep on him.

Her eyes remained closed.

"Delia?" he asked again.

Silence.

Could it be true? He tested her, the perfect test on an immobilized woman, one which audiences always believed: He touched her breast. If she was conscious, human nature dictated he'd get a reaction. But she didn't move.

Gilbert couldn't believe he'd succeeded. Delia was hypnotized, in his car, in the dark! A double, triple dream come true. He felt the full and corruptive thrill of the voyeur.

"Can you hear me?" he asked.

". . . Yes." It hardly seemed to be her voice.

It was true, he reassured himself. She was completely under.

She was not playacting and his arousal was sexual: Delia was at his disposal, a willing servant. If she were a corpse he could not have felt more free, for it was the uncritical aspect of a corpse that he longed for—a desired body which could not wake up on him. She couldn't say that he stank, which had happened with another girl, nor that his breath was putrid; nor could she act as if he were too ugly to look at, and wince when he smiled. Confident that he could be neither rejected nor reproached, he slipped into the uncensored world of the libido.

But what should he do with all this beauty now suddenly inviting him? What? What would the great Olivier Samuels from England do, the onion man? Perhaps he would make Delia desire Gilbert and then wake her, a willing and promiscuous partner. But he wanted her asleep. He couldn't face her. He needed her to be still. If only he had a clue what to do next.

"Okay," said Gilbert. "Can you hear me? Delia . . . ?"

". . . Mmm."

Years of rejected desire and repressed dreams were incarnate, but the reality of it suddenly intimidated him. Delia sat there, eyes closed, her subconscious unlocked, awaiting his suggestion.

"Okay," he said. He was sweating torrentially now, and had to turn away from her to clear his thoughts. He looked into the darkness, seeking inspiration as his head swam with suppressed urges and elaborate fantasies which grew ever more erotic.

Seduced by the knowledge that he could be this lucky only once in his life, he instructed her to visualize an object. And out in the night Gilbert saw his theme.

"Can you see it?"

Delia replied, "Mmm," and then she smiled. It was an open invitation, a sign of consent from a sixteen-year-old angel.

, , , , ,

Outside Gilbert's house, Phillip leaned on the mechanic's car to catch his breath: With revulsion he looked in at the front seat where Gilbert had worked his crooked magic. And he saw the spaceship as she had visualized it, realizing why, in contrast, it had to be so beautiful. Now he was able to fathom Delia's story, and understand why her spaceman had been all-encompassing, dazzling and commanding her full attention.

, , , , ,

Delia saw a spaceman.

Delia could not take her eyes off him. The leader—whom she had once described to Phillip—spoke to Delia by name as though she'd been expected. He asked Delia if she wanted to put down the package she was holding: He spoke English very well. She said yes, and he reached out and took the bag of chips from her to put them gently on the ground. Then he proceeded to take off her clothes. He was patient when her actions were no faster than the slow motion of an underwater diver. He seemed infinitely kind and graceful, even beautiful in an unconventional way. She was aware of his intelligence at once. Would she permit herself to be examined? She could only reply: "Mmm." And soon she found herself having sex with the leader. This created in her a hallucinogenic state of such intensity that she forgot she was on the spaceship and was oddly transported to a car where she was alone with an unknown man, and the sex that was taking place was not like that on the spaceship at all: It was unpleasant and painful, and made her cry and murmur "Stop." But this horrible hallucination faded, returning her to her real body, and she realized that the most lovingly pure creature imaginable was engaged with her in heavenly parliament. And then when her mouth moved, and the last pleading words "Stop" or "No" escaped, they were so drained of fury that they ceased to be protestations. To someone from another world her tears could only be interpreted as tears of pleasure.

Phillip walked away from the vehicle, caring nothing for the survival of the unconscious man he was leaving behind.

, , , , ,

Delia saw a spaceman.

Gilbert climaxed with a grunt and climbed off her, rolling back into his own seat, gasping for breath, pulling up his trousers, giving first thought to covering his own partial nudity. So erotically intense had the encounter been that he'd lasted only a minute, a mere sixty seconds, his loins succumbing instantly to the lethal combination of illicit magic and her welcome indifference. He'd had sex a few times before, but nothing rivaled the appeal of Delia in her stupendous lethargy.

Delia didn't stir or open her eyes, so expertly was she hypnotized. He could hardly believe that such vigorous intercourse had not broken her trance. He called her name several times as he did up his fly and tucked in his shirt.

"Delia? You hear me? You okay?"

He leaned over and closed her white uniform over her breasts as she was making no effort to cover herself. His big fingers fumbled with the buttons in the dark. Her panties wouldn't clear her immobile hips. Trying to tug them up, he talked to her constantly, forgetting that she was reliant upon him to wake her. "C'mon, Delia. . . . I can't do this unless you . . . lift . . ." Failing, he got out of the car, saying, "I can't drive you home either, Delia. You know what your father's like." As he rounded the hood another vehicle came up the river road, and a second later headlights lit the trees.

Gilbert pictured Delia's father armed with a shotgun. In the split second before the car took the bend, he ran to take cover in the bush. Crouching out of sight, oblivious to the implications of Delia's continued trance, he waited, thinking that if she needed to, she could perhaps talk her way out of it. But the driver passed diplomatically, not wanting to disturb what seemed a lovers' tryst.

When Gilbert returned to the car he opened the passenger door to discover that Delia was gone.

He called out for her, and in a panic ran fifty meters in three directions before starting through the trees toward the highway where more lights split the undergrowth. He kept branches from his eyes with his forearms as he ran. He reached the road only in time to see Phillip's Ford pulling away.

He stirred, woke from his delirium on the carpet and with great effort tried to crawl toward the telephone across the room.

FUGITIVES

Phillip had managed to wash most of Gilbert's blood from his clothes and to clean the cuts on his face and hands. He had made an anonymous phone call to the hospital, a stupidly amateur gesture, to report a man in need of an ambulance, and now he prepared to leave by the library's back door. He intended to turn himself in, in a crazy reenactment of events two years earlier. That time too, he had initially run for cover, seeing sense once his intelligence had returned. This time he would drive to Watson's place, interrupt the man at home and tell him everything he'd done, just as once he'd crossed the parade ground, knocked on the lieutenant's door and said, "I'm here."

Just then the telephone rang. Instinctively he picked it up.

"A book? Yes. Yes. Where did you say you were calling from again? I see. Okay. What's the title?" Phillip's pen froze on the notepaper. "How did you get it? Did you see the young woman who left it behind? Can I have your address, please. No. I'll come now. I'll come and get it. I know it's forty kilometers. Thank you very much. Good-bye."

Phillip put down the phone and altered his plans. It was not a difficult decision. Before he placed himself in custody, he would retrieve one more book and renew his search for the borrower.

He drove toward New Plymouth at well above legal speed, a journey memorialized only by the speed camera whose magic eye blinked once as his car shot past in the dark.

Harvey Watson arrived at the library too late and found it locked. He thought perhaps Phillip was hiding inside, and so smashed a window and wasted a quarter of an hour moving among the aisles. When he emerged he felt like a moth.

, , , ,

Delia went to use the sink in the hallway. Returning to her room she was stopped by a *Pssst* from the end of the hall. It was one of the crew-cut twins who, with a jerk of his head, invited her to approach.

"I know who . . . who you are," he said, stuttering slightly.

"Who?"

"You're the . . . the spaceship woman."

Delia nodded but begged him not to tell anyone.

"Okay," he said. "I d-don't have to, if you don't want."

"Please, don't." The look of distress in her eyes was real.

"Don't worry, I won't. If-if-if-if . . ."

"What?"

"If-if you do something for us. Us."

"Who?"

The man shrugged, then tried to smile, stepping backward into his room to reveal his identical twin sitting on the bed. With his palms flat he invitingly tapped the mattress twice.

Delia laughed at the gesture. "No," she said, but in a second she was pushed into the room and the door was closed behind her. The room was filled with a flotilla of model ships hugging the shelves and squadrons of plastic planes which were suspended by cotton threads from the ceiling. Such was the number of toys, they spoke to Delia of another harmless hobby that was out of control.

"We promise not to t-tell," the first brother said.

"One kiss . . . each," said the second. The door wasn't locked, but his back was pressed against it, barring her exit.

"J-just one kiss each. From the . . . the spacelady."

"Don't be disgusting. Open the door." Delia was alarmed by the ludicrous request.

"Otherwise we'll tell." The second brother grinned hungrily.

"I'll scream," she threatened.

"No one'll hear you. Now, then . . . one each. Each." He seemed at pains to make this clear: His sardonic brother was not to miss out.

"You don't think anyone's ever going to kiss you, do you?" she said.

"I can find s-someone to kiss. Anytime I-I"—his voice trailed off—"want to."

Delia thought rapidly. From a shelf she grabbed the largest battleship of the lilliputian fleet, and held it above her head.

He shook his head. "No!"

"Open the door. Otherwise I'll smash it." His prize piece wobbled in her giant hands.

The twin had no choice, gestured that she shouldn't do anything rash, and slowly backed away from the door. Delia ran out of the room and dropped the model ship in the hall with a clatter.

From this moment on, her hotel ceased to be the sanctuary it had promised to be. She was back down the stairs, out of the building and halfway down the street before she stopped running.

. . . . .

The half-hour journey to New Plymouth in search of Delia took Phillip twenty minutes. He quickly found the grocery store he was seeking, just as it was closing.

"What can I get you?" the woman behind the counter asked brightly.

"I'm from the Opunake Library. You rang, about half an hour ago—"

"That was you."

"I've just driven up from . . ."

"Oh! That's awfully quick, isn't it? You library people must have really smartened up your act, eh? Hang on, then. Just wait there." And with that she turned and parted the straps of rainbow-colored vinyl which hung in the doorway.

Phillip was left alone to survey the cluttered counter: a vibrant assortment of chocolate confectioneries, magazines, gums and newspapers. His library could benefit from such an efficient use of shelf space.

"Here it is," she said as she returned with the familiar octavo volume which he had lent Delia four months earlier. "The girl, that's the preggie one, is it? . . . She's been in a few times and left it here the last time."

"Any idea where she might be living?"

"No idea, love, none at all. She doesn't talk. But she must be in the area. She's always on foot. Looking for her, are ya?"

"Yeah."

"Oh. So . . . you're the dad, are ya?"

It was a strange conclusion to jump to, but was not far off the mark.

"Yes," Phillip replied. "I am, actually."

It surprised him what pleasure he found in saying this. He had long since assumed the role of father, but had spent very little time preparing himself for the reality, and this acknowledgment became a departure point, a defining moment. He then thanked the woman warmly, and left the shop with the recovered book pinned under his arm, less a single man than a man of the world.

He began a search of hostels and hotels in the vicinity. The Belgravia was the third hotel he tried. He was told that Delia Chapman had just rushed out minutes before but the hotel had a ten o'clock curfew, so she could be expected back soon. He stationed himself on the Belgravia's front steps, his mind spinning with the facts he had learned that evening and with the prospect of confronting Delia with his knowledge. He feared she would not want to see him. The last time they had been together she had ejected him from her home. Perhaps she would not even come back to the hotel. But his apprehensions vanished when he saw the familiar combination of cap and T-shirt walking toward him.

Delia looked at Phillip without the smallest hint of surprise, and said flatly, "Sorry I took your money—I'll pay you back."

If he expected her to look destitute or sickly and half out of her wits, he was mistaken. She was the picture of good health. Her skin glowed, her hair was shining and she radiated a new aura of control.

"So," she said. "How did you find me?"

He held up the library book.

She smiled. "Should have been a detective. What happened to your face?"

"It's a long story."

. . . . .

A traveling carnival had established itself in a vacant lot on a back street. Phillip paid their entrance fees. As they walked side by side around the makeshift attractions, he tried to find a moment in which to reveal what he knew. But he was in no real hurry to become her enemy again, now that he had found her.

After all, why was it urgent for her to know that Gilbert Haines probably lay in a hospital bed in New Plymouth?

They had completely circled the fairground when he spoke.

"That time when you asked me to leave your flat . . . I'm sorry. I didn't mean that I doubted your story."

"That's all right," she said. "Why should you believe it? I wouldn't either if I were you." This was Phillip's moment.

"I talked to Gilbert," he said.

"Gilbert?"

"Gilbert Haines?"

"Oh, that little twerp. Is he still going around saying he's the father?"

"Isn't he?" Phillip was earnest.

"You what?"

"I . . . I think he is the real father of your child."

"You *believe* him?" She laughed.

"We talked. He told me a few things. He told me he . . . he slept with you one night in his car." Phillip was surprised that the subject seemed to upset him more than it did Delia. She appeared unruffled and superior.

"Ha! As if I'd ever have sex with Gilbert Haines!"

"He said he hypnotized you first. He had books."

She laughed again, louder. "Actually, I think anybody would *have* to be hypnotized to have sex with Gilbert Haines. Gilbert Haines couldn't hypnotize a flea. He's been trying to hypnotize people for years. He's never done one magic trick in his entire life that's ever worked. And you think he managed to *hypnotize* me?"

"Yes, I do. Just before I met you that first night. I think he managed it, Delia. And in the trance he put you in, I think he made you see a spaceship, and now that's all you want to remember."

She looked at him as if he had just uttered the most ridiculous words in history. "It was always his fantasy to hypnotize someone. He saw some famous hypnotist once, or something. Did he tell you about that too? At school it was all he talked about." She turned on him again. "Phillip, he's just jealous. He's not the father. He's had a crush on me since we were kids. He just told you all this to irritate you."

Phillip was speechless. He remembered the mad look in Gilbert's eyes, but Delia's effortless dismissal of his theory undermined his certainty.

"I hope he didn't make you do anything stupid," she said.

He saw the mechanic lying against the TV set, blood trickling from his nose. "I beat him up."

"Oh, God," she said. She laughed one last time and walked off, but Phillip could not follow at once. He stood for a moment and reviewed the various possibilities.

He tried to decide whether she was burying a grim reality, and if so, could Jean-Paul Sartre be wrong? He had read and endorsed the existentialists' view that the self-deceiver was morally justified in seeking refuge from the truth under certain human circumstances. After all, who would choose to sacrifice a beautiful dream for a nightmare, exchange a starry spaceship for a beaten-up station wagon, turn an iridescent pool of celestial light into mere headlights, replace gentle attenuated fingers with the greasy black digits of a mechanic?

Or was it perhaps that he had leaped on his quick solution about Gilbert out of frustration? Gilbert was an incompetent and Delia had discredited him in a second. If Phillip was wrong, he had just put an innocent man into the hospital.

Or perhaps the truth was a strange combination of his own and Delia's stories; or even a different possibility altogether, something he had not yet considered?

In this whirlwind of scenarios, Phillip's exhausted curiosity finally disappeared. His revised position was that the best magician in this story was Delia herself, with her instinctive abracadabra: Now you see it, now you don't.

He ran after her, intent on apology. She refused to speak any more about the past, and Phillip, with no idea of how to proceed further, agreed.

He suggested they ride the old-fashioned ghost train, but she had seen a more sensational ride called the Octopus. In the chaos of merriment the machine hoisted children skyward and flung them shrieking on parabolic journeys, metal arms swishing the air, the sky filled with meteors, steel buckets orbiting like asteroids.

They waited their turn, arm in arm.

SWIMMING WITH THE TIDE

Vic Young unlatched the wooden gate. A white hen flapped toward him across the sunlit lawn, clucking and jabbing its head. An old woman with white hair came to the door. She held in her hands the knitting he had interrupted. She told him the young woman he was seeking was to be found around the back.

The small yellow hut was set in the corner of the garden between plum trees, their twisted branches covering the windows. He walked to the door across a sea of white daisies.

Delia Chapman was expecting him—indeed, was happy to see him. He was not surprised by this reception. She herself had invited him to visit her at her new address in New Plymouth, where she had apparently moved to be close to a friend, and had told him to bring his notebook.

Vic guessed who this friend was. He knew of the hospitalization of the mechanic and the arrest in New Plymouth, a day later, of the librarian, a man whom he remembered meeting once but with whom he had never exchanged words. Phillip Sullivan had been found by police sleeping in the back of a car in a farmer's field with Delia Chapman locked in his arms. He had already appeared in the New Plymouth District Court charged with grievous bodily harm, and had been placed in the city prison on remand.

"Thanks for coming," said Delia.

She asked him to sit down in a small room already benefiting from the tasteful placement of a few objects; a vase, seashells, candlesticks, a crystalline wind chime which tinkled in the window almost of its own volition. She had wrapped her head in a towel after her shower, and the residue of talcum powder was still on her neck. Vic looked at Delia only when necessary, refusing to refuel the addiction which had kept him sleepless all those months ago.

"I'll give you whatever it was you wanted before, if you like. That deal you talked about."

"A deal?"

"You know what I mean." She adjusted the towel.

Vic prized his eyes away from her, lest she transform herself into the twelve-year-old of his fixation. "Okay," he said. "What have you got?"

"I want to talk about the money first." She seemed a changed person.

He nodded, catching a whiff of soap. "How much do you want?"

She had already decided on the amount. "Ten thousand dollars."

She had calculated it carefully: It would be enough for Phillip's bail and to engage the best Auckland lawyer to defend him in his imminent court hearing.

"What do we get for the money?"

She looked at him. "I'll tell you everything you want to know."

"You mean about what *really* happened?"

"Everything," she said candidly.

And Vic Young's heart skipped a beat, his dormant professional curiosity returning in an instant, as if it had never abandoned him. "For instance?"

"Everything," she said calmly, willing to give him the sneak preview he desired. "Everything about the aliens."

"Oh." Young could not conceal a monumental note of disappointment in his voice. "Aliens. Christ!"

Her eyebrows knitted. "Isn't that what you want?" She was prepared to change her story on demand.

He nodded bitterly. It was of course the story his newspaper would pay any amount for, but any interest he himself may once have had was long since snuffed out by disillusionment, guilt and the continual barrage of mystical details from his lover. Personally, he wanted to know the truth. He'd had enough of concocted nonsense.

"Okay, then," Delia continued. "I'll tell you what the spaceship looked like. Everything that happened inside. Stuff like that. How many I had sex with. Everything you want to know."

Young gave a jaded nod. His employer would be delighted, he said.

"Oh, yeah," Delia added brightly. "And I saw another spaceship last night. They said they're gonna come back regularly to check on their kid."

Young didn't blink. He realized at that historic moment that he had become a victim of his own creation. He had sent something into the world which had taken on a life of its own and no longer resembled his original idea; he was a Frankenstein of the UFO business, a witless begetter of a stitched-together beast which was turning on its creator.

"Yes. I'm sure they'll pay you for that kind of story."

"Shall we start now, then? Or later?"

He shrugged, knew he should make a phone call to authorize the deal but knew also that the money was available, and so picked up the pen as if it weighed a ton, sighed and wearily looked at Delia.

"So tell me about last night. I s'pose—"

"I want a check," she said.

"You'll get it."

"Okay. So what, exactly, do you want to know? How tall they were? What they said? What they did to me?"

"Let's start," said Young, feeling ill, "with how many there were."

. . . . .

The editor of the *Sunday Enquirer* could not have sounded more excited when Vic Young phoned him a half hour later from inside the main house.

"How soon till she gives birth?" Hungerford asked, when the journalist had finished reading him his notes.

"Three months or so."

"What about the other two girls?"

Young paused to consider his reply. "Not sure about them."

"Why not?"

"One's been hushed up by her parents, and the other . . ."

"Yes? Vic? Are you still there?"

"She's . . . a bit behind schedule."

It took Young ten full minutes to explain this obscure comment in such a way as not to betray his lover.

Remand prisoners were permitted to wear their own clothes, and Phillip was escorted into the visitors' room in his old jeans and a cotton shirt Delia had seen him wear many times. They had given him a haircut.

"It doesn't look too bad here." Delia had prepared herself for the worst.

He agreed that it was not all that different from the army.

He did not, however, look at all happy. He was on speaking terms with another remand prisoner, a man arrested for cultivation of cannabis eight months earlier who was still awaiting trial.

She reached across and grasped his hand which he quickly covered with his own. She told him she was raising the bail of $5,000. There would hopefully be enough money left to engage a good lawyer. She had even received a number of checks from strangers via the newspapers. She held one up to show him.

"And I've got my own philosophy now too!"

"Have you?"

"Well it's one of Mum's actually. I'm not sure if it's a great idea to adopt the philosophy of a person who killed herself, but there you go. I remembered it the other day. Anyway, it's pretty basic. Not sure whether it's a philosophy or just a saying."

She told him, and waited nervously as he pondered it. She had remembered it as she took a seaside walk a week before, recalling her mother's advice that if you were ever caught in a riptide you must turn and swim back out into the raging sea before it exhausted you. As terrifying as this would be, it was your only chance. And you shouldn't just be carried along by the tide either, her mother had cautioned, you should swim faster than it! This was how you escaped the sea's terrible grip.

This belated whisper from the past had come to Delia at a moment when she was so exhausted by her own endless struggle that she was on the verge of surrender. Immediately she felt lighter, excited, hopeful; the example of her mother's life, with all its futile swimming, spoke through those unheeded lines and across the years.

Phillip happily confirmed that this easily qualified as a philosophy, and that its simplicity was its great strength. She grinned. She had a philosophy of her own.

"So, does that make me an intellectual too?"

"Better than that. It makes you smart."

Her decision to go to the press, in return for the money they promised, had been the first act based on her new philosophy, and her eyes sparkled with future possibilities.

"Did you find somewhere to stay?" he asked, clenching and unclenching his fists, eager to visualize somewhere other than his cell or this sterile room.

She told him she had found a place within easy walking distance of the prison, a hut surrounded by plum trees in a spinster's backyard where she paid no rent in exchange for two days' domestic work per week. She'd made it quite attractive, she said, furnishing it slowly, and had even gone home to rescue a mirror of her mother's, an heirloom promised her as a child. She had been nervous about seeing her father again, but when she arrived she found him in the darkened living room. He did not speak to her. Sullen, unwilling to rise from his armchair, he watched daytime television. The man had become a victim of soap operas, and was so ensnared in them that the farm was falling into dilapidation. Gates were falling off hinges and paint was peeling loose as Marty lost himself in the fates of fictitious characters and their fabricated passions. When Delia left he didn't take his eyes off the set.

Phillip could see that Delia had changed. She sounded confident and detached when describing her father.

Then she found the courage to break her worst news. "Somebody burned down your library. I'm sorry."

It was true. The damage to the library was major, and a long-term reclosure seemed inevitable. An arsonist had set a fire against the front door. The area's volunteer fire brigade had stumbled from their beds in time to save most of the building, justifying their annual stipend in a single night of feverish amateurism, but they were unable to save the bulk of the books. Most of the damage had been done to the new reference section, the encyclopedias, the *Great Books*, the romances and the classics. In a strange irony of fate, however, the oldest books, the war and gardening titles, were barely touched.

Phillip didn't flinch at the crippling news and listened with the same implacable expression he had worn since they first met. He showed no sadness, nor did he say anything about returning to

Opunake some day to try again. His only comment was a banal proverb which Delia interpreted as philosophical: You can lead a horse to water but you can't make it drink.

He leaned forward and kissed her. It was a strange sort of bond between them. Dignified, not yet passionate; perhaps it would never be love—but then perhaps it would. It was pure, however. This was how Delia felt.

She left him as she always did, feeling refreshed, clean, clear and a little more hopeful.

Heavy doors clanked shut behind her.

, , , , ,

At the end of autumn, a meeting in the town hall called to protest the temporary closure of the Borthwick's Freezing Works went almost unattended. Even the most disadvantaged workers began to see the changes as inevitable.

Great trucks bearing the new robotics drove up the main street at an insidious five kilometers an hour. The smallest children could walk abreast of the transports. Their bodies were no bigger than the hubcaps. Curiosity about the actual shape of the robots was not satisfied. The trucks turned into the Borthwick's gate and deposited their metal containers in growing stacks which were hastily covered by tarpaulins, forming a vast and mysterious pavilion.

The future seemed hopeless.

In this climate, Delia's new newspaper articles were a release from a dark age. And so extreme were the claims that the articles were quickly augmented by national radio shows and TV news items.

On the first Sunday morning of this new era, Harvey Watson sat in Whittaker's barber's chair reading all about Delia, an entire page of incendiary speculations and impossible promulgations, all conveyed in familiar no-nonsense phrases. But he was not dismayed by what he read. It was clear that she was going to be all right from now on. How he knew this was that she had taken the unprecedented step of mentioning the spacemen's names in the article, a revelation made more striking by the fact that principal among them was Watson's own. The sergeant roared with laughter. "Oh yes!"

The laughter quickly drew the barber to his shoulder. On a list of earthly pseudonyms, arguably contrived on the night by the visitors to substitute for their own phonetically unspeakable ones, was not only the policeman's but also that of the mayor, her own father, as well as several local identities, all dragged on to the stage with Delia in a grand burlesque. But while it was a tour de force, Watson also saw it as a subtle piece of cryptic code on her part, which proved to him not only that she was in full charge of her wits once more but also that she had these journalistic jackals by the snout prior to shoving them in the shit, where they belonged!

He breathed an especially deep sigh of relief and decided to celebrate the redemption of his protégée.

"Whittaker? Get your scissors before I change my mind."

He reopened the paper with a snap and to the melodious *snip-snip* of Whittaker's rejuvenated scissors, he roared again at the idea of an alien civilization so ordinary that it would allow its citizens to be seen dead with names like Jim, Marty, or, heaven forbid, Harvey.

The first televised pictures to be aired nationally showed Delia, nearly six months pregnant, smiling at a famous interviewer who, plainly unimpressed, asked Delia Chapman what she was playing at.

She answered simply. "Having a baby."

The interviewer, accustomed to tales of misguided passion, asked, "But it's not just a normal type of baby, is it?"

Delia agreed that it was not. Asked to be more specific, she replied that the father was the commander of a spaceship, he was particularly civilized and would probably even be able to pick up this broadcast. She was asked if she had any words for him. "Yes," she said, and turned to the camera quite calmly. "If you can hear me, we're doing okay."

There was time for one last question.

Opunake watched and waited.

What were her plans for the future? Did she have any?

She thought for a moment, then looked at the interviewer and announced, "I wouldn't mind doing a movie."

, , , ,

Father O'Brien's white collar told the story as well as anything. Once a tight and rigid band giving rise to rashes around his neck, it had progressively slipped, passing through an intermediate stage where it loosely rimmed his neck, and now suddenly it was gone altogether. So too were his visits to the tobacconist. His candy-floss hair had thinned alarmingly.

The priest strode to the church of Our Lady of Perpetual Succor in civilian clothes and opened the front door with a large key. For the first time in the church's history, he had begun locking the great doors following a significant incident a week earlier when a condemned cow, spilling from Borthwick's overflowing stockyard, had found its way onto the main street. Strolling in a daze as if Opunake were Delhi and she were sacred, the doomed animal had taken refuge in the church, causing considerable damage. Many parishioners felt the locking of the church in the wake of this incident to be directly connected to the impending closure of the freezing works, and added it to their unchecked list of grievances.

The priest stood in front of the Infant of Prague and irreverently smoked a cigarette. In such apocalyptic times Opunake was in desperate need of salvation, but he no longer had the strength to be of use. On his mind was the announcement of his carefully considered decision to leave the priesthood. His position was no longer tenable. With his intestines knotted with remorse, he eventually took up his position in the confessional box, and crossed his hands on his lap. In the darkness, on the other side of the screen, he was soon visited by a mutual sinner.

The voice was soft and therapeutic. "Bless me, Father, for I have sinned."

He responded to it through the gauze. "Hello, Yvonne."

"Can we talk where we can see each other, at least?"

In the vaulted privacy of the sacristy, the priest listened to the pregnant girl.

"I couldn't tell my parents, but I did as you said."

"You wrote the letter?"

"I felt stupid," said Yvonne. "But, yeah. I did. I wrote it down. It was like a confession."

"And you posted it to them?"

"Yes. It was the only way I could tell them."

The priest sighed heavily. "Then that makes two letters," he said gloomily.

She looked at him through the lattice of the confessional box, puzzled.

The graven priest turned his unshaven face toward her. "I wrote to the bishop this morning."

"You didn't!"

"I'm getting out, Yvonne. I am. I decided."

"You can't."

"It's done."

Yvonne stared at him, shocked that the immovable mantle of the priest could disappear in a second and leave behind just a man. She looked at him for the first time in this new light. A middle-aged bachelor. He had refined hands. His already graying hair was a thinning bird's nest. His eyes were gentle. He looked like an old painting.

She left her side of the confessional and joined him, taking his hand in hers. He looked in more need of comfort than she did. Together, they stood at a calm point from which a breeze would soon begin, an eddying breeze which would spiral slowly around them and outward, building hour by hour to create what would become a typhoon of argument, of condemnation and quite terrible disapproval.

She wanted to get out of the church. She wanted to go for a walk. Together. Just walk somewhere. It would be good for the baby, and good for them.

He wasn't sure that it was the right time for them to be seen doing that. And then he thought, If not now, when? The priest held the hand of the young woman and wondered about making her his bride.

, , , , ,

In the days which followed, days in which Father O'Brien was unfrocked and discreetly married to Yvonne McKay in a sparsely attended garden ceremony, days in which the town struggled to redefine itself as a record 1,500 cattle a day were butchered in a final death throe before the temporary closure of the freezing works, days in which the giant plastic cobra of a high-tech hydra-slide was seen uncoiling into the sky above the town, the mayor withdrew into a twilight of his own invention.

It was the pseudo-retirement of a dictator: not so much an abdication as a growing invisibility. Hiding out in his chambers, he became a silhouette at the window, looking out onto the streets with his arms behind his back, accepting his own verdict that he had failed in the battle to save eight hundred jobs.

From there he could see the CLOSED sign which sat permanently in the window of the blackened library. It represented a last straw, a final insult to a man already stupefied by defeat. It was not that he had ever been a prime advocate of the library, being no great believer in higher learning, but the institution was not without status, and it brought a certain respectability to the factory town. But even this simple objective had run foul, conferring on him a new dose of humiliation when it was officially learned that his nephew had squandered the entire annual library budget in one vast shipment of useless intellectual claptrap un-leavened by a single readable potboiler! When he himself had discovered this, he blamed himself for taking up his nephew's case in the first place and added it to his long list of critical mis-calculations of the past year.

He viewed as strange, therefore, the arrival the day before of a green notification card that advised a book was waiting for him at the unmanned library. He let himself in with a janitor's key and among the cinders found his name on a note tucked into a large tome that had survived on the front desk.

Back in his office, he opened the scorched book. The author was Spengler, and a page was dog-eared for him. He did not expect much and took from his reading even less.

And then begins the gigantic megalopolis, the city-as-world, which suffers nothing beside itself and sets about annihilating the country picture. Woods and pastures become a park, mountains become tourists' view-points, an imitation of Nature, fountains in lieu of springs, flower beds, formal ponds, and clipped hedges in lieu of meadows and ponds and bushes. Costumes, even faces, are adjusted to a background of stone. And the yokel stands helpless on the pavement, understanding nothing and understood by nobody.

He snapped the book shut and tossed it into the trash.

When the time came for the grand opening of the new Aquatic Center, not a single journalist in the area could be persuaded to attend the ceremony.

With much more at stake than could ever have been predicted, the main pool had been filled a week before. It waited glistening and blue, and after early trouble with the filters, was fully opera-tional. The public was admitted, and the weather was providential.

The final structure stood at over twenty meters, outdoing the town's previous tallest building, the clock tower, by three meters. The mayor, trying to overcome his deep depression, felt justified in declaring that at last Opunake had acquired a skyline. Defiantly, Opunake had for the first time in many years thrown up a monument, albeit a lime-green one made of tubular plastic.

The entire council, plus a good number of local people, had gathered to hear the mayor's speech, which was a potted history of the project, and to see him apply cement around a plaque at the base of a statue of Peter Pan. Waiting foremost to try out the hydra-slide, the children were already in their togs, pressed against the ribbon with their eyes popping in anticipation of their first downward assault. The mayor, wearing a beach robe and sandals, was to take the first ride as planned, a popular gesture, and when he removed his robe, revealing tight trunks and a voluminous pot belly, he received a hearty cheer. He climbed the steps to the top of the tower and the people continued to applaud this show of pioneering spirit as their heads craned upward. Finally, with the jaunty wave of a prime minister about to board a plane, he stepped into the launching enclosure and out of view. Waiting, the crowd smiled, eyes flicking between the top of the slide twenty meters above, where the mayor prepared for his ride, and the bottom where a funnel of water flowed out of the tube into the small splash pool—the very water which would lubricate the mayor's artesian descent.

When Sullivan set off, the onlookers knew it because the sound of his body thumping against the wall of the first turn was impressive, and the whole structure shook. Indeed, they could track his invisible progress, following the thuds and quakes through the first twists and turns, so that by the time he turned for the loop-the-loop section, it was obvious to all that he had attained the speed of a missile, his body booming against all the walls of the slide with devastating force.

When he was finally ejected back into daylight, Mayor Sullivan was unconscious and floated facedown in the splash pool like a dead man.

The Hydra-Slide was quickly closed, pending refinements to the breakneck speed it generated, and amid an air of collective shock the mayor was resuscitated at the water's edge. The kids, meanwhile, were permitted to jump into the main pool and baptize it with their urine.

The council would have to wait some time to see whether its plans to resuscitate the town with this futuristic park would be as effective as the efforts just then being applied to the mayor's chest.

A NIETZSCHEAN SUPERMAN

Delia found the exercise book in the back of Phillip's car. The title, "A Psycho-Philosophical Enquiry," was written in his own hand. She believed she was reading the diary of his innermost thoughts, written in moments of inspired anguish, and passages struck her at once with their intimacy:

> What of the self-deceiver, who takes refuge behind their passions, who hides the truth out of fear? They are not to be judged morally, but I define the self-deception an error. Draw back the curtains.

Phillip, she learned, believed everything in the universe to be divine. His voice was quite often pretentious, and it varied from passage to passage as if he had many personalities. Sometimes his voice was grand and sometimes it was simple, but two themes were repeated: Where was the individual who would come and protect us from ourselves; and, If that individual never existed, how would we begin to create him?

Someday, in a stronger age than this decaying, self-doubting present, he must yet come to us, the redeeming being of great love
and contempt, the creative spirit whose isolation is misunderstood
by the people as if it were a flight from reality—while it is only
his absorption, immersion, penetration into reality, so that, when
he one day emerges again into the light, he may bring home the
redemption of this reality and restore its goal to the earth and his
hope to man.

Delia was lying asleep on her bed. Phillip's obscure handwrit-
ten journal lay open on her chest. And the first contraction came.

, , , ,

The nurses in the maternity ward never liked to mention the
term infant mortality. The loss of highly premature newborns
was too close to abject tragedy to merit discussion. There was a
procedure, however. They knew what to do. Little baby coffins
often rolled down the corridor, and there was no denying it. But
for the most part the nurses tried to keep it out of their consciousness. And for Delia Chapman the nurses silently prepared the
neonatal unit. How long the baby would require it, nobody
could say.

Delia's labor was in its sixth hour.

The slow transformation of the lobby into a press gallery was
the other feature of the morning. One TV camera team and several journalists smoked their cigarettes idly but were prepared at
any time to push record buttons, hike cameras onto shoulders and
scribble Pitman's shorthand onto empty pads. The main prize
would be to get the first pictures of the baby. Was it normal, as
everyone expected it to be, or was there just a chance, an unthinkable possibility, that it would be green, or transparent, or special
in some other way? The staff cafeteria was put under pressure to
meet the abrupt demand for cappuccinos.

The charge nurse of the maternity ward appeared, and the

throng cornered her, only to be told, "She's still in labor. And it could be a while yet. Things seem to have slowed down."

The encampment returned to its unextinguished cigarettes and tepid coffees.

Vic Young took this opportunity to slip away. He wanted to visit the mechanic Gilbert Haines, convalescing in the same hospital, from whom he had just received an urgent but confusing note. As Young fully expected the baby to be human, he wanted to preempt the welter of anticlimactic stories with his own tale of human tragedy, the project he had never quite given up on. Perhaps the mechanic would somehow be of use.

. . . . .

Surrounded by fruit and flowers from his employer, central among them a pineapple, Gilbert Haines had regained consciousness, swum to the surface of his dream and awoken into a tropical paradise.

With his head heavily bandaged he was more than eager to talk to the press and to solve, for his visitor, an outstanding mystery, all for a moderate price and the prize of fame.

First Gilbert pulled up his shirt to reveal a purple scar the shape of South America on his chest. "Burned myself singeing the grass circle with barbecue starter fluid. See?"

"What about the cow then?"

"What about some money?"

"Money?"

"I want a few grand first."

The journalist shook his head. "After. Tell me the story first, then we can talk about money."

"Okay. Two-hundred-kilo animal, squashed flat like a pancake. And no sign of how it got into the middle of the landing pad. You newspaper people loved that bit. Wanna know how I did it?"

Young nodded.

"By accident. Do you believe that? Perfectly by accident. I went out there to Philpott's place that night, didn't I—only place growing barley you see—with an idea of how to help Delia out, since she was saying what she was saying and all that, and I got a speed up, turned off my engine and my headlights as I rolled past the farmhouse so I wouldn't wake them. Well, I musta been going about sixty k's an hour, in near darkness! I couldn't see a thing!"

And with that Gilbert began to elaborate on his most perverse attempt to impress himself upon a world equally determined to ignore him. Unable to see beyond the hood of his station wagon he could not have hoped to see the piebald cow standing in perfect camouflage on the road ahead. The bars on the front of his wagon crushed its ribs instantly, propelling it sideways and stopping the vehicle in its tracks. Before Gilbert could lift his head from the wheel, the dying cow eerily rose to its feet under its own steam. Hopelessly crippled, with blood trickling from its mouth, the unfortunate animal crept off into the barley, emitting low moans of terminal distress. Gilbert followed it, shocked and nauseous. Where it finally fell, pulverized on the ground, became the site for Gilbert's mad scheme, a plan to lend weight to Delia's flimsy spaceship story: a favor to his beloved.

The success of the mission amazed no one more than Gilbert himself, who had felt personally embarrassed by the low quality of the fabrication. He had walked away thinking it a washout, and was stunned by the reactions which followed, concluding that so frenzied was the public desire for the site to be authentic that everyone, including Young himself, had overlooked a welter of evidence to the contrary.

Gilbert lowered his shirt, saying the purple burn over his ribs would be his lifelong proof that everything he'd described was the complete and unadulterated truth.

But the journalist was barely listening by this time, his mind having drifted into other thoughts.

"Let's talk money," Gilbert said.

"What?"

"The money."

Young closed his notebook, in which he had written nothing. "No, I don't think so," he said.

He had been bombarded one too many times by young people trying to get their faces in the newspaper at any cost. This story lacked a ring of truth; and what's more, he had disliked the mechanic on sight.

What he also had to admit was that he had begun to grow accustomed to the fantastic conjectures of his lover, and in comparison this scenario seemed dull, lifeless and too simplistic.

By the time he left Gilbert behind in his Arcadia of fruits, he had not only judged his story unworthy of reportage but also decided to forget everything he had just heard. He was anxious to return to the maternity ward where his real interests lay.

, , , ,

At 1 A.M. on June 25 the charge nurse came through the doors and announced to the crowd of journalists that a baby had been born to Delia Chapman exactly at midnight, a tiny infant who weighed 1,065 grams, or two pounds of butter. "It is a troubled little boy," she said, "and it's a miracle he's even alive at twenty-four weeks. He's a gift from God, and we're all praying for his survival." The baby's condition was critical, she said, and it wasn't certain whether the little chap would live more than a few hours. She asked for their cooperation and their understanding.

The nurse was besieged with questions, most of which she ignored. She was able to explain, however, that the infant had been placed in intensive care as it had not yet produced its own surfactant—pens raced to follow the requested spelling of the word: little bubbles which prevented the complete collapse of the lungs between each breath—and so an artificial substance was being injected into the infant lungs.

Before the journalists could learn whether the baby resembled an alien, the nurse was gone.

Delia's baby was in an incubator, and she could not yet hold him in her arms. In the bubble of a closed hygienic atmosphere, everything was being done to encourage his little elfin heart, but it was a precarious thing when every beat could just as easily not occur. They waited and hoped that life would become a habit.

A chaplain had been called to the neonatal unit. Delia didn't want last rites, but had asked, instead, that her baby be baptized. She knew what his name was: James, after James Dean. She'd decided this a long time ago, and even when she'd talked to him in the womb she had called him Jimmy. It had always felt right.

The chaplain wore a surgical mask and gown, and conducted a simple baptism. Unable to physically anoint the baby's head because of the danger of infection, he performed the ceremony in the air above the plastic capsule. Delia sat quietly, her gloved hand on the side of the incubator, never taking her eyes off the tiny movements of her son, who was still curled up, not fully formed.

And Phillip had been right: The child had come to earth in human form. Yet, small and embryonic, he reminded Delia of the gentle alien in the library book. The chaplain pronounced the infant James Christopher, and sprinkled two drops of holy water which sat on the lid of the incubator over the child's forehead.

After the christening, Delia could not be persuaded to leave the room for many hours.

She sang songs and talked to her baby all night, certain that he could hear her. The heart monitor, showing little green peaks at regular intervals, gave no promising signs. Why had he been born this early? Just because of the occasional cigarette she'd smoked? Or was she being punished for her unfitness as a mother? Did she deserve to lose this child?

Throughout the long night she would cry, then recover for a moment, dry her eyes, and then cry again in the unparalleled sadness of a grieving mother, until early the next morning, swollen-eyed and exhausted, she collapsed into her bed.

, , , , ,

An orderly, his arms loaded with flowers, approached a nurse outside Delia's room. "There's more flowers coming in for the Chapman woman," he said.

"Put them on her bed. She'll see them when she wakes up," the staff nurse told him.

He didn't move. "I think you'd better come and take a look at this."

At the end of the hall he opened the ward door. The hallway beyond was a Garden of Eden.

"Deliveries coming all the time, from all round the country," he said.

The nurse shook her head in disbelief. She didn't have an immediate solution.

While they were debating what to do with the flowers, three young women slipped past them unnoticed. Access to all but close family was prohibited at this hour.

Deborah Kerr, Suzy Jackson and their new friend Mara Maxwell scoured the ward, peeking into rooms of sleeping mothers with cots drawn up to their beds. They stopped at the viewing window of the neonatal unit, and crowded side by side, their noses close to the glass, peering at the small incubator on the other side.

Inside was a child so small that a face cloth had been used as a diaper.

The young women whispered to each other until the orderly walked toward them.

Deborah turned. "Excuse me, is this the Chapman baby?"

He nodded. "Poor little thing is so premature that its heart isn't fully formed. It keeps stopping."

The girls had not heard that the baby was in so much danger. Suddenly shocked, Suzy asked, "How would anyone know if its heart stopped?"

"They monitor the heartbeat through a special pad that it's lying on, which is attached to a kind of alarm. But the doctors won't know for a couple of days whether it's going to survive. It's fighting for its life right now."

The girls had just come up from Opunake for a bit of a laugh, just for a look-see at the baby which they had expected to be nothing more than a bit small and a helluva lot stupid, like Delia's mother. But primarily they just wanted to lay eyes on the kid to say I told you so.

The orderly left them, and as they stood looking silently at the heartbreaking slip of a child, they were thoroughly ashamed of themselves. When they spoke now it was with the penitential tones of the humbled, and as the baby quietly fought for its life Deborah confessed, "I feel terrible."

No one said anything more for several minutes until Suzy whispered, "Is he sleeping, do y'reckon?"

"No, he's not." Mara Maxwell knew more about infants because her sister had just had a baby. "His eyes haven't developed enough yet to open."

This information lent even more weight to what they were already feeling. "Poor little fella," said Deborah.

Suzy was shaking her head. "I've never seen a baby so small. Look how tiny his little diaper is."

Suddenly the alarm on the incubator went off. A light flashed and a loud buzzer sounded. It took everyone a second to realize what was happening.

The girls grabbed each other's arms, their hearts leaping to their mouths.

"Oh, my God!" gasped Mara.

"What is it?" screamed Suzy.

"The bloody alarm's gone off!" shouted Deborah. "Get a nurse! Quick!"

The corridor was completely empty. Deborah started to run first, heading one way, Suzy the other. Mara was lost, and just stood there, white as a ghost. The alarm screamed. The baby didn't seem to move.

Deborah found a nurse first. She seemed reluctant to run, so Deborah shouted, "Run, for God's sake!"

"Settle down, settle down."

The nurse raced to the incubator. The girls regrouped at the window, breathless. After a second's rapid inspection of equipment and hoses, the nurse rapped on the incubator's meter with her knuckle. The alarm didn't stop, but with a second rap it promptly fell silent. The nurse turned and gave the girls an okay sign: faulty equipment. She pointed at the monitor, which had shown no interruption in the child's heartbeat throughout the emergency.

Six eyes looked as if they would pop out of their heads, and remained riveted on the baby. None of the girls permitted herself another breath until she saw the infant twitch again, which it mercifully did.

"Fuck me," Deborah Kerr said.

"I need a fresh pair of knickers," Mara chimed in.

They had resumed their grips on each other's forearms.

"I think I need to check into this hospital myself," Suzy remarked.

Mara and Deborah laughed, and the nurse came out of the incubator room.

"Sorry about that, just old equipment."

She disappeared again and the girls were left alone in the unexpected role of guardians.

Deborah, Suzy and Mara lit up an illicit cigarette, took several purely medicinal drags each, then prematurely stubbed it out in a planter. They returned to the window to watch over Delia's baby. There they remained, taking turns in a protective vigil which continued for most of the day.

When Delia awoke, the nurse asked her if she was well enough to have some visitors. Three girls were waiting outside.

They came in, grinning, and crowded around the bed. They had brought presents: a baby's bottle, a tiny sheepskin and a plastic tray of little cakes, items they had hurriedly purchased. They placed them on the end of the bed.

"We just wanted to tell you," said Deborah, speaking first to her old friend, "you're out of the team."

"Yeah," said Suzy. "And we're out too. Borthwick's have pulled out of sponsoring us. Harvey told us yesterday."

Delia nodded in her railed bed.

"Unless we find another sponsor," added Suzy.

"We're thinking of putting some money in ourselves," said Mara.

"Okay," said Delia. "Count me in."

"Yeah?"

"Yeah. But you better give me a chance to recover first."

There was an awkward silence. Months of unkindness, cruelty and jealousy were absolved in a few moments of guilt, shame and compassion.

"We saw the baby," said Deborah.

"Did ya?"

"Just before."

The girls didn't tell her that they had been at the hospital for three and a half hours and were ready to drop.

"He's beautiful," Suzy said. Mara nodded. And Deborah added, "We reckon he looks like you."

"Yeah," the others agreed, subtly hoping to communicate that their interest in the baby's paternity was a thing of the past.

"Got a name for him yet?" asked Mara.

"We had the idea of Cosmo," said Suzy. "Waddaya reckon? Just a joke, eh?"

"No!" said Delia, "He's already been christened James Christopher. I call him Jimmy. Just in case, you know, he doesn't make it."

They all had tears in their eyes and hugged Delia as much to comfort themselves as their friend.

When Delia said she was getting tired, the girls asked if they could come again.

"Course you can. It's good to see ya. And thanks a lot for the presents."

"He's on nine," said Suzy, who had talked to the nurse. "The nurse told us. We don't know what that means but fifteen is normal, so it might take a while."

, , , ,

Twelve days later, Harvey Watson, Vic Young and Mayor Sullivan arrived at the hospital simultaneously, each carrying a bouquet of flowers: red poinsettias, sweet-smelling roses and a perfumed arrangement of lilies.

They stood at the viewing window together, but could not tell the Chapman baby from the others. Alarmed, thinking they had arrived too late, they sought a nurse only to be told that, because of a slight improvement in the child's condition, the Chapman incubator had been moved into the mother's room.

Allowed to briefly pay their respects, the men greeted Delia, placed their flowers on the end of her bed, and crept to the incubator, peering inside, almost reverential and making sonorous whispers.

Delia watched them, amused by their formality, and told them that they could speak normally, that this wasn't a library, and her baby was a little stronger today. She had been told that every hour he lived, the better his chances were of survival.

The men smiled, relaxing, and the mayor, speaking for all of them, said he was eager to have her return to Opunake when the baby was well. Opunake was on the move, he said, on the verge of a new era of prosperity, on the golden cusp of good fortune, and Delia and the next generation would play a vital part in that. She thanked them, and an awkward silence descended. Watson, Young and Sullivan turned back to the incubator.

"Poor little mite," Harvey said. He was struggling to find the correct level of sympathy: not sadness, but tenderness scented with hope.

"Fighting though," added the mayor, meaning that there was a good lesson in this for everyone, and especially himself. "Makes you feel guilty."

Harvey was nodding already, acting like this was what he had intended to say. "We take things for granted, until they're not there," he said. "Then you see something like this."

"Superman," murmured Vic Young abstractly, and everyone looked at him for the first time. "Looks like Superman." He blushed, surprised by the level of sudden attention, and searched their faces for support. "In the comics? When he arrives on earth. As a baby, you know, from . . . in a capsule. Looked just like that. The capsule thing. You know?"

The vacant stares of the other men made him feel he had been disrespectful when he had not intended to be. Only Delia put him at ease.

"I know what you mean," she said.

When the visit ended, the mayor hung behind for a last word. "Just thought you'd like to know. If you talk to Phillip"—Delia already knew, from her numerous telephone calls with Phillip, that no one apart from her had tried to contact him in prison— "if you do, tell him that there's a certain willingness in the past couple of days to try and get the, ah . . . the library back up. We had a little spontaneous working-bee on Sunday. Quite a few people showed up, actually. And about the other thing: Harvey reckons there was a degree of provocation in this attack business, and some extenuating circumstances in his running off, so just tell him . . . why don't you just tell him to give me a call sometime."

Delia nodded, not wanting to prolong the mayor's obvious discomfort. She understood.

When the men had gone, Delia opened Phillip's journal, which she kept on the bedside table, and read from it, going over the same passages many times until they offered up a meaning, not necessarily their intended one, but a meaning all the same.

And what rough beast, its hour come round at last,
Slouches toward Bethlehem to be born?

She slid out of bed and sat down in the low chair beside the incubator. She tried to contact her son through the plastic walls of the chamber, frustrated and upset that she still could not hold him, see his eyes which would not yet open, or touch the tiny pink fingers hopelessly clutching the air in a world it had not yet seen. She tried to whisper to her baby in his vacuum, humming little tunes, leaning her cheek against the casing whenever he seemed anxious, watching his tiny heart palpitating as fast as a lizard's under his near-translucent skin.

Three hours later Delia's face broke into a shining smile and tears slid down her cheeks. Finally, she felt she had discovered a delicate framework of interaction, a clairvoyance which new mothers possess but which had taken her a long time to discover. Her forehead rested against the shell of the incubator in supersensible communication. Then she closed her eyes and was able to rest, optimistic and reassured that, in an esoteric language, she had at last received a tacit agreement from her child that he would soon be ready to confirm his glorious presence on this planet.

ABOUT THE AUTHOR

Besides being a novelist, Anthony McCarten is one of New Zealand's foremost playwrights. He has written eleven widely performed plays, and co-wrote the hugely successful *Ladies Night*, which has been translated into four languages. His collection of short stories, *A Modest Apocalypse*, was runner-up in the Heinemann-Reed Fiction Award in 1991, judged by Angela Carter; and a selection of these appeared in Faber & Faber's *Introductions* series. He is also a filmmaker, and has adapted one of his plays, *Via Satellite*, into a feature film, which he directed, and which had its world premiere at the 1998 Cannes Film Festival.

Born in 1961, Anthony McCarten grew up in New Plymouth, and spent two years as a reporter on the *Taranaki Herald*. He currently divides his time between Wellington and London.